STATE OF REMAINS

VIRGIL JONES MYSTERY THRILLER SERIES
BOOK 18

THOMAS SCOTT

Copyright © 2023 by Thomas Scott. All rights reserved. No part of this book may be reproduced in any form or by any electronic or mechanical means, without written permission from the copyright owner of this book. This book is a work of fiction. Names, characters, places, governmental institutions, venues, and all incidents or events are either the product of the author's imagination or are used fictitiously. Any resemblance to actual persons, living or dead, businesses, companies, events, locales, venues, or government organizations is entirely coincidental.

For information contact:

ThomasScottBooks.com

Linda Heaton - Editor

VIRGIL JONES SERIES IN ORDER:
State of Anger - Book 1
State of Betrayal - Book 2
State of Control - Book 3
State of Deception - Book 4
State of Exile - Book 5
State of Freedom - Book 6
State of Genesis - Book 7
State of Humanity - Book 8
State of Impact - Book 9
State of Justice - Book 10
State of Killers - Book 11
State of Life - Book 12
State of Mind - Book 13
State of Need - Book 14
State of One - Book 15
State of Play - Book 16
State of Qualms - Book 17
State of Remains - Book 18

JACK BELLOWS SERIES IN ORDER:
Wayward Strangers

Updates on future novels available at:
ThomasScottBooks.com

Those of you who have been with me throughout the entire series know I have a character who shows up every now and again: Detective Jack Grady. I borrowed that name from my nephew, a fine young man we call G.J.

His name is Grady Jack.

So, this one's for you, G.J. Keep it cool in Kansas, or wherever life leads you.

Remains:
/rəˈmānz/

Continue to exist, especially after other similar or related things have ceased to exist.

Be left over after others or other parts have been used, or dealt with.

"What we have done for ourselves dies with us; what we have done for others remains immortal."
—Albert Pike

"You're my hero, Small. You always will be."
—Murton Wheeler

CHAPTER ONE

THE DAYS AND NIGHTS, LONG AND SEEMINGLY WITHOUT end, rolled beneath both a deep blue sky and a hard rising moon backlit by star clusters that all went unseen under a cover of concrete, steel, and razor wire designed to keep the participants of death, destruction, and greed at bay. Most of the incarcerated—many of whom had long ago made the kinds of decisions that managed to turn them into their own worst enemy—spent the time convincing themselves that a cell the size of a broom closet was cruel and unusual punishment.

Everyone else essentially shrugged, called it justice, and looked the other way.

But the looking away…it'd come back at them with teeth, a bite that wouldn't let go because justice, like its participants on either side of the bar, was a living, breathing machine. And if someone knew which valve to adjust or which screw to turn, eventually a buzzer would sound, a lock would click, and a door would slide open—the deep blue sky and the hard rising moon visible once again.

It wasn't very hard if you knew the inner workings of the machine. It should have been, but it wasn't.

Roy Landry was beginning to think his past was built around a house of cards, one where the deck was always stacked against him. What he could never fully comprehend was the simple fact that the house plans were self-drawn, and the faulty construction process and shoddy workmanship was a nightmare of his own design.

As a former prison guard for the Indiana women's correctional facility, his boss—a nasty female bureaucrat with thin hair and big teeth—after hearing multiple rumors over Landry's conduct, decided enough was enough. She set up a sting and managed to catch him in the act of servicing one of the female prisoners after lights out, which was, for reasons Landry never really could understand, against the rules. When he tried to talk his way out of the situation, his misogynistic attitude assured him of three things: He'd lose his job, his pension, and despite his training and qualifications, he'd never be allowed to work in the state prison system again.

But Landry knew a guy who had a friend, introductions were made, and after weeks of pressure, the guy's friend finally relented and gave him a new job as a Department of Natural Resources officer for the state. After he'd been given the job, Lester Poole, the director of the DNR, sat Landry down and said, "I've looked at your track record. You're not exactly blazing a new trail when it comes to your work ethic."

Landry tried very hard not to roll his eyes. "I don't know what to tell you, sir, other than sometimes things go your way, and sometimes they don't. I've had a bit of a bad run lately."

"Based on what I've been able to gather, it's been luck of your own making. You're getting a chance here, and a good one at that. There's nothing wrong with a fresh start."

"Thank you, sir."

"Don't thank me because it's my way of saying you better not screw it up."

"I won't. I promise."

"I mean it, Landry. I've got plans. Big plans which have been in the works for a very long time. What I don't need right now are distractions…of any kind. Are you hearing me on this?"

"You won't get any trouble from me, sir."

"Good. Make sure I don't. Get out in the field and make sure everyone has their fishing license up to date, write a few citations to prove you're doing your job, and everything will be fine. It's a pretty laid-back atmosphere out there. Let's try to keep it that way."

"Got it," Landry said.

"If you've got it, why are you still sitting there staring at me?"

Landry got up, walked out the door, gently pulled it closed, and muttered, "Asshole."

THE DNR GIG LASTED LESS THAN A YEAR. HE'D WRITTEN two citations for a couple of cops who'd abandoned their campsite, and when he tried to hand them to their boss—some dickwad detective by the name of Virgil Jones—the guy started throwing his weight around and spouting off about his wife being the governor. Big fucking deal. But then the dickwad's partner all but threatened his life when Landry refused to destroy the tickets. When he filed a formal complaint with his supervisor, it got kicked upstairs to the director, who ended up having a meeting with the acting governor over the entire matter.

But as Landry soon found out, the acting governor was the boss of the cops who'd threatened him to begin with. By the time it was all said and done, both Landry and the director had been fired.

And that led him to where he was today. Working as a

security guard for a psychiatric hospital located in Madison, Indiana, way down at the southern end of the state, just north of the Ohio River.

The job was about as lame as it could be…standing around all day and half the night watching a bunch of goony birds drool all over their shoes. But it wasn't all bad. He had his eye on a female patient. He'd known her back when he was still working the prison. They'd had some good times, so…

Landry found her sitting on the ground under a maple tree. He'd been watching her for a few days, waiting to see if she would recognize or acknowledge him. So far she hadn't. When he approached her she held a vacuous look in her eyes and was mumbling to herself, saying the same thing over and over. Something about a bag? It didn't make any sense.

Landry walked over and said, "Hey, baby-doll, remember me? I see they finally let you out of lockdown. I know it wasn't for good behavior. Or maybe it was. You always gave me good behavior, if you know what I mean."

The woman stared straight ahead as if Landry wasn't present. "Cash in a bag. Cash in a bag."

Landry knew the prison system…and he also knew

getting transferred to a psych facility wasn't an everyday occurrence. If he could get a reaction out of her, he'd know if she was truly messed up in the head or running some sort of game. With the crazies, sometimes it was hard to tell. "What'd you do? You putting on some kind of act?"

When she didn't respond in any way—other than to repeat the bag comment—Landry snapped his fingers in front of her face a couple of times. "Yoo-hoo…anybody home in there?"

"Cash in a bag. Said said. Cash in a bag."

Landry didn't know much, but he knew one thing. If someone had cash in a bag, he was going to find a way to get it, especially if it was a big bag. Then the system could take their twelve bucks an hour and shove it up their dick.

Yep, that was Landry.

"WHO HAS CASH IN A BAG, CHARLENE?" HE USED HER proper name because she once told him how much she hated it. "If you tell me, maybe we could work something out. What do you say, Charlie? We had some good times after hours, remember? How'd you get all those scars on your arms?"

Charlie Reed was many things, chief among them the former CFO for MedCap, a now defunct pharmaceutical hedge fund that had been bankrolling a company called Freedom Pharm. She ended up in jail after MedCap's founder and his wife were horrifically murdered, then mutilated after the fact. Reed hadn't done the actual killings, but she'd been involved up to her neck in the illegal manufacturing of Schedule One narcotics. When she was finally captured and convicted, they locked her in a cell the size of a broom closet and all but flushed the key down the toilet.

"Remember, remember. Cash in a bag. Cash in a bag. Said said so, so cash in a bag."

"You're not making any sense, Charlie."

When she didn't respond or make eye contact, Landry rolled his eyes and turned to walk away. She was still a fine looking woman, so maybe he'd try to screw her brains straight when he got the chance. That would probably make her talk.

He'd only made it a step or two away when he heard Reed make a clicking noise with her tongue. When he turned back, Reed looked around to make sure no one was watching, then wiggled her index finger in a come-over-here gesture.

Landry walked back and said, "So you are in there after all."

Reed gave him a wicked grin and said, "If you fuck me up, I'll find a way to kill you."

As a former prison guard, Landry had heard it all

before, so the comment barely registered with him. "And if I don't?"

"Then I'll make you rich."

"How rich?"

Reed wrinkled her nose. "Based on the way you smell, richer than you are now. What are they paying you here?"

"Ah, you know…the going rate."

"Right. It looks like you've reached the bottom of the barrel, Roy."

"I've had worse jobs," Landry lied.

Reed laughed at him. "Like what? Street sweeper in Shitsville?"

"Never mind all that. How much?"

"Your cut would come in somewhere in the neighborhood of at least a half million."

That got Landry's motor running. "What would I have to do?"

"Do you know how hard it is to convince somebody you're crazy?"

"No, I don't."

"It's not really very hard at all if you know what you're doing," Reed said, a violent look in her eyes.

"Are you going to answer me or not? What would I have to do?"

"For starters? Get me the hell out of here."

Landry let Reed tell him the story. She spilled it out so fast Landry had trouble keeping up. "Hey, slow down, will you? It sounds like you're trying to qualify for the fast-talker championship or something."

"That's because we don't have all day. Now shut up."

Landry ignored her. "Tell me again about this Said guy."

"He was a billionaire, you dope. Or at least he used to run a billion dollar company. He's dead now. Forget about Said. He's not the guy we're after."

"So, who are we talking about?"

"Said had a property not far from here down in Kentucky. Huge place. Big private estate with its own lake. I saw it once when I was still at MedCap. Met the caretaker too. A guy named Roger Getz. When we were all down there I saw Said give Getz an envelope full of cash. When I asked my boss about it, he told me Said pays the guy ten grand a month under the table. Called it cash in a bag."

"Big deal," Landry said. "Ten grand isn't exactly what anyone would call being rich. How do you get from ten thousand to half a mil?"

"Shut. Up. And. Listen. I was the chief financial officer of MedCap. We were always looking for investors, so I pulled Getz aside while I was at the estate and asked him if he needed someone to handle his cash. Told him I could invest it and get him close to twenty percent. He wasn't interested. Said he wanted to keep it in cash. Wouldn't tell me why. When I asked him how long he'd been keeping his cash, he told me it'd been ten years. Do the math, Roy. In case you can't, I'll do it for you. It amounts to one point two million bucks, and that was some time ago. I'll bet he's got close to one point five by now."

"And what? We're just going to waltz into his place and take it?"

Reed let out a genuine smile for the first time. "Why not?"

CHAPTER TWO

Landry thought about it for so long that Reed noticed his eyes were starting to glaze over. When she'd finally had enough, she looked at Landry and said, "What I need to know is this: How much cash can you get your hands on. I mean, like right now?"

Landry did some quick and simple math in his head. "I lost my pension when the Bureau of Prisons fired me. Didn't get anything out of my last job, and the pay here is pretty thin."

"Or you could just give me a number," Reed said.

"Why do you want to know?"

"Because we need to plan. We'll need a place to stay in Kentucky. We'll need some cash to get us going."

"I've got almost three hundred in checking. About half that in savings."

Reed let her chin drop to her chest. "Are you kidding

me? It wasn't long ago that if I didn't have at least twenty grand in my checking account I considered myself broke. How's your credit?"

Landry turned the corners of his mouth down. "Believe it or not, it's pretty decent. Didn't have any trouble getting my new apartment."

"You got a computer?"

"No."

"Can you buy one?"

"Not if I want to eat."

"That's why I asked about your credit, you moron. Go to BestBuy, open an account and get one."

"Why? And how about it on the derogatory names?"

"Because I've got a few bucks tucked offshore the feds never found. It's in a numbered account, and there isn't much left, but if I can get to it, we'll have what we need to get started. What do you say?"

Landry thought about the question, and its implications. If he was caught, he'd end up in the joint, and as a former prison guard, he'd probably last about ten hours before someone shanked him in the shower. But, Landry being Landry, decided to fabricate another house of cards, his shoddy workmanship never quite making it to the frontal lobe of his design process.

"I'll help you, Charlie, but I'm going to need your help with my own little project. There's a guy I'd like to wipe off the map."

"Why?"

"It's personal. Are you in or not?"

"I don't have any problem with map wiping," Reed said. "When can you get me out of here?"

"With the level of security at this place? How does tonight sound?"

Reed gave him another genuine smile. "Like we're about to be free and easy." Then, just to make sure the hook was set: "I've missed you, Roy. I really have."

LANDRY WAS WORKING A DOUBLE, WITH A TWO HOUR break between shifts. He used the time to go to a place called Scrubs-R-Us—the R itself was backward on the sign, which Landry thought was about the stupidest thing he'd ever seen—and used a precious fifty dollars or so out of his savings account to make the purchase, then went back to work at four in the afternoon.

When he passed by Reed's room, she was right there waiting.

Landry had the scrubs rolled up tight, stuck under his arm. He passed her the outfit and said, "Five minutes," then kept right on moving down the hall and into the security office.

The day shift security supervisor looked at Landry and said, "What up, Roy, my boy?"

"Same O, same O," Landry said. "Listen, I went home during my break but accidentally left my keycard behind. I can either go back and get it—probably take an hour or so for the round trip—or you could just code a temporary one for me. I'm good either way."

The supervisor, who might have been somewhere in his late twenties, looked at his cool black Apple Watch, and said, "You're supposed to cover for me, remember?"

"And I am. But I gotta have a keycard to do it."

"Hang on, I'll code one right now, but then I need to get out of here." He unlocked the desk drawer that held the spare keycards for the magnetic door locks, pulled one out and stuck it into a slot next to the computer monitor. Then he typed in a short series of codes and when the computer beeped at him, he pulled the card from the slot and handed it to Landry. "There you go."

"Thanks for the assist. Have a good night." Landry took the keycard, walked back down the hall and found Reed once again waiting right inside her door. He slipped her the card, and said, "Be ready at midnight. Take the south hall, keep your head down, and don't run. Remember, you've got to look like you're part of the nursing unit."

"What if someone tries to stop me?" Reed said.

"No one will. I know the routines around here. After lights out, the nurses sit around and bitch about their boyfriends and husbands, and the security—that'd be me

—will be non-existent. I'll be waiting in my car right outside the south hall exit door. Walk out, don't look back, hop in, and we'll be gone."

WHEN THE CALL CAME FOR LIGHTS OUT, LANDRY WALKED into the security office, killed the cameras that monitored the south hall exit door, then made a note in the log about the malfunction. After that was done, he sat and waited for nearly ninety minutes.

At 11:50 pm, he went to the nursing station and spoke with the head nurse. "Looks like it's all quiet on the western front. I'm gonna take a quick smoke break." He wiggled the radio clipped to his belt and said, "I'm on channel two if you need me. Give me a beep and I'll come running."

The nurse nodded without looking up. "No problem, Roy. Take your time."

"Roger that," Landry said. He walked down the hall, went out the door using the keycard he hadn't really forgotten at home, hopped into his car and pulled right up to the south exit door. He only had to wait three minutes before the door opened and Reed—just as she'd been told—walked over to the car without looking back and climbed right in.

Two minutes later they were cruising south, headed

toward the Ohio River and down to Kentucky. Landry took the radio from his belt and tossed it out the window, along with both keycards.

Reed laughed, buzzed her window down and looked up at the night sky, the hard rising moon visible once again.

When they arrived in Kentucky at the trailer Landry had arranged—a single wide dump on the outskirts of a town called Eminence—they went inside and the first words out of Reed's mouth were, "Jesus, this is the best you could do? My room at the loony bin was better than this."

"Beggars can't be choosers. You wanted out, you're out. Besides, it's only for a week or so, right?"

"Yeah, I guess. But still."

"I'll tell you what works about this place, even though it is sort of a shit hole."

"What's that?"

"It has everything we need and nothing we don't. There's an internet connection for the computer, a wood burner if it gets too cold, hot water for the shower, and best of all, it's basically out in the middle of nowhere. No one could ever find us here."

Reed, while not happy with the accommodations,

knew she really couldn't complain. "How'd you find this dump anyway?"

"When I was with the prison I knew a guy…this was one of the other guards. It belongs to him, and he told me he only uses it for hunting and drinking. So I called him up and asked if he had any hunting or drinking plans in the near future. He told me he didn't, and I could use the place for as long as I wanted."

"He didn't ask what you wanted it for?" Reed said.

"Nope."

"Well, I hope he didn't charge you very much."

"Didn't charge me a dime," Landry said.

"Now I know where the phrase, 'you get what you pay for' comes from."

Landry waved her off. "Ah, what's the matter? Didn't you ever go camping when you were a kid? This is practically the same thing."

"Whatever. I assume you got the computer?"

"Yep. Got it in the trunk. Want me to bring it in?"

Reed let her eyes do a little half roll, and said, "No, let's just run an extension cord out to the car."

Landry looked away for a moment. "Right. I'll go get it."

Once they had the computer set up, Reed went online and logged into her numbered account and checked the balance. Landry was leaning over her shoulder and when he saw the amount, he said, "Wow. I thought you told me there wasn't much left."

"There isn't. The 20K you're looking at? It used to be ten times that amount."

"What happened to the rest of it?"

Reed told him the story of what happened with MedCap, and finished with, "I had a gut feeling things were going to go bad, so I pulled most of the money, converted it to gold, then sold off the gold for cash in case I had to run."

"But you got caught," Landry said.

"No shit," Reed said, rather dryly.

"So what happened to the cash?"

"Forfeiture laws, you dope. When they busted me, the feds took everything I owned, right down to the kitchen spoons."

"How about it on the name-calling?"

Reed logged off and shut the computer down. When she looked at Landry, she wasn't sure where to start. Finally, she said, "Okay, there's something we need to talk about. Actually, there are a number of things, but let me start by saying this: I know you provided a, umm, service, let's say, to myself and a few other women in the pen. And while those services were appreciated, going forward, I'd like for you and me to keep things on more of a business type relationship. I'm sorry about the name calling. I do it when I'm nervous, and I don't want you to be disappointed with any of this, but our past is our past, Roy. It's not our future…or our present, for that matter."

Landry looked at her like she was from outer space. "That's a lot of words. You could have just said, 'I don't want to sleep together.' One of the reasons I picked this place is because it has two bedrooms, Charlie. You've been free for what…two hours, and you've already climbed up on your horse?"

"No, I'm trying to clear the air, is all. I'm hoping you're okay with what I said."

"Look, we're here to do two things. We're going to take care of the asshole who fired me, and then we're going to get the cash from this Getz goon. Afterwards, we'll go our separate ways and you can find someone else to butter your bread. I know I won't have any trouble."

"Good," Reed said. "Now, let's get some sleep. I'm exhausted, and we've got a busy day tomorrow."

CHAPTER THREE

A WEEK AFTER LANDRY SNUCK REED OUT OF THE PSYCH ward, Virgil Jones, lead detective with the state's Major Crimes Unit, was, on a mid-Monday afternoon, sitting on his back deck enjoying a cup of coffee with his friend and business partner, a Jamaican named Delroy Rouche.

Years ago, Virgil's late father—a retired Marion County sheriff—decided to open a downtown bar, and Virgil agreed to go in on the deal with his dad. It hadn't been easy because neither Virgil nor his father had ever managed—much less owned—a bar.

But the hand of fate tapped Virgil on the shoulder one day as he was vacationing down in Jamaica. He'd cut a tire on his car, and turned into a roadside beer and chicken stand run by Delroy and his lifelong friend, Robert Whyte. After they'd helped him change the tire and filled him with food and drink, Virgil convinced the men to help him and his father run the bar back in the States. And in doing so, as the years rolled on, the bar became one of the most popular Jamaican-themed joints in the Midwest. But, much like history, the hands of fate had a fickle side as well, and Virgil's father, Mason Jones, was shot to death inside the bar.

Shortly after Mason passed, the family attorney informed Virgil his father's will stipulated that the majority of Mason's half of the bar would go to three people; Delroy and Robert were two, and Virgil's adoptive brother, Murton Wheeler—who had been a part of Virgil's family ever since childhood—was the third. Murton also worked side-by-side with Virgil as a detective for the MCU.

Delroy looked at his friend and noticed he was fixated on a particular spot in the backyard. "You tink and tink all you want, Virgil Jones. It don't change da outcome."

If Virgil's response surprised Delroy, he didn't let it show. Virgil took a long slow sip of his coffee, then looked Delroy in the eyes. "I feel like death follows me wherever I go. Maybe my dad was right. Maybe you've been right all these years as well. I'm beginning to think I should hang it all up and come run the bar with you and Robert."

Delroy chose his words with care. "But Sandy okay, no?"

Virgil's wife, Sandy, who happened to be the governor of the state, had been shot in her own backyard at the tail end of the MCU's last major case only weeks ago. She hadn't been the actual target, but she was standing next to the former governor—who *had* been the target—and when she saw the gun she shoved Mac to the ground and ended up taking a bullet in her side, destroying both her kidneys.

Except the fickle hand of fate stayed with the game, seemingly never able to choose a particular side, and the person who shot Sandy turned out to be a perfect donor match, and the kidney transplant had gone off without a hitch. How *that* all came about was known to only five people in the entire world. Sandy didn't even know. Neither, of course, did Delroy.

Virgil set his coffee cup down on the deck railing and said, "Her recovery has been…a challenge. The doctors, they make it sound like after a few months everything will be just fine, but they tend to gloss over the specifics. Is she okay? Yes. But the road ahead isn't going to be as easy as we'd hoped it might be."

Delroy's lover, Huma Moon, a modern-day free-spirited bohemian sort with long, shock-white dreads tied up in a scarf, stuck her head out the back door. "You guys need anymore coffee?"

Both men told her they were fine, then Virgil said, "How's she doing?" He was speaking of Sandy.

Huma was Virgil and Sandy's live-in nanny to their sons, Jonas, and Wyatt. Since Huma and Delroy were lovers with a child of their own—a wonderful little toddler named Aayla—they all lived with the Joneses in their own wing of the house. Virgil had added the wing a few years ago because neither he nor Sandy ever wanted to lose Huma…or Delroy. Besides, they could afford it. Virgil and Sandy were sort of rich.

"She's sleeping right now," Huma said. Then, picking up on the vibe, added, "She's going to be okay, Jonesy."

Virgil nodded and looked away at the same time. Delroy picked up the slack for Virgil, gave his lover a wink, and said, "You beautiful, Huma Moon. Tru and tru, you."

Huma stepped all the way out the door, then walked over and gave Delroy a kiss on top of his bald head. Then she moved to the side, gently wrapped Virgil up in a choke hold from behind, leaned down close, and repeated herself. "She's going to be okay."

Virgil reached up and patted Huma's arm near her elbow. He nodded again, but didn't say anything. The words…they just wouldn't come.

After Huma went back inside, both men sat in silence for a few minutes, then Delroy said, "Were you serious about what you say a few minutes ago?"

"You mean hanging it up?"

"Yeah, mon. What else?"

"Maybe. I'm not sure. You want to know something?"

"What's dat?"

"I don't know why I keep doing it. Wait…that's not exactly true. I do know why. I do the job because I like it. I like the action, the mystery, the chase, the danger. I like it all. It's like I'm some kind of junky, or something. I like it almost as much as…" He let his thought float away, but Delroy, one of the wisest people Virgil had ever known, snatched the thought back before it was completely out of reach.

"As da pills." It wasn't a question.

Virgil paused before he answered, then said, "Yes. Looking back, it was one of the most selfish things I've ever done to the people in my life. This feels like the same thing."

"Dat not exactly tru, mon."

"You're telling me how I feel, now?" Virgil said with a whiff of irritation.

"No, mon, no. Delroy know better dan dat, me. But I tink you mixing your feelings up with da facts."

Virgil was frustrated, not with his friend, but with the situation. "Oh yeah? How's that?"

This time it was Delroy who looked away…not out to the backyard where Sandy had been shot, but out toward the road, where they'd almost lost Huma to a madman a few years ago.

"Because Delroy been there myself, me. Maybe you forgot about da argument we had at da hospital when it time to bring Huma home."

"Of course I haven't forgotten, Delroy. It wasn't one of my best moments."

Despite the nature of their discussion, Delroy actually laughed. "You can say dat again. But you make Delroy's point for him. Da whole ting was my fault because I couldn't see the other side of da situation. Too many tings to worry about at da time, no?"

Virgil didn't respond right away. When he finally did, he said, "You're the one who's been after me for years to walk away from the job and come work the bar with you and Robert. If I didn't know any better, it sounds like you're trying to get me to stay with the MCU."

"I'm not doing either one, me. I'm trying to get you to see dat no matter what Mason wanted, no matter what Delroy want, da choice belong only to you. I can tell you someting, though."

"What's that?"

"You won't figure it out sitting on your deck staring at a spot in da backyard where Sandy almost die. You figure it out by doing…by moving forward. How much time do you have left before you go back?"

"I told everyone it'd be at least another week or so."

Delroy glanced at his watch. "Den come tend bar with me, mon. It be just like da old days. See how you feel. Or don't, but no matter, it time to get off your butt, Virgil Jones. Sitting, staring…neither of those tings help a beautiful soul dat trying to heal."

"I don't see how it can hurt."

Delroy stood, then leaned down and placed his hand on Virgil's chest, right over his heart. "Dat because you not listening, mon. Sandy not the only soul I'm talking about." He glanced at his watch again, then said, "I have to get down to da bar, me. Maybe I see you there, den again, maybe I don't. Either way, what Huma said is true. Everting irie, Virgil Jones."

Except, it wasn't. Not by a long shot.

AFTER DELROY LEFT, VIRGIL SAT BY HIMSELF FOR A while, then went into the house to check on Sandy. He found her in their bedroom, still sleeping, though Virgil knew—both from what Sandy had told him, and his own personal experience with severe injury and surgery—that the sleep, while vital to the healing process, wasn't exactly what anyone would describe as peaceful.

He stood for a moment and looked at the bottles of medication on the nightstand, then walked closer and looked at the individual containers and read the labels:

Prograf: *Take twice a day...*

Cyclosporine: *Take twice a day...*

Rapamune: *Take once a day in the morning...*

Cellcept: *Take two to four times a day...*

And, of course, Percocet: *Take one tablet two to three times a day for pain...*

Virgil held the Percocet bottle in his hands, then glanced down at Sandy to make sure she was still sleeping. When he saw she was, he opened the bottle and shook the pills out into the palm of his hand and counted how many remained in the amber-colored plastic container. When he saw there were more than there should have been, he inwardly smiled.

His wife was raising the bar.

Virgil looked at the pills for a moment and realized he didn't really want them, but neither could he deny the feelings he had either. He likened it to walking down the street and having a chance encounter with an old lover from decades ago. The memories were there, but the flame had turned to ash. He dumped the pills back into the bottle before putting them on the nightstand and walking out of the room.

When Sandy heard the door close, she reached for the bottle of pain meds, then did what Virgil had just done. She shook the pills out of the bottle and counted how many were left. Then she smiled and went back to sleep.

Virgil made his way back toward the front of the house, and when he walked into the kitchen, he glanced at the microwave clock and did a little time zone math in his head. The equation worked out like this: If, let's say, he currently found himself in the central part of Greenland, or—simply for the sake of argument—anywhere along the eastern edge of Brazil…like Rio de Janeiro or São Paulo, it would, in fact, be happy hour.

And while the rationalization might have been a little sketchy at best, everyone knew, including Virgil, that math didn't lie. So he said to hell with it, reached into the fridge and grabbed a bottle of Red Stripe, cracked the top, then went back outside to the deck.

His phone was still sitting on the table where he'd left it, and the damned thing was buzzing at him. He glanced at the screen, saw who was calling, took a long hard pull on the beer, then hit the Answer button. His greeting, while less than cordial, did manage to get right to the point.

"I'm not available for at least another week. Everyone at the MCU knows it, and I know you know it as well. Whatever it is, call Murton and let him handle it."

"Hello, Jones-man," Murton said. "Cora handed me her phone and suggested I make the call. Your greeting alone tells me it was probably a good idea. She's standing right next to me, by the way…Cora. She'd like you to come down to her office, and based on the way she's looking at me right now, I'd like you to as well. In fact, I'd like you to hurry."

Cora LaRue was exactly three things to Virgil: The current lieutenant governor of the state—although at the moment she was the acting governor in Sandy's absence—a genuine friend, and his boss…although if mapped out on a flowchart, the hierarchy of those things seemed to change positions with great regularity.

"Not gonna happen, Murt. I've got too much on my mind right now. Besides, I've already had something to drink."

Murton, who knew his brother—and his rationalization skills—better than anyone said, "Are we talking about Sierra Leone, or Caracas, Venezuela?"

Virgil closed his eyes, brought up a mental vision of the world map, then said, "I'd say you could split the difference. My actual point of reference was Rio."

"Good. That means you've only had one beer."

"Murt—"

"Is Small okay?"

Virgil loved his brother…so much so that a few years ago he and Sandy had deeded half their land over to Murton, and his wife, Becky—who also worked with the Major Crimes Unit as their researcher and computer expert. The land was on the far side of Virgil's pond where Murton and Becky built their dream home. Virgil happened to be staring at their house when he spoke.

"You left your back porch lights on again. What's your electric bill running you these days?"

"Answer my question, Jonesy."

"She's sleeping. I think that's the best answer I can give you right now."

"Is Huma home?"

"Of course. What's going on, Murt?"

Murton lowered his voice a notch. "I need you here, Virgil."

Whenever Murton addressed Virgil by his proper name it tended to mean something serious was happening. "Tell me what's going on. Lay it out for me in ten words or less."

"I'll only need four," Murton said. "You should recognize them because they're your words, not mine."

"So what are they?"

When Murton spoke, the words he used caused Virgil

to lose his grip on the beer bottle. It landed on the deck, then cracked clean in half as if the bottle had been scored by an expert glass cutter. It also made him feel like his heart had just been etched with the same blade.

"You left a trail…"

CHAPTER FOUR

THE FORMER GOVERNOR OF INDIANA, HEWITT (MAC) McConnell, sat in his office reviewing the latest financial reports of Said, Inc., the company he now ran. Mac, along with his love interest, Nichole Pope—a former pseudo criminal turned businesswoman and philanthropist—had taken Said's corporation from public to private a number of months ago, nearly a year after its founder, Rick Said, had been murdered by two of his executive committee members, Frank Odom and Holly Novak. The whole mess was discovered after Novak herself was killed…the subsequent investigation by the state's Major Crimes Unit revealing that while Odom had been the one who actually murdered Said, the plan had been Novak's all along. It was all in the past now, but, history…

Ah, such a fickle bitch.

Mac's executive assistant stuck her head in the doorway, gave the jamb a polite little knock, and said, "Patty is on line seven."

Mac set his report down atop a pile of other paperwork, thanked his assistant with a smile and nod, then hit the blinking button on his desk phone. "Hello, Patty. How are you?"

Patty Stronghill was Rick Said's niece and only living relative. Shortly after Said died, Mac had the honor of officiating her marriage to Tony Stronghill, a Bureau of Indian Affairs agent who worked alongside his wife at the Shelby County Cultural Center.

"I'm well," Patty said. "And you?"

Mac barked out a laugh, a brief snort that might have said more than he wanted it to. "I'll tell you something, young lady, and there is absolutely zero cow dung in my next statement: After running the state for nearly two terms, I thought I knew what paperwork was like. I saw mountains of it. But this job and the amount of paperwork that gets generated? It is absolutely insane. Ask me what I'm doing right now."

Patty decided to play along. "Okay. What are you doing?"

"I'm reviewing a five-hundred page financial report."

Patty was completely underwhelmed, and her tone said so. "Part of the job, Mac. You run the place."

"I don't think you get it. The report is a mere summary of the other individual financials. At the rate we're pushing paper around here it won't be long before I'm literally buried up to my neck in the stuff."

"Maybe you should reconsider the harvesting contract with the Hoosier National Forest."

"Like I need that kind of grief. Anyway, I'm glad you called. Not only is it good to hear your voice, but my eyes were starting to bleed from all the reading I've been doing. If I don't take a break, I'll be carrying them out in a bag."

"Interesting choice of words," Patty said.

Mac paused before he spoke, a brief lull as his brain tried to digest Patty's statement. Finally, though he was loath to admit it, he said, "I'm afraid I don't understand."

Patty ignored his comment and asked a question instead. "How's the jet?"

"In my line of work these days? Fueled up and ready to go at a moment's notice. Why do you ask? Do you need to use it?"

"No, I don't, but let me ask you something: Have you ever been to the company's lakeside retreat down in Kentucky?"

"That's the one where Holly Novak was killed, if I'm not mistaken."

"It is," Patty said.

"Well, to answer your question, no, I've never been. Although I understand it is quite nice. I'll get down there eventually, I'm sure."

Patty laughed in a kind way, then let a whisper of corporate authority slip into the back of her throat. "I'd say you'll be seeing it sooner rather than later. I'm driving down there as we speak. There's someone you should meet, and a situation that needs to be addressed before things get any further out of hand. I'd like you to get on the jet and fly down to the Capital City Airport in Frankfort. If you leave now, the timing should work out perfectly."

"Listen, Patty, I'd love to. I really would. God knows I could use a break, but—"

Patty wasn't playing. "Mac?"

"Yes?"

"Who runs my uncle's company?"

"I do, Patty. You know that."

"Mmm, yes, I suppose I do," Patty said, the back of her throat staying in the game. "And while the death of Uncle Rick still saddens me to no end—and probably always will—now that he's gone and the corporation has been privatized, who actually holds the majority of shares in the company?"

Mac could feel the cartilage at the back of his jaw

starting to knot. "You do." He tried to say it without clenching his teeth but failed.

"Great," Patty said, her voice taking on a lighter tone. "How does two hours sound?"

"Like I don't have a choice if I'm reading the situation correctly."

Patty laughed like she didn't have a care in the world…mainly because she really didn't. "It seems to me you are."

"You're starting to sound a lot like Nichole. Has anyone mentioned that to you lately?"

"No, but thank you. Do you need directions to the lakeside property?"

"I'm sure my assistant can provide them."

"Wonderful. Oh, and Mac?"

"Yes?"

"The summary report you mentioned? Bring it along, will you? I'd like to page through it while you're here. Fly safe, and all that. I'll see you in a couple of hours."

Mac said he would, then, not one who often let his emotions get the better of him, he gently set the receiver back into the cradle. Then he pulled out his cell, called the airport, and got his chief pilot on the line. "It's me. I'm on my way. I should be there in about forty-five minutes or so."

"Yes, sir," the pilot said. "Destination?"

"The Capital City Airport in Frankfort, Kentucky."

"Very good, sir. Will you be traveling alone?"

"It sure doesn't feel like it."

"Sir?"

"Yes, yes," Mac said. He snapped it at him; the difference between often and rarely. "I'll be alone."

The pilot ignored the snap, as gainfully employed corporate pilots tend to do. "And how long will we be staying, sir?"

"Probably for however long it takes me to locate my nut sack. Be ready." Then Mac stabbed at the phone's End button so hard he chipped his fingernail.

It was a new role for Mac. Being summoned. He didn't like it.

MAC SPENT THE SHORT FLIGHT DOWN FROM INDIANAPOLIS to Kentucky trying to calm his nerves and wondering why Patty had used the statement, 'Interesting choice of words,' after he'd mentioned carrying his eyes out in a bag. By the time the plane landed he still hadn't figured it out, but three fingers of Johnnie Walker Blue Label—served neat, of course—managed to help take the edge off.

The pilots had arranged for a rental car, and once he was on his way, Mac was surprised to discover he was actually smiling, the smile stemming from the fact he hadn't been allowed to drive much over the last eight years. But now that he was a free man—so to speak—he discovered driving through the Kentucky countryside was a wonderful way to relax.

Except the relaxation went away when he almost missed a Stop sign that was partially obscured by an overgrown tree branch. When he hit the brakes—much harder than necessary—the rental's right front wheel slid off the shoulder, got sucked into the weeds, and scraped the entire side of the car against the sign's metal pole. When the pole collapsed, the sign itself hit the passenger window, and left a huge crack.

Mac sat there for a minute, then, out loud to exactly no one, said, "Fuck it. That's what insurance is for." Then he laughed, drove away, and a mile later turned into the drive of the lakeside estate, his cardio for the day complete.

Patty was waiting in the drive, her arms over her chest, her butt parked on the front fender of her own car, her ankles crossed. She looked, Mac thought, like a woman with an agenda.

CHAPTER FIVE

Virgil went inside and did his level best to remain quiet while he changed clothes. But Sandy was awake and when she sat up in bed, Virgil heard the sheets ruffle and came out of the closet. "Hi, Baby. I'm sorry if I woke you." He leaned down and gave his wife a kiss.

Sandy scratched at the back of her head, then said, "You didn't. I was already awake. Are you going somewhere?"

"Yeah. Murt called and said he needed me for something."

"I thought you were going to take another week."

"I am. Or at least I intend to."

Sandy stood carefully, then checked the time. She shook her head with a measure of disgust, reached for one of the pill bottles, and downed a capsule with a long drink of water. "I can't believe I have to do this for the rest of my life…the anti-rejection meds."

They'd been talking to each other for weeks about the medications, and Virgil knew Sandy was struggling with it. "It's better than the alternative."

"I'm beginning to wonder."

Virgil audibly swallowed. "Hey, sweetheart…"

Sandy waved her own words away. "I'm sorry. I didn't mean that. You know I didn't. It's simply something I'll have to adjust to."

"A lot of people have to take some sort of medication on a permanent basis. It won't be long before the whole thing will seem second nature. I'm sure of it. How's the pain?"

"I'm managing."

Virgil instinctively glanced at the Percocet bottle. "I can see that."

"I was awake when you came in earlier," Sandy said. "I worry about you, Virgil. I know having those particular pills in the house can't be easy for you."

Virgil sat down on the bed, and Sandy joined him. "Believe it or not, it doesn't bother me. The truth is, at any given time I may see them either on the street, or in a bag down in the evidence lockup."

Sandy took her husband's hand in her own. "I'm sure that's true, but do you look inside the bag and count them?"

Virgil opened his mouth to answer, closed it, then tried again. "No, I don't. I only did today because I want to make sure you don't end up on the same road I did."

Sandy gave his hand a squeeze. "I won't. I give you my word, Virgil." Then: "Hey, what's with the look on your face? What'd I say?"

Virgil blinked a couple of times, then said, "Uh, nothing really. I was just thinking about something Murton told me a few weeks ago."

"Why do you need to go in, again? I don't think you answered me."

Virgil didn't want to lie to his wife, but he also knew excessive stress of any kind was a known precursor for organ rejection—no matter the meds—so he chose his words with care. "I'm not entirely sure. He was with Cora, so something is probably happening that I'm not aware of. But don't worry. I'll be back as soon as I can. Promise."

"Since you're going to see Cora anyway, get an update from her on how things are going, will you?"

"You're not supposed to be worrying about the state right now."

"I'm not worrying. I'm curious. There's a difference."

"Are you okay?" Virgil said.

Sandy arched her back slightly, and Virgil knew she was trying to keep her muscles from tightening up. "I thought I'd be further along by now."

"It was a major surgery, sweetheart. It takes time.

You'll get there." Then with no segue whatsoever: "Listen, how about we put the Percocet someplace where the boys won't find it. You hear these stories…"

Sandy nodded. "I agree. I'll put them in the gun safe." Then with little segue of her own: "When do you have to leave?"

Virgil gave her an evil little grin. "When I'm damned good and ready. What are they going to do? Fire me?"

Sandy laughed, and Virgil was glad to hear it. "They might, seeing as how you don't have me to protect you right now."

Virgil kissed his wife, then stood from the bed. "Let 'em try. I had a long conversation with Delroy earlier this afternoon about quitting anyway." He was only half joking when he said it, but Sandy took him seriously. "We should talk about that…the quitting."

Virgil kissed her again. "We can talk about anything you like when I get home, but right now I better get moving or Cora will have my head on a pike."

"I'm not joking, Virg. I want to talk about it."

Virgil was backing out of the room. "We will. I promise. I'll see you later tonight."

VIRGIL TURNED OUT OF HIS DRIVEWAY, KEYED THE microphone in his Range Rover, and said, "Unit one is outbound on the gate." By the time he reached the highway, the state troopers tasked with guarding Virgil and Murton's private road had their squad cars backed out of the way. Virgil had plans to install a motorized gate, but hadn't gotten around to it yet.

He gave the troopers a friendly wave, then spent almost the entire drive over to the statehouse thinking about what Sandy had said…the quitting. It confused him because his wife had always been an advocate of Virgil's job and the work he did. And while both of them recognized it was dangerous, Sandy—a former state cop herself—knew how much Virgil loved it. Why would she want him to quit? Her injury aside, it simply didn't make much sense.

But while those thoughts circled through Virgil's brain on the periphery, at the core, what was really going through his head was what Murton had said over the phone and the implications of it all.

"You left a trail…"

The bottom line? Virgil knew he might not have to quit. For all he knew—given what Murton, Becky, and the Pope crew had done to save Sandy's life—they were going to put him in prison for murder as an accessory after the fact.

When he licked his lips, they tasted like salt.

Virgil turned into the statehouse parking garage and slipped the Rover into a visitor's spot. He thought about parking in the space reserved for the governor—he was married to the woman after all—but Emily Baker, Sandy's personal security guard, already had her own vehicle parked there. He got out of the Range Rover and when he made it over to the elevator he found Murton waiting for him.

"How bad is it?" Virgil said.

Murton wrinkled his nose. "I'm still trying to figure it out, but it's not good. I think Cora is getting squeezed...I have no idea by who, and she's parsing the intel very carefully. So far all she's told me is she knows I was in Toronto and when. She has, however, implied she knows who was with me and why. Also, I don't know if this matters or not, but apparently someone from the Treasury Department was in with Cora while I was waiting to see her. I was in the outer office, so I couldn't hear what was said, but I could hear the tone. It was pretty unpleasant."

"Cora unpleasant, or unpleasant, unpleasant?"

"The latter," Murton said. "I think."

"Well, let's go in and see what we can see, huh? Maybe it's not as bad as it seems."

"Not so fast, Jones-man. There are things you don't know about what happened the night Small got her new kidneys, and I'm also aware you've been smart enough not to ask."

Virgil looked away and thought back to the conversation he and Murton had after Sandy's transplant surgery. He'd been reviewing account expenditures for the Major Crimes Unit and noticed Murton had used his MCU credit card to pay for dinner at a bistro in Toronto. Becky, along with Wu and Nicky Pope, were there as well. Their time in Canada coincided with the exact time Sandy's kidney donor—Lisa Young, the former Brown County sheriff—died of respiratory distress when the machines that were keeping her alive, along with the magnetic door locks which gave access to her room all mysteriously malfunctioned for exactly twelve minutes. But Murton, Becky, Nicky, and Wu—and by extension, Virgil—knew there was nothing mysterious about it at all. Murton was right; Virgil didn't have all the details, and he'd done his level best to ignore them, although it hadn't been easy.

"Should I be asking now?" Virgil said.

Murton thought about the question for a few seconds before answering. "My gut says no."

"Lay it out for me."

Murton looked around the garage area as if someone might be listening in on their conversation. "We've spent most of our entire lives together, Virgil. You're one of the smartest guys I know. That means I'm all but certain you know what happened when I went to Canada with Becky and our two favorite computer freaks. You even thanked me for going after the fact, which was an admission all in itself. But as any lawyer in the world would tell you—especially the ones sitting at the prosecutor's table—there's knowing, and then there's proving."

Virgil rubbed the bottom of his nose with his index finger. Then he took a deep breath, and said, "Well, if you're about to get jammed up, there's no way I'm going to let you go down alone."

"And there's no way I'm going to let you fall on your own sword at my expense," Murton said. "You've got a family to think about."

"And you don't?"

"Of course I do," Murton said. "Why do you think you're here? Cora is about to get her hooks into me, she thinks you're involved, and it's my job to make sure she changes her mind."

"Do you really think she'd do that?"

"What? Hook me…or change her mind?"

When Virgil didn't answer, Murton pushed the call button on the elevator. Then he held up a key. "We're going down, by the way. Not up."

And Virgil thought, *That's not good.*

VIRGIL AND MURTON GOT OFF THE ELEVATOR AND WALKED down the hall, then made their way into the state's version of the White House Situation Room, a richly appointed secret area in the statehouse very few people knew of. There was a large conference table in the middle that was big enough for eight people to sit comfortably, and in front of each seat was a small viewing monitor, with two larger monitors hanging from both side walls. It looked like something right out of a Hollywood movie set, but it wasn't.

Cora was sitting at the head of the table at the far end of the room. As usual, she didn't look happy. Once both men were seated, she looked at Murton as if Virgil wasn't present. The words that crossed her lips so surprised Virgil he almost laughed.

"I'm afraid I've made a terrible mistake."

CHAPTER SIX

Mac grabbed the report, then got out of the rental and walked over to greet Patty. The look on her face was suggestive of someone who might have overplayed their hand, and her initial comment matched her expression.

"Mac, I'm sorry. I've been thinking about our phone conversation, and I'm afraid I might have sounded a little more aggressive than I intended to." Then, before Mac could respond, Patty saw the condition of his rental, and said, "My God, what happened to your car? Were you in some sort of accident?"

Mac had been a politician for most of his adult life, so he knew a thing or two about diplomacy. In other words, he knew when to hold 'em, and when to fold 'em. He gave Patty one of his best political grins, wrapped her in a hug, then held her—somewhat awkwardly because of the report in his hand—at arm's length. She wore simple blue jeans, a flowing white linen shirt, and purple Chucks without laces that matched the color of her eyes and the violet streaks in her hair.

"Forget about the car," Mac said. "It seems I'm a little out of practice when it comes to emergency vehicular maneuvers. As for the phone call, I'll tell you something, young lady: I learned long ago if you've got a winning hand, you play the cards. Don't apologize for being at the top of your game."

Patty gave her friend what she considered her third best smile, then said, "Nice try. I could tell by the tone of your voice you weren't very happy about being called down here."

Mac wouldn't hear it. "I'm afraid you're misreading the situation. I am happy to be here, but admittedly, I'm still getting used to command performances, as they say." Then, before Patty could respond, Mac let it all go, and said, "My God, this place is stunning."

Patty stuck her hand in the crook of Mac's elbow and steered him down toward the water. "It is, isn't it?" When they got to the edge of the lake, she slid her arm free and swept it out in front of them in what could only be described as a perfect Vanna White, Wheel of Fortune gesture. "The property itself is forty acres. The lake and the woods beyond take up about half that."

Mac looked across the water and said, "That's where they discovered Holly Novak's body."

Patty turned from the water and faced Mac. "Yes, it is. It's one of the reasons I wanted you to come down here today…to meet the man who discovered she'd been murdered."

Mac kept his expression as neutral as possible. "Then I may have wasted a trip."

"In what way?" Patty said.

"In that I've met Jack Grady, the lead detective with Kentucky's Criminal Apprehension Bureau any number of times while I was governor."

"I'm not speaking of Detective Grady. He ran the investigation down here as I understand it, but it wasn't actually him who discovered someone had been killed."

Mac switched the report he held from one hand to the other. The damned thing was heavy enough it was causing his fingers to cramp. "Then who was it?"

"He's waiting inside," Patty said.

Mac naturally turned and looked back and studied the cabin. When he didn't respond, Patty pointed at the massive cabin and continued with, "The house is almost seven thousand square feet. There are ten bedrooms, each with its own master bath, a chef's kitchen so nice that if you weren't a chef it'd make you want to enroll in culinary school, and just about any other amenity you could ask for in a place like this. The boat house itself is clean enough to live in."

Mac had seen his share of nice properties and had to

admit the one where they stood was very impressive. "So, who's this guy, and why am I meeting him?"

Patty slipped her hand back into the crook of Mac's elbow again and said, "Let's go inside and get everyone introduced." Then: "Here, let me take that report for you."

PATTY LED MAC INTO THE CABIN'S GREAT ROOM, WHERE they found a slightly overweight man sitting in one of the high-backed leather chairs that faced the water. He was dressed in clean outdoor work clothes, and wore a faded green John Deere hat that covered most of his short gray hair. When Mac and Patty stepped into his view, he stood, gave them both a polite tip of his chin, then stuck out his hand to Mac. "It's a pleasure, Governor."

Mac shook the man's hand, and said, "I'm afraid you have me at a disadvantage, sir."

"That's easy enough to fix…just as long as you stop calling me sir. When you get to be my age, it's another indicator of how there's less road ahead of you and much more behind, if you take my meaning. Name's Roger Getz. I've been the caretaker of Mr. Said's estate for over ten years now."

Mac looked a question at Patty, but she didn't see it because she was thumbing through the report. He turned back to Getz, and said, "It's nice to meet you, Roger. And please call me Mac. I'm no longer the governor, so that doesn't really fit anymore."

"Whatever you say, Mac. I just thought it was proper…you know, the way everyone still calls someone Mr. President, even though they're out of office."

Mac rolled his shoulders slightly. "I know some former governors do prefer it. Depends on how big their ego is, I suppose. I try to keep mine in check. Anyway, it seems our lovely Patty, here, wanted us to meet although she wouldn't tell me why."

"That might be mostly my fault," Getz said. "I told her if we were going to have the talk it'd have to be face-to-face, and you needed to see the place anyway."

Mac was still confused. "What talk would that be?"

Patty found what she was looking for in the report, and before Getz could answer, she looked at both men, and said, "Why don't we all sit down?"

They pulled three chairs into a little triangle and Patty set the report on an end table, one of the pages folded back to mark her place. She looked at Mac and said, "Roger has a story he'd like to tell you."

Mac tipped his head at Getz and opened his eyes a bit wider.

"I guess that's my cue," Getz said. He jerked his thumb over his own shoulder and said, "That wood burner in the corner? You see, a little over ten years ago I ran into Mr. Said at the hardware…"

Mac listened as Getz told the story of how he and Said had met, how the wood burner went in, and how it all led to the job offer as caretaker of the estate.

When Getz was finished, Mac looked at him and said, "So you'd like to have the job back?"

Getz let out a friendly chuckle and said, "No disrespect, Mac, but I already have the job. You can inspect the house and the grounds and you won't find one single fork out of place inside, or a single weed out in the lawn. I work here six days a week in the spring summer and fall, and half that during the winter months. You know… keeping the drive and sidewalks clear, and whatnot. I love every minute of it."

When Mac took charge of Said's corporation, he knew he'd never be able to meet every single employee across the various companies under his umbrella of control. There were simply too many people…thousands of them scattered all across the Midwest. So it didn't surprise him he'd never heard Getz was the caretaker of the estate. "Well, based on your attitude—not to mention the level of care you put into this place—I don't know what to tell you, other than the job is yours for as long as you want it."

Getz opened his mouth to answer, but the words felt like they were stuck at the back of his throat. When he glanced at Patty, his expression was one that simply said, 'help me.'

Patty caught the glance and its meaning. She looked at Mac, and said, "It's not the job that's the problem. It's the compensation."

"What about it?"

"The man hasn't been paid since Uncle Rick died."

Mac felt his face redden slightly. "What? How can that be?"

Getz and Patty took turns telling the story. They told Mac about Getz's disability, the monthly envelopes Said would personally deliver, the amount of money the envelopes contained, and how it all stopped once Said was gone. Getz finished with a chuckle and said, "No one ever told me to stop taking care of the place, so I just kept at it. Problem is, no one ever showed up with any more envelopes. Mr. Said called it cash in a bag."

And Mac thought, *Ah, the bag comment.* Then: "And you'd like to keep your current arrangement?"

Getz nodded with enthusiasm. "If I could. I don't know the particulars regarding the ownership of the estate since Mr. Said died, but I'm not an idiot either. I'm guessing it's either the company, you personally, Patty, or some odd combination of the three."

Mac tilted his head back in thought for a few seconds, then looked at Getz, and said, "Would you mind if I had a word in private with Patty?"

"Not at all. I've got plenty to do today as it is. I'll be down at the boathouse if you need me." Then he slapped his thighs with both hands, stood, and walked out of the room.

Once Getz was outside they got down to the nut cutting. Mac looked at Patty, and said, "I like him, but ten grand a month—in under-the-table cash no less—seems a little steep. We could probably get someone half his age for half as much."

Patty twirled her index finger through her hair the way women do, then said, "Ever hear the expression you get what you pay for? No wait, let me finish. I've personally witnessed what the man does around here… and I'm not just talking about keeping the lawn mowed and the carpets vacuumed. Whenever Uncle Rick had an event here, or guests of any kind, he'd give Getz the information and the man would run with it. No one ever left this place disappointed…Holly Novak notwithstanding."

"I'll give you that," Mac said. "But ten a month?"

Patty gave him a look like he'd just farted in public. "I've seen the books, Mac. The amount we're talking about doesn't even rise to the level of a rounding error. The man's been doing the job unpaid for eighteen months.

It's time to get him his back pay, and keep the arrangement in place."

Mac let his jaw unhinge slightly. "You want me to hand over nearly two hundred grand in cash to a guy I just met?"

Patty picked up the report Mac had brought with him, flipped to the proper page, then held it out. "Take a look at the figure on line seventeen, under the heading of Estate Property Management Petty Cash. What's the amount?"

Mac knew he was fighting a losing battle but soldiered on anyway. He snatched at the report, ran his finger down the page, saw the amount, then tossed the paperwork back on the table. "It says one-ninety."

"There you go," Patty said.

Mac shook his head and let a bit of sarcasm seep into his voice. "No, there I don't go. I'm afraid I'll have to think about this."

"What's there to think about? It's not our money. It's his. He did the work, so we owe it to him."

Mac raked his tongue across his bottom teeth, then said, "When Rick died, I remember you saying something to the effect of he left you all his personal property. Do I have that right?"

"You do."

"Then it seems to me the owner of this property—namely you—are the one who should pay the man."

Patty pulled out her second best smile. "Yes, but you

might also recall once the will was straightened out, the holding company you now run—at my behest, by the way—agreed to lease this property from me in perpetuity. In doing so, the responsibility of caretaker compensation falls back on the company…not me personally."

Mac was getting frustrated. "Then I'll break the goddamn lease."

Patty leaned forward slightly, her second best smile still in place. "No, you won't. Get the man his money, Mac. It's what Uncle Rick wanted, and that means it's what I want."

Mac was beat, and he knew it. Patty held the majority of shares in her uncle's company, and if she wanted something, it was his job to make it happen. "Okay, okay. Christ, I've got two women in my life and they both have me by the balls…one literally and one figuratively."

"Look at the bright side, Mac."

"I will if you'd be so kind as to show it to me."

"I'm pretty sure I just did," Patty said.

"How's that?"

"This meeting was a courtesy. I'm trying to save you some money."

"How did this trip save me money?"

"I was going to double his pay. What did you say earlier? Something about if you've got the winning hand…"

They went outside and found Getz in the boathouse, tinkering with the engine on one of the Evinrudes. Mac got right to the point. "Mr. Getz, I'd like to apologize for the oversight and also assure you that going forward your original agreement with Mr. Said will remain in place. You'll also be compensated at the same rate for any back pay you are owed."

"Appreciate it, Mac."

"I only ask one thing."

Getz wiped his hands on a shop rag, and said, "Sure. What's that?"

"I won't be coming down here every month with cash in a bag, as Said called it. You'll have to come up to Indy and collect it."

"I can do that, Mac. I'm grateful for your attention to the matter."

"Don't mention it…to anyone."

Getz laughed and assured him he wouldn't. "C'mon, I'll walk you up to your car. You look like you're ready to get outta Dodge."

As the three of them walked up from the boathouse, Mac looked at Getz and said, "If you don't mind my asking, where, uh, do you keep all this cash?"

"Don't mind at all. I used to keep it in a safe deposit box at the bank. Then I started worrying about it because I had over a million bucks in there, and banks make me nervous."

"So what'd you do?" Patty asked.

"Went out and bought me the biggest, most expensive safe I could find. Had it professionally installed in my basement. It's bolted to both the floor and the wall, and it is completely airtight and fireproof. It's every bit as good as the safes they use out in Vegas."

The more Mac listened to Getz speak, the more he began to like him. By the time they got to the driveway, Mac discovered he was glad he'd made the trip down to the estate after all. But when he looked at where he'd left his rental car it was gone, and a different one sat in its place.

"What the heck happened to my rental?"

Getz laughed and said, "That's the same question the agency rep asked me when he delivered this one as a replacement. I didn't think you'd want to drive a dinged up car with a busted window back to the airport. Who needs that kind of grief in their life?"

"You did this for me?" Mac said.

Getz shrugged it off. "Part of the job, *Sir*. I like to make sure the guests leave happy."

Patty turned to Mac, caught his eye, then gave him her first best smile. "Told you he was worth it."

CHAPTER SEVEN

Murton touched eyes with Virgil, but neither man said anything…at least not to each other. Then, like the detectives they were, they simply continued to sit in silence until Cora spoke again. When she did, she sounded more like her usual self.

"Knock it off with the sweat 'em in silence routine. In case either of you might have forgotten, I used to be a cop."

Virgil tried on a smile. "I don't think either of us has forgotten, Cora. And no one is trying to sweat you. We're here at your request. What seems to be the problem?"

Cora laughed and scowled all at the same time. "*What seems to be the problem,* he says. In this building? Throw a dart. I guarantee you'll pop a balloon."

"You mentioned something about a mistake?" Virgil said.

"Yes, I did. I also used the adjective 'terrible' as a modifier. Try to keep up, will you?"

"I am keeping up," Virgil said. "And it sounds like you're feeling better already, or at the very least, more like the kind of boss I know you to be. Tell us what's happening and we'll do whatever we can to help."

Cora tugged at an earlobe and said, "I'm not sure where to start."

"I've found the beginning usually works well," Murton said.

Cora looked at him like she wanted to rip his eyeballs out. Then the look went away and she focused on a point about six inches in front of her nose. "I know both of you have a deep personal relationship with Mac. I do as well, but God bless me, that man was ten times easier to deal with when he was in office."

Murton felt himself relax just a bit. If they were talking about Mac—no matter the problem—at least they were staying clear of Lisa Young's mysterious death. But Murton also knew Cora could spar with the best of them, so he kept his gloves up and ready, just in case. "Jonesy mentioned something to that effect shortly after Sandy took office. It had to do with the Hoosier National Forest and the Buffalo Springs Restoration Process."

Cora looked at Virgil, her expression softening. "How is she doing?"

Virgil gave his boss a flat, toothless grin. "It hasn't

been easy, but she's getting there. She asked for an update, by the way."

"I'm not surprised," Cora said. "And don't worry, by the time we're done here, she'll have plenty to mull over."

Virgil very diplomatically cleared his throat, then said, "Although we are trying to keep her stress level down to avoid any rejection issues."

"Jonesy, the conversations you have with your wife are your business, not mine." Then, as if her own statement put a period on the conversational diversion, she looked at both Virgil and Murton, and said, "You wanted it from the beginning? Here goes: Does the name Lester Poole ring any bells?"

Murton felt his gloves drop a fraction more. He glanced at Virgil who shook his head. "Never heard of the guy."

"Same here," Virgil said.

"He was the director of the Indiana Department of Natural Resources. I fired him two months ago."

"Why?" Murton asked.

"Because as the director, he serves at the pleasure of the governor, which for the time being, would be me. I wanted him to let something go, and he refused. We went back and forth over it for a few days but he wouldn't budge. In the end, I said to hell with it and told him to either resign, or I'd sack him. He held his ground, so I let him go."

"What was the issue?" Murton said.

Cora looked him right in the eye and said, "In a word? You."

Murton got his gloves back up in a hurry.

Virgil, who could spar every bit as well as his brother, tucked his chin, and said, "Murt? What the hell did he do?"

Cora let her eyes go flat. "In a minute. When are you coming back to work, by the way? You're running out of vacation days."

Virgil ducked under the jab, set his mental feet, and countered with a roundhouse. "I'll come back when I'm ready. You'll be the third to know."

Cora let that slide, and said, "Do you guys remember Roy Landry?"

Virgil rolled his eyes. "If you're talking about the fish dick who tried to write up Mayo and Ortiz when they had to abandon their campsite, then yeah, I remember him well. He's an asshole. What about him?"

"He filed a complaint with Poole, the basis of said complaint being Detective Wheeler threatened his life by implying the MCU's resident sniper, Detective Andrew Ross, was going to take matters into his own hands over the way Landry interacted with your operations manager,

Sarah Palmer. How's that relationship working out by the way? We have rules against those kinds of things, you know."

"A rule I squashed," Virgil said. "The relationship is fine, not that it matters regarding this discussion."

Cora let that go as well, and continued with, "In any event, Poole didn't take the threat—or implied threat—seriously, so Landry went over his head and brought it to my attention. The three of us ended up sitting down together, and I discovered what kind of director Poole was. It wasn't too hard to get a read on Landry, either. I tried diplomacy, I tried tact, I tried damn near every arrow in my quiver, but Poole didn't care about Landry, and Landry didn't care about anything except the run-in he had with the two of you. Eventually I put my foot down and told them both to drop it. Landry got pissed and started ranting and raving, so Poole fired him right there on the spot…in my office. Then he looks at me and says if I ever tried to get involved with the DNR's business again, I'd come to regret it."

"A threat in and of itself," Murton said.

"Exactly," Cora replied. "That's why I fired him."

They sat silently for a few seconds, then Virgil looked at Cora and said, "You once told me I don't miss much, and I'd like to think that's true. But clearly I'm missing something here, because I don't see how that amounts to a terrible mistake. Indiana is an at-will state when it comes to employment. The law also extends to state employees. They essentially worked for you, and you let them go. So what?"

Cora laughed without humor, turned to Murton, and said, "How was Toronto last time you were there? As I understand it, you didn't go alone."

Murton could have chosen his words with a bit more care, but instead he went the other way. "If you're trying to put on a show, Cora, open the curtains and dim the stage lights, will you? We've already had this part of the conversation before Jonesy arrived. I told you that the Popes were in town, and since the case with the Buffalo Springs Restoration Project was closed, Becky and I accepted an offer of dinner from Nicky and Wu. It was all very last minute, and in typical big money fashion, they flew us up to Toronto where we had a lovely dinner at a fine little bistro on the water. The whole thing was Nicky's idea."

"All while your brother's wife was in the intensive care unit, with her condition listed as critical?"

"I'm not a doctor, Cora," Murton said. "What should I have done? Stayed home and paced around the house? There wasn't anything for me to do. We got a dinner invitation and accepted."

"And you used your MCU card to pay for your meal."

"It was an oversight on my part…one that Jonesy brought to my attention, and also one I rectified. Is the state's budget so tight they couldn't go without a couple hundred bucks for, what was it? Three days?"

"Don't get cute with me, Wheeler."

Virgil had almost had enough. "It seems like you're the one who's playing games, Cora. We're all on the same side here. I've got a sick wife at home who needs me, so I don't have all night. What, exactly, is the problem?"

"I might not be the sharpest tack in the box, but I'm not an idiot, either," Cora said. "And watch your tone when you're speaking to me, Detective. We're friends, and I'd go to the mat for you, Jonesy, but I won't tolerate any disrespect."

Virgil held up his hands, palms out. "You're right, of course. I'm sorry. Things have been a little tense lately."

Cora acknowledged Virgil's apology with a wave of her hand. "I understand tense. In any event, certain information—some of it fact, some of it speculation—has come to light and we need to find a way to deal with it before we all end up as the lead story on CNN."

"What kind of information?" Murton said.

Cora opened a binder, looked directly at Virgil, and said, "Former Brown County Sheriff Lisa Young was shot and critically injured at your home by one of your detectives."

Virgil shrugged it off. "And you know why. The woman was deranged. She tried to assassinate Mac, so Rosencrantz took her out. What would you have him do? Stand there and watch?"

"No. I'm not being critical of Detective Rosencrantz's actions. And please stop interrupting me." Cora turned to Murton and continued with, "You and Becky left the country—along with two world-class hackers—and were gone at the exact same time there was some sort of systems failure at the hospital where Young was being kept alive on a ventilator. The system failure caused Young's death, and Sandy got her kidneys as a result. That's quite a coincidence, wouldn't you agree?"

Murton kept his face blank. "They do happen…coincidences."

"I'm aware," Cora said, dryly. "But as I mentioned a moment ago, I'm not an idiot. Or maybe I am, because it wasn't me who pieced all of it together. We'll get to that little nugget in a moment."

"How about we get to it now?" Murton said.

"Okay, we'll do it your way, Wheeler. When you paid the state back for your unauthorized use of funds, someone in accounting got curious. They looked at your card statement and started asking questions…questions like, why would a state detective be using his state-issued card while out of the country? The questions made it all the way to the superintendent of the state police, who, instead of asking me about it, decided to handle the matter himself. He put in a call to Franklin over at Homeland, who put him in touch with Customs to verify that you had, in fact, been in Canada at the time.

"Customs looked at their records and reported back that you and your lovely wife, Becky, along with Nicky and Wu, arrived in Toronto but didn't leave the airport right away. In fact, none of you left until the system failure at the hospital was somehow mysteriously over and Lisa Young was declared dead. Then you went out to dinner, and when it was time to come home, you did so on a different plane. Why was that, Wheeler?"

Murton, still playing his part, shrugged, and said, "How the hell should I know? I do remember Nicky saying something about a satellite component needing to be repaired. I think it was some sort of navigational issue. Anyway, another plane was ready and waiting when it was time to go. I didn't give it much thought."

"Uh-huh. I'm guessing whatever equipment the four of you used on the original plane to remotely disable the hospital's systems was either destroyed, or wiped, or whatever it is computer nerds do to make something disappear. If I'm right, this whole fiasco is starting to look like a state-sponsored hit, perpetrated by employees of the state while working from another country. That's the kind of thing DHS likes to call terrorism."

"It's also the kind of thing anybody with more than

two functioning brain cells would call pure speculation," Virgil said. "Because other than the fact that Murt and Becky went to dinner with friends, took their time getting off the aircraft, and, due to mechanical difficulties, were forced to take a different plane home, that's all it is. Pure speculation. There's no actual proof of any wrongdoing."

Cora gave Virgil a look like he'd just broken her heart. She reached into her purse, pulled out a handheld digital recorder, set it on the table, and said, "Think again, Hotshot." Then she pressed the Play button.

CHAPTER EIGHT

Murton quickly reached across the table and hit the Pause button, and Cora let him. Then he turned to his brother and said, "Virgil, I need a favor."

Virgil instinctively knew whatever happened in the next few minutes would chart a course for not only Murton and Becky, but for he and Sandy as well. Nevertheless, after everything they'd been through together, Virgil wasn't going to let Cora take Murton apart at the molecular level. He knew what Murton wanted, so he said, "Not going to happen, Murt."

"Virgil, please. You need to step out of the room for a couple of minutes."

Virgil looked at Murton and said the only word he could think of which would have an impact on his brother. He pointed his finger at him, and said, "Family." Then, when no one moved or said anything, Virgil reached over and hit the Play button on the recorder. The voices that came from the speaker were crisp and clear, and everybody in the room knew who they belonged to.

MURTON: *I'm going to ask you guys to do something, and it has to stay between the three of us. I need your word on that. No one can know. Not Nichole, not Becky, not Jonesy...no one. Can you do that?*

NICKY: *In case you haven't noticed, we know how to keep a few secrets. What do you need?*

MURTON: *I need a power failure in a particular room at the hospital. Specifically on the holding cell floor where criminals are kept while receiving medical care. I'll also need the magnetic door locks jammed for a period of time so no one can enter the room. Can it be done?*

NICKY: *When do you need this to happen?*

MURTON: *The sooner the better.*

WU: *Why do Wu want this?*

MURTON: *Because my brother's wife is going to die if the woman who shot her doesn't. She's brain-dead as it is. All we'll be doing is helping the process along.*

NICKY: *Meet us at the Million-Air facility tonight at eleven. Bring your passport.*

MURTON: *Why?*

NICKY: *Eleven o'clock, Murt. Don't be late.*

Murton put his elbows on the table and his face in his hands. Cora turned the recording device off, then sat and stared at nothing.

Virgil stood and walked out of the room.

A few minutes later when Murton stepped out into the hallway, he found Virgil leaning against the wall and staring at his shoes.

"Jonesy…"

Virgil jerked his head up, pointed a finger at his brother and let his teeth show. "You stood on my back deck and gave me your word. *You said we were good.*"

"I honestly thought we were. I wasn't trying to deceive you in any way, Virg."

Virgil took a deep breath to calm himself. "I know it. I don't think you were. But we've got a hell of a problem. Where did that recording come from?"

"If you're asking how Cora got it, I have no idea. But I do know it originated in the office over the bar," Murton said.

"So the office is bugged?"

"Yeah, but it was Becky who did the bugging. When Nicky and Wu walked in I made a grand show of removing the battery from my phone, and they got the message right away. Once both of them did the same, Wu turned off all Becky's equipment, and then we had the conversation you just heard."

"Why would Becky bug her own office?"

"Wu put it down to paranoia. You know how computer geeks are. I love Becky with my whole heart, but she does have some safety-related security issues."

"Is that how she ended up on the plane?"

"In a manner of speaking. I went home to get what I needed, and she played the recording for me. She also tricked me with my own passport, and made it clear if I was going, she was too."

Virgil ran his hands through his hair. "Christ, Murt, this could be the end of us."

Murton wasn't buying it. "My gut tells me there's more at play here. And I'll tell you something else: We've been in tighter spots than this before, Jones-man. We'll figure it out."

"How?" Virgil said.

Murton pointed behind himself. "By going back into that room and getting the rest of the story from Cora. I still have the feeling she's being squeezed somehow."

"What makes you say that?"

"The nature of the conversation, if nothing else. She mentioned Mac, that Poole guy, and Landry. She also said she made a terrible mistake."

"I heard her, Murt, but I don't see the connection."

"That's because what I told you earlier is true. She's

parsing out the intel in her own way. Why not let her? She's the one who said if we don't figure it out we'd all end up on CNN. The way she said it made me think she's either in trouble herself, or she's willing to back our play. She said as much just a few minutes ago."

"Should we come clean with her?" Virgil said.

Murton considered the question carefully because it was a good one. "I'm not sure. On one hand, she has all the pieces, so it's not like we can hide it any longer. But on the other—as acting governor—she may want to feign ignorance as a way to insulate herself."

"And leave us twisting in the wind?" Virgil said.

Cora had opened the door and heard the last part of Virgil and Murton's conversation. "Do you guys really think I'd do that to either of you?"

When Virgil turned toward the sound of Cora's voice he couldn't remember ever seeing such an expression of hurt cross her face.

WHEN THEY WERE ONCE AGAIN SEATED AT THE conference table inside the room, Cora took a deep breath, looked at Murton, and said, "You saved my life, Wheeler. You also killed the man responsible for shooting me in the parking garage. When someone owes you their life, you don't turn your back on them."

"So what are we going to do?" Murton said. "And how did you come to be in possession of the recording?"

"We'll address those questions in just a moment," Cora said. Then she turned her attention to Virgil. "I know I already asked you this, but I'd like a detailed answer…if you can."

"I'll try, Cora. What is it?"

"How, exactly, is Sandy doing?"

Virgil took a few seconds to consider the question. He looked at nothing when he spoke. "I'm guessing after you were shot, you remember what the recovery was like."

"I do," Cora said. "It wasn't easy, and it wasn't pleasant, and the whole process frustrated the hell out of me. I also remember it took much longer than I thought it would. I kept thinking it was never going to be over…that I'd never get back to where I was."

Virgil turned away from nothing and focused his gaze on Cora. "That's where Sandy is at right now. I don't think I could add anything to your own statement that could give you a clearer picture of her condition, or her state of mind."

"Fair enough," Cora said.

Virgil had the impression she was about to move on, so he asked a question of his own. "I know most people aren't fond of this, so forgive me in advance, but why do you ask?"

"Because Sandy stepped up via constitutional succession after Mac resigned from office. So far, she's done a stellar job as far as I'm concerned, but what she hasn't done yet is made any sort of commitment going forward. You yourself said you're trying to keep her stress level down due to rejection issues. Unfortunately, it won't be too many more weeks before the election cycle starts to crank into gear. Will she be able to handle that sort of pressure?"

Virgil wasn't sure and said so. Then he remembered what Sandy had said before he'd left earlier in the afternoon, but he kept that little nugget of information to himself. "I'll talk to her about it tonight, but I can tell you this: If there's any risk to her health, and I mean any at all, I'll do everything I can to convince her not to run. It simply isn't worth it."

"I agree, and I don't want you to think less of me for what I'm about to say, but if she isn't going to run, then the next logical step would be—"

"For you to do so in her place," Murton said, keeping his voice as neutral as possible.

"What did I tell you about interrupting me, Wheeler? But, yes. Given my experience with Mac and the other connections I've made over the years, I believe I'd have a good chance of coming out on top. *Very good.*" Cora picked up the digital recorder and examined it like she'd never seen it before. Then she gave it a little wiggle, slid it across the table toward Virgil, and said, "But none of it matters until we get that particular problem addressed."

Virgil slipped the recording device into his jacket pocket and said, "Murton asked you a question a moment ago. I'm hoping you'll answer it now. How did you come to be in possession of the recording?"

"That doesn't matter," Cora said.

Virgil tapped his index finger on the table. "I think it does."

"I sort of agree," Murton said.

Cora disagreed with both men. "Wrong question, guys. It was dropped off via courier in the mail room, where it eventually ended up on my desk this morning. No return label, in case you were wondering."

Virgil rolled his neck. "So, the right question would be who sent it, and why."

Cora didn't completely agree. "Yes, and no. I already know why. Someone is leveraging us…all of us. It doesn't matter if Sandy can go forward or not, because once that recording goes public, her career would be finished. The same is true for me if I step up in her place during the election cycle."

"And Murton, Becky, and me all go to jail," Virgil said.

"I get the bottom bunk," Murton said.

"Can it, Wheeler," Cora said. "This is serious."

"I know," Murton said. "I'm not joking."

Cora ignored the comment because she knew it was the best way to keep them on track. "The person who holds the master copy of that recording is going to be able to put whoever they want in the governor's chair."

"And you want us to figure it out?" Virgil said.

"You've got the motivation, if nothing else," Cora said. "And I can even give you a good place to start. Care to guess who recently filed with the state's board of elections as a candidate for office of the governor?"

"Who?" Virgil said.

"It all goes back to my mistake," Cora said. "It's the guy I fired…the former director of the DNR, Lester Poole. And don't forget who offered Poole the position to begin with…"

"Mac?" Murton said.

"Who else?" Cora replied. "Poole's father and our former governor go way back. Much further than any of us."

Virgil didn't see it. "If you're implying Mac is somehow involved—"

Cora did the one thing she hated when done to her; she interrupted Virgil. "I'm not. I'm simply pointing out there's a connection."

"Fair enough," Virgil said. "But based on what I've heard about this Poole guy, he doesn't sound like the brightest bulb in the lantern."

Cora huffed. "He's not. If it was just him, I think we

could clean this mess up rather quickly. Except the problem is a little deeper than all that. He has a brother who works for the federal government, and his father, John Poole is a former United States Senator from Kentucky. As I understand it, the senator—while no longer in office—was the chair of the intelligence committee, and he is still very active in the political arena. In any event, it seems our previous DNR director was the runt of the family. Either that, or he didn't have federal aspirations."

"Maybe he does," Virgil said. "The quickest way to the White House—your Barack Obamas notwithstanding—is via a governorship. And with family members already operating at the federal level, he might very well succeed."

Cora gave Virgil a dull look. "Believe it or not, the thought occurred."

Murton leaned forward. "Earlier today while I was waiting outside your office, you were meeting with someone from the Treasury Department. It sounded a little…tense."

Cora let her jaw hang open, exposing her bottom teeth. "Yes, it was. They've asked for our help…specifically the Major Crimes Unit's help."

"What do they need us for?" Virgil said.

"The specifics were a little thin. That's my way of letting you know he wouldn't say until he could speak with the entire squad. I'd like to do a full briefing tomorrow morning at the MCU. The Treasury agent will be there to delineate the particulars."

"We can do that," Virgil said. "Be nice to know what we're walking into, though."

"I don't know what we're walking into, Jones-man," Cora said. "But I do know the name of the Treasury agent who'll be briefing you. It's James Poole…Lester Poole's brother." Then she turned to Murton and said, "That's why it was tense."

CHAPTER NINE

Virgil followed Murton over to the MCU facility where they dumped his squad car for the evening. He'd leave it there overnight and ride back home with Virgil. They needed to talk.

Once both men were in the Range Rover, Murton looked at Virgil and said, "I'm sorry, Jonesy. I don't know what else to say, and I sure as hell don't know how this happened."

"Don't apologize, Murt. What you guys did? It saved Sandy's life. I'd have done it myself if I knew about Young."

"So what are we going to do?"

Virgil thought before he spoke. "I'm not sure. I think one of the first things we need to accomplish is to let Becky, Wu, and Nicky know what's going on."

"I'll get with Nicky and Wu tonight. Becky as well, obviously. What about Small?"

Virgil shook his head. "We can't do that, Murt. The stress would consume her. If she rejects those kidneys…"

"Okay, it's your call, but don't forget, I know the woman, Jonesy. The longer you keep this from her, the worse it's going to be."

"And you think I don't know that?" Virgil said, his jaw tight.

"Of course I do. I'm just trying to look at all the angles."

Virgil didn't respond to his brother's comment. Instead, he asked a question. "Tell me something: What exactly did you guys do in Toronto?"

"You already know, Jonesy."

Virgil waved his own words away. "That's not what I meant. What I'm asking is, how did you cover your tracks?"

Murton took a deep breath. "Apparently we didn't…at least not well enough. Nothing actually happened until after we landed. Once we got through Customs, we all went back on board the plane, Nicky and Wu did their thing, then we went out to the bistro. Wu took his laptop with him, which, by the way, was the only computer we had with us, and at some point during dinner he ditched it. He didn't say anything about doing so, but it was clear that's what happened. As for the plane…Nicky told me there was some sort of system failure in the satellite uplink computer and the entire unit had been damaged beyond repair."

"So Wu ditches the computer, and Nicky made sure the satellite uplink system was wiped, or whatever."

"That's the gist of it," Murton said.

"Why do you say it that way?"

"Because there's more to the sequence, Jones-man. There must be. It's that damned recording. Think about it…Becky had her own office bugged, and that's where it originated. Nicky took care of the plane, and Wu took care of the laptop. But somehow someone ends up with the recording. It's not too difficult to imagine who…my money is on one of the Pooles, by the way."

"Mine too," Virgil said. "Especially since two out of the three Poole guys are hooked up at the federal level." Then: "I know this is a ridiculous question, but I'm going to ask it anyway. Does Becky still have a copy of the recording?"

Murton laughed without humor, then keyed the microphone as they approached their private road. "Unit One, inbound on the gate." Then he looked at his brother, and said, "It's not a ridiculous question. Want to know why? I never bothered to ask her."

Virgil took out his phone and gave Sandy a quick call. "How are you?"

"I'm feeling…weird," Sandy said.

Virgil didn't want to hear that. "Weird how?"

Sandy caught the worry in her husband's voice. "It's nothing new, Virg. I just feel like my insides are rearranging themselves. I'm also tired. Are you going to be home soon?"

"Probably fifteen minutes or so. I've got to drop Murton off, and I need a quick word with Becky, but I'll be right there. The boys okay?"

"Yes. Huma's getting them ready for bed right now."

"Okay, fifteen minutes, sweetheart. I'll see you then." Virgil ended the call just as he turned into Murton's drive. He killed the ignition, then looked at his brother. "I guess I should have asked this already, but does Becky know what we're up against?"

Murton shook his head. "Not yet. I have a feeling it's going to be a long night."

Once they were in the house, Becky walked over and gave Murton a kiss, and Virgil got a hug. "Where the heck have you guys been?"

"We had a meeting with Cora," Virgil said. "In the secure room at the statehouse, if that tells you anything."

"Uh-oh."

Virgil scratched at the back of his head. "That about says it. Listen, Becks, there are some things happening, and I'll let Murton fill you in because I've got to get back home, but I have a quick question."

"Sure," Becky said. "Whatcha got?"

"At one point you had a recording of a conversation between Nicky, Wu, and Murton. I assume you know which one I'm talking about."

Becky touched eyes with Murton, who said, "It's okay. He knows the whole story. There wasn't any way around it."

Becky turned her attention to Virgil and said, "Yes, I know what you're referring to."

"Did you destroy it, or erase it, or whatever you do to make those kinds of things go away?"

Becky gave Virgil a look like he'd just insulted her. "Of course I did."

"When, exactly? And how?"

Becky bit into her bottom lip, then said, "It was the day after we returned from our dinner in Toronto. We didn't get back until very late...I think it was something like three or four in the morning, but I took care of it as soon as I was up and around."

"Why'd you wait?" Virgil said.

"Because I wanted to make sure I did it right. You can delete anything you want from your phone, Jonesy, but if you give it to me, chances are I can still recover the information."

"So what'd you do differently…other than delete the recording?"

"That's why I had to wait. I went into the shop, did a complete wipe of the phone, then destroyed it…with a hammer, in case you were wondering. Then I grabbed a new one from supply, restored everything I had prior to the recording being on my phone, and that was that."

"Except that wasn't that," Virgil said. "Was your phone ever out of your possession?"

"No, I'm certain of it. What the heck is going on?"

"I'll let Murt explain, but the bottom line is this: Cora has a copy of the recording. It was delivered via courier to the mail room in the statehouse, where it eventually ended up on her desk."

Becky rolled her shoulders forward and tipped her head to the side. "She can't have a copy. That'd be impossible."

"Apparently not," Virgil said. He reached into his pocket and pulled out the digital recorder and hit the Play button.

When Becky heard the voices coming from the tiny speaker, her expression was one of a woman who'd just stepped into the abyss, her future certain, her final destiny preordained.

When Virgil got home he found Sandy resting in bed. He walked into the room, gave his wife a quick kiss, then said, "Let me go say goodnight to the boys. I'll be right back."

Sandy said, "Okay, but Virgil?"

"Yes?"

"Your guns…"

"Right, right." Virgil walked over to the bedroom's gun safe, got it open, then put both his Sig 226s and his shoulder rig into the safe. Then with little forethought, he put the digital recorder inside as well, all the way in the back, next to a box of ammunition. With that done, he looked at Sandy and said, "Hang tight. Two minutes."

It wasn't two…it was more like ten because both boys wanted to download their day on him. Virgil tried not to rush them, but even as he walked back into his own bedroom, he knew he'd just failed on more than one count. The boys probably felt like he wasn't interested in their daily lives…and Sandy was fast asleep.

Virgil decided to let Sandy sleep, even though he knew she wouldn't like it. But the fact remained, she needed her rest, so he'd take the heat later on if he had to. Then he thought he'd pick up where he left off before his day had taken a hard left turn into the ditch, so he went into the kitchen, grabbed a Red Stripe and went out on the back deck.

He sat for a while and did the thing Delroy had asked him not to do: He stared at the spot in the backyard where Sandy had been shot and almost died. But during the staring process something occurred to him. He took out his cell phone and called Rosencrantz. "Hope I didn't wake you."

"You didn't," Rosencrantz lied.

Virgil knew he was lying because he could hear the sleep in his voice. "Uh-huh. You sound like a bear that just came out of hibernation."

"Ah, I just dozed off watching the game. What's up?"

Good question, Virgil thought. "Nothing much. Just checking in to see how you're feeling these days. Looking for a work update as well."

"Is Sandy okay?"

"Thanks, Tom. She's resting. It's a battle, but she'll make it…thanks to you. Anyway, I was asking how you're doing."

Rosencrantz gave Virgil a chuckle that sounded hollow and false. "Same answer. It's a battle, but I'll make it."

"I know you will. Did you and Ross clear the catalytic converter case?"

"Yeah. Mayo and Ortiz worked it with us. I've never seen so many junkyards in my entire life. I'll tell you something, Jonesy: The criminals are starting to get creative."

"Not creative enough, apparently."

"That's true. Listen, is something going on with Murton?"

"Why?"

"Because you guys live within spitting distance of each other. I thought he'd be keeping you in the loop."

"Ah, he is. That's not really why I'm calling."

"So what is it?" Rosencrantz said.

"Need a favor."

"Name it."

"Get in touch with Ross, Mayo, and Ortiz, will you? Everybody gets the morning off tomorrow."

"No kidding?" Rosencrantz said.

"None whatsoever. Relax and take your time coming in. Make sure everyone else does as well. Anyone who shows up before noon is fired."

"You won't get any argument from me. Probably anyone else either, so consider it done. And listen, I'm not one to boot an endowment donkey in the teeth, but is there something going on?"

It took Virgil a few seconds, but he finally got it. He laughed, then said, "Ah, it's nothing to worry about. You guys have been working your tails off. Just take a little breather tomorrow morning, huh? Make sure everyone knows."

Rosencrantz said he would.

Virgil had no sooner finished his call with Rosencrantz when Sandy stepped outside wrapped up in a blanket. She sat down next to Virgil and said, "What happened to two minutes?"

Virgil gave her a smile and said, "Sorry. It was the boys. The older they get the more they want to talk about what's happening in their lives. By the time I finished you were already sleeping. I didn't want to disturb you."

"Mind if we go inside?" Sandy said. "I'm a little chilly."

"I was thinking you're sort of hot."

Sandy smiled with her eyes and said, "Even though I'm all scarred up?"

"Maybe especially," Virgil said. "I'd wear them like a badge of honor. It shows you're a fighter."

Sandy looked out across the backyard to the same spot Virgil had been staring at for weeks. Then, with a voice full of regret, she said, "Maybe I'm not the fighter everyone thinks I am."

"What do you mean?"

"Let's go inside, Virg. We need to talk about something."

"Sure," Virgil said, even though he'd had his fill of conversational surprises for the day. "Here, let me help you up…"

CHAPTER TEN

Murton told Becky everything he knew, and after she'd heard it all, while not exactly panicking, she was dealing with her fair share of anxiety. Becky ran her hands through her long black hair and tied the strands up in a knot. It made her look like she was about to go for a run.

"I don't understand it, Murt. There's no way anyone could have gotten that recording."

"Well, not to overstate the obvious, but clearly there must have been at least one way, because Cora had it. She doesn't know who sent it, but we do have a few suspicions. Is there any way at all someone could be in your system, either at the bar or the MCU?"

Becky walked over to the giant window of their living room—the one that looked out toward the pond—and saw Virgil and Sandy sitting on their back deck. When she spoke, it was to Murton's reflection in the glass. "There is always a chance, but I have so many traps and alarms set up it would take someone with a very special skill set to get past everything. Even then, it wouldn't be something they could just sit down and do."

"What do you mean?" Murton said.

"This isn't something like you'd see in the movies, or read about in some ridiculous spy novel. Haven't you ever noticed when you or Jonesy or anyone else asks me to sneak a peak inside a database, it doesn't happen right away?"

"Yes, I have noticed. But sometimes it does happen rather quickly."

Becky turned from the window and faced her husband. "You're right. Sometimes it does. Kentucky's Criminal Apprehension Bureau would be the very good example. It took me a long time to wiggle my way in, but once I had, the hard work was over. Getting back in the next time is much easier because the groundwork has already been laid. As long as they don't go looking for a trail, they'd never know I was there."

Murton thought about that for a few seconds. "So, it's no different from what Nicky and Wu said about the hospital that night when I asked them how they got in so quickly. They said after helping Carlos escape they never left the system."

"That's right," Becky said. "And while all that is good

information, it really only tells us three things: Either someone has managed to get into my system and has been there for a very long time, or the office over the bar is bugged—by someone other than me—or there's something else I'm not seeing."

"How likely is that," Murton said. "The bugging?"

"Like my system, I'd say all but impossible. I've got video cameras on the stairs, and in the office. Everything is motion activated, and even if someone found a way around all that, the computer logs would tell me if any of the monitoring systems went offline. I check them every single day, and so far, nothing out of the ordinary has happened."

"Well, somehow we've got to find out what's going on," Murton said.

Becky took out her phone and after pressing only a few keys, sent out a text.

"What are you doing?"

"What you just said. I'm going to try to figure it out." Becky held the phone up so Murton could see the screen. The text message contained only one word: *Burn.*

"Who'd you send that to?"

"Who else? Nicky and Wu. I need to call them and it isn't going to be with this phone. I'll have to use one of the burners, and if they don't recognize the number, they won't answer. Grab your go-bag, will you?"

Murton went into the office and a few minutes later he

returned with a never-before-used burner phone. Just as he came back into the room, Becky's phone dinged at her. The message simply read: 'Send last two, and wait.' Murton looked at the message over his wife's shoulder, and said, "What the heck does that mean?"

"It means they want the last two digits of the number I'll be calling from, and I'm supposed to wait for a number they'll send." Becky took the burner from Murton, powered it up, then sent the information back to either Nicky or Wu. She didn't really know who she was communicating with…yet. Then she looked at Murton and said, "Kill the Wi-Fi for me?"

ONCE THEY WERE SEATED COMFORTABLY IN THE LIVING room, Virgil looked at his wife and said, "What's on your mind?"

Sandy laughed, and the laugh made her wince. Once the wince was put away, she looked at Virgil and said, "Plenty. Believe it or not, lately I've been thinking about Decker, and what he did to me."

Sandy's statement caught Virgil off guard. "Decker? Why?"

"Because this isn't the first time I've had major surgery. To be honest, it's not actually Decker I've been thinking about, but what happened afterward. I recovered from that incident much more quickly than I am this time. I don't really understand why."

"I think the answers, while not very complicated, aren't exactly what you're going to want to hear. One of them, anyway."

"What are they?"

"The first is simple. Every time you have a major surgery, the recovery is harder than the time before. I've talked to a lot of cops about it, and the answers are always the same. It gets harder as you go…not easier. Those scars you mentioned just a few minutes ago? They're on the inside as well. The scar tissue builds up, and when they go back in, it makes the next recovery more difficult, or longer at the very least."

"I can see that," Sandy said. "What's the other reason?"

"That's the one you're not going to want to hear. It's age, sweetheart. You're a little older now than you were when Decker shot you."

That got Virgil a look…a wife look. Virgil caught Sandy's expression and quickly added, "But you're so much more beautiful now."

When Sandy spoke next, Virgil thought her voice sounded like that of a little girl. "Am I?"

"Of course you are."

"I sure don't feel that way," Sandy said. "In fact, I feel used up."

Virgil nodded. It was a feeling he could relate to. "There is an emotional element to the healing as well."

"I know, Virgil. I probably know it as well as anyone. But that's not really what I'm talking about. Want to know why it didn't bother me when you spent a few extra minutes with the boys, even though you knew I was waiting for you?"

"Sure."

"It's because I can feel the time slipping away. How many chances do we get in our lives to do the one thing we're here to do?" Then, as if the question she'd just put forth was rhetorical in nature, she asked her husband something else before he could answer. "What did Cora have to say?"

Virgil wasn't sure how to respond. He didn't want to lie to his wife, but he also knew the stress she would have to endure surrounding the truth could literally kill her. And even if he only told her the parts that were easily digestible, a lie of omission was still a lie. Virgil was stuck. In the end, he went with the lesser of two evils. "As far as the day-to-day operations and everything else down at the statehouse, it all seems to be business as usual. It sounds to me like Cora has the place running like clockwork. She knows you're not supposed to be worrying about any of it, and I get the impression she's doing a pretty good job of making sure you don't have to."

Sandy blew out her breath and said, "Boy, that's a lot of words to say everything is okay. What aren't you telling me?"

Plenty, Virgil thought. Then once again Sandy said something that surprised Virgil.

"It's okay, Virg. I know the truth. I know what's happening, and I know why Cora wanted to meet with you."

And Virgil thought, *Oh, shit…*

ONCE ALL THE CODED TEXTS BACK AND FORTH WERE complete, Becky made the call and put them on speaker. And because Nicky and Wu were good, when the call was answered, the only word spoken on their end was, "Yes?" It was Nicky.

"No names," Becky said. "You might be secure on your end, but we are not. You're on speaker with my better half."

"You may have the equation backward," Wu said.

Despite their situation, Becky smiled. "A discussion for later. We need to ask some questions. If you can't or don't feel it's safe to respond, remain silent and we'll understand."

"Continue," Nicky said.

"I was thinking of the last time the four of us were together," Becky said.

"We remember it well."

"It was only going to be a party of three," Becky said. "But as it turned out, it was four."

"Yes," Nicky said. "Someone brought their plus one, as I recall."

"And do you remember how all of that came about? Every last detail?"

"Of course."

"There's definitive proof of outside involvement," Becky said. "The method I used to make it a party of four has found its way into other hands. We don't yet know who…or how it happened."

There was a slight pause before Wu said, "This is somewhat troubling."

"Extremely," Becky said. "Listen, I'm going to do something I'd only ever do for the two of you. I'm going to open a secure socket layer on my end, and I want you both to go in and see if you can find out if someone has been snooping around in my system. Will you do that for me?"

"We could," Wu said, "but we must refuse. There is a better way. A safer way."

"What is it?" Becky said.

"We'll be in touch," Nicky said. And then he killed the connection.

"Now what?" Murton said.

Becky looked at him and said, "Grab mommy a hammer, will you?"

Murton gave her a wink and was back in thirty seconds with a hammer. Becky removed the battery from the phone and set it aside. She also pulled the SIM card from its slot and stuck it in her pocket. With that done, she took the phone out to their back deck and smashed it with the hammer until it was reduced to scraps.

When she walked back inside, Murton said, "What about the SIM?"

"It's going to get flushed down the toilet in about ten seconds."

Murton gave her a bemused look and said, "Hope the septic guy isn't in on any of this."

VIRGIL TRIED VERY HARD TO KEEP HIS EXPRESSION neutral, but he wasn't quite sure if he pulled it off or not. "What truth are you referring to?"

Before she answered, Sandy did something Virgil hadn't seen her do in a very long time. She stood, walked into their home office, and came back carrying her father's turn-out helmet. Virgil kept the helmet on a credenza in the office as a reminder of Sandy's father and the ultimate sacrifice he'd made decades ago so Virgil could live.

When Sandy sat back down, she held the helmet in her lap. Then she looked at her husband and said, "This is how you and I came to be together. It was my first experience with death, and it remains one of the saddest days of my life."

"Sandy?"

"Please, Virgil, just let me get it out. I have to do it my way."

"I'm sorry. Go ahead."

"There's no need to apologize," Sandy said. "I simply want you to know how strongly I feel about what I'm going to tell you. Growing up without a father…without his presence in my life changed me deeply, so much so that I don't have the words to actually describe it. But no matter how terrible that day was, had it not happened, where would I be now? You would have died in the fire, and that means we wouldn't have each other, our boys, or any of the other people we call family. Based on what I know about his father, Murton wouldn't have survived childhood, which means we wouldn't have Becky, or little Ellie Rae. I guess what I'm trying to say isn't very complicated, but the fact is, a single act by a man I barely remember changed countless lives for the good."

Virgil held his wife's hand, but remained silent.

"Earlier today, before you had to leave, we talked about quitting. I'm not trying to control the universe, Virgil. I'm simply saying I recognize that fate and everything that happens from this moment forward is largely out of our hands. But I do know one thing, and I know it right down to my core: I'll do everything in my power to make sure Wyatt never has to go through what I did as a child…losing a parent. Jonas has already been through it with both of his biological parents. Can you imagine the outcome if he had to relive it all over again with one of us? I've almost died twice since you and I have been together. How many chances does a person get?"

Virgil thought about all the tough spots he'd been in over the course of his life. "Some more than others. And listen, I understand how you feel, and what you're asking, but I'm simply not ready to hang it up. The day will come when I'll walk away from the job. Hell, it might not be too far down the line, but someday I will. Let me ask you something: What does any of this have to do with Cora and the meeting?"

Sandy set her father's turn-out helmet aside and said, "I know you love your job, Virgil. I'm not asking you to quit. Haven't you been listening? I've made a decision which affects us both, and while that's not entirely fair, I intend to stand by it."

"What decision?"

"I'll go down in history as the state's first female

governor. I'll also make the books for the shortest term. I'm not going to run for re-election."

And Virgil thought, *Thank God.*

But what Sandy had told him only moments ago—that fate and everything else moving forward was largely out of their hands—it was all true. Virgil just didn't realize the depth of it yet.

CHAPTER ELEVEN

The conversation between Virgil and Sandy continued well into the night, and the next morning during the drive over to the Major Crimes Unit facility, Virgil shared the details with Murton.

"How do you feel about the whole thing?" Murton said.

"Relieved. I know the boys will be happy about it. I'll tell you something else, Murt: After everything Sandy has been through, I think it's a wise decision."

"It's hard to argue the point. But I'm wondering if she hadn't been shot and lost her kidneys…do you think she'd feel differently?"

"Based on the way she laid it out for me last night, I'd have to say no, especially if you factor in what Cora told us yesterday. Sandy hasn't done one single thing to prepare to run for re-election. I don't think getting shot is her excuse, but I think it did help her realize what she wants out of life moving forward."

"Probably more alone time with me," Murton said.

Virgil let out a laugh. "Yeah, I'm sure Becky would love that." Then, out of nowhere: "Let me ask you something, if you don't mind."

"Sure," Murton said.

"How would you describe the relationship between Sandy and Becky?"

Murton frowned and said, "Where is this coming from?"

Virgil looked over at his brother. "Why are you answering my question with a question?"

"You mean like you just did?"

"Murt…"

"Okay, okay, I'm just messing with ya. Keep your eyes on the road, huh? I'd like to make it to the shop without an extended layover in the hospital. Anyway, they're solid. As sisters-in-law go, I don't think either one of them have any complaints."

"Let's hope it stays that way," Virgil said.

"What do you mean?"

"Well, Becky wiggled her way into this mess, and it wasn't even necessary. I don't understand why she did it."

"Why else? She loves Small as much as I do. Becky isn't the type of woman to sit around and let others decide her fate. If I was going—and as you know, I did—she was going to go as well."

"I wish she would have stayed out of it," Virgil said. "We'd have one less person to worry about."

Murton disagreed. "I think you're wrong, Jonesy."

"In what way?"

"Because even if she hadn't gone with me—all things being equal—we'd still need her now. If we don't get out from under this thing, accessory after the fact is just as bad."

"Yeah, I guess you're right. How'd it go last night?"

Murton took his time answering. "It wasn't too terribly bad. I think you saw the worst of it before you left. At the very least she took it better than either you or I did."

"She have any thoughts?" Virgil said.

Murton explained the cryptic conversation with Nicky and Wu…and how it ended. "I get the feeling they want to help, and I'm even pretty sure they're going to, but I have no idea how or when. They essentially hung up on us."

"What's she going to do today? Becky."

"She's going to go through her system at the bar and see if there are any holes, or leaks or whatever they're called. Said she'd be there all day."

"Good," Virgil said as he turned the Rover into the MCU's parking lot. "I'd like to keep her away from the shop for a while. By the way, I called Rosie last night and told him to let everyone know they could take the morning off."

"Not a bad idea," Murton said, "at least until we figure out what this Poole guy wants from us…or has on us."

"Only one way to find out." Both men got out of Virgil's SUV and started walking across the lot. Then Virgil looked at Murton and said, "You know, the way we keep referring to Poole…"

Murton got it right away. "I know. It's like looking out the window and saying, 'Hey, the pool guy is here.'"

ODDLY ENOUGH, AGENT POOLE DID BEAR A STRIKING resemblance to an actual pool guy. They found him having what appeared to be a pleasant conversation with the MCU's operations manager, Sarah Palmer. He was much younger than Virgil expected, had blonde hair that was long for a federal agent, and he wore casual pants and a canary yellow golf shirt. Were it not for the fact that he was standing inside the Major Crimes Unit facility, he looked like he might be ready to hit the links.

When Sarah saw Virgil and Murton, she turned from Poole, and said, "Good morning. Detectives Virgil Jones and Murton Wheeler, meet Agent James Poole with the Treasury Department."

Given what Murton had told him about what he'd

overheard outside of Cora's office yesterday, Virgil was ready for a fight. But Poole surprised both men by offering a warm smile that appeared genuine, along with a strong handshake.

"Detectives, it's a pleasure," Poole said. "Thank you for taking the time to meet with me. I understand I'll be briefing your entire team, along with the acting governor."

Virgil and Murton exchanged a quick glance, then Virgil looked directly at Poole and said, "I'm sure Cora will be here any minute. I'm afraid the rest of our unit is tied up for the morning. I'll bring them up to speed later in the day."

Poole didn't seem to mind. "Fair enough. To tell you the truth, I may have overstepped by asking for all of your detectives to be present. The acting governor wasn't too happy with me. I'm certain I owe her an apology."

Murton laughed through his nose. "I have a tremendous amount of respect for the woman, but our acting governor is never very happy with anyone."

Poole's expression let both Virgil and Murton know that he knew the type. Then he said, "In addition to overstepping, I also might have unintentionally offended her by saying I assumed that I'd be meeting with the actual governor…not the woman who fired my brother."

"Sounds like our gal," Murton said.

Poole looked at Virgil and said, "As I understand it, sir, the governor is your wife."

"That's right," Virgil said.

"I've also been made aware of Governor Jones's recent…mmm…difficulties. I hope she's doing well."

"As well as can be expected." Then Virgil decided to do a little fishing. "If you don't mind me asking, how did you happen to hear of my wife's incident?"

Poole gave Virgil a warm smile. "When one of the nation's governors is shot by a former county sheriff—in her own backyard, no less—it tends to make the news cycle."

"I guess so," Virgil said.

Poole seemed to look at nothing for a few seconds, then said, "I have a bad habit of sticking my nose where it often doesn't belong, so I hope you'll forgive my next question. Is your wife handling the anti-rejection meds okay? That's not something you want to fool around with. Miss more than a few doses and it could mean real trouble."

Virgil very diplomatically sidestepped the question. "It sounds like you have some intimate knowledge of the subject, Agent Poole."

"Indeed, I do. More than I care to, actually. My father went through it some time ago. It's not quite as simple as the doctors make it sound. In any event, he had a little liver problem…which is a polite way of saying he had a little drinking problem. He damned near lost his new liver when he got behind on the meds."

"And he's doing well now, I take it?" Virgil said.

Poole nodded. "Yes, very well, in fact. His recovery took some time, though, if I'm being honest with you. He now spends most of his day talking back to Fox News. I can never quite tell if he's in agreement with them or not."

Murton caught Sarah's eye and tipped his head toward the conference room. Sarah, who'd learned the nuances of the MCU in short order caught on right away. She stood from behind her horseshoe-shaped desk, and said, "Agent Poole? If I could show you to our conference room, I'm sure Detectives Jones and Wheeler will be right in…just as soon as the acting governor arrives."

"Yes, of course," Poole said. Then as they were walking down the hall, "I do hope she'll accept my apologies. I was simply having one of those days…"

Virgil and Murton went upstairs and once they were out of earshot, Virgil looked at his brother and said, "What do you think?"

Murton leaned against the wall and crossed his arms over his chest. "I gotta tell you, Jones-man, he wasn't what I expected."

"Me either. In fact, he was the polar opposite of what I expected. Think it was an act?"

"If it was, the guy should take the next flight out to Hollywood."

Virgil raked his bottom lip with his teeth. "What about the questions regarding Sandy's health? Think he was trying to get a reaction of some kind out of us?"

Murton kept his arms crossed and raised his shoulders. "In all honesty, I didn't get that impression."

"Me either," Virgil said. "The problem is, I don't know if that's good news, or bad. On one hand, it'd be nice to know where our little problem is coming from, and I had my money on Poole. If that's not the case…" Virgil let his statement hang.

Murton picked up the slack. "Then we're running blind." He tipped his head over Virgil's shoulder and finished with, "Here comes Cora."

Virgil turned and gave Cora a wave, then both men started back down the stairs. Once they reached Sarah's desk, Cora looked at them and said, "Is that Poole guy here?"

"In the conference room," Virgil said.

"Good, let's go see what the man has to say. What are you guys smiling about?"

"Nothing," Virgil said. "Inside joke. Listen, before we go in, I wanted to let you know I'll need a few minutes with you after Poole is gone."

"That's probably all I'll have," Cora said.

"All I'll need. By the way, I gave the rest of the squad

the morning off."

Cora gave Virgil a sharp nod. "Good thinking. I'd like to keep this whole thing as compartmentalized as possible."

"Is there something going on?" Sarah said.

Cora turned around, almost as if she wasn't aware that Sarah was at her desk. "I think we're about to find out." Then: "My God, I'd kill to have hair like yours."

WHEN CORA, VIRGIL, AND MURTON WALKED INTO THE conference room, Agent Poole stood and went straight for Cora, his hand extended, his face slightly red, his expression full of regret. "Madam Acting Governor LaRue—" That's as far as he got.

"Look, how about we just go with ma'am?" Cora said. "No one needs to use nine syllables to address me."

"Very well," Poole said. Then he started over. "Ma'am, I'd like to offer my sincere apologies regarding the way our initial meeting went yesterday. As I mentioned to your detectives, I was having a difficult day and managed to lose sight of not only my manners, but my emotions as well. I hope you'll forgive me."

Cora, who could play along with the best of them when she needed to, waved Poole off and said, "That's not necessary, although I accept if it makes you feel better. I know about bad days. I also know about busy days. Today happens to be one of them. We're all here at your request, Agent Poole. If you don't have any objections, I suggest we get started."

"Of course." Once they were all seated, Poole looked around the table, then let his gaze rest on Cora. "I'm a special investigator for the Treasury Department. My job is mainly administrative…looking into fiscal irregularities regarding security concerns as they relate to our nation, and other things of that nature…none of which I can really talk about. But essentially I push paper all day. And while I'm known as an investigator inside certain circles at the federal level, I don't do the kind of work your people do. I majored in finance, so I'm basically an accountant with a badge."

Cora let out a weary sigh, then said, "While we appreciate the delineation of your vitae, Agent Poole, if your agency has a specific request for the state's Major Crimes Unit, now would be the time for you to go ahead and make one."

"That's the problem," Poole said. "It's also the reason I'm sort of beating around the bush. The request isn't coming from Treasury. It's coming from my father and myself, personally. Shortly after my brother, Lester, filed the necessary paperwork with the state to run for governor, he went missing. No one has heard from him in over a week. My father and I really need your help."

CHAPTER TWELVE

Once they were finished, Murton escorted Poole out of the building. While that was happening, Cora pulled Virgil aside, and said, "What do you think?"

"Are you asking about our ability to help him, or if he's involved in our other problem?"

Cora turned the corners of her mouth down. "Both."

"As far as his request goes, we have the means, and if I'm being honest with you, as it stands right now I don't think we have a choice."

"Why not?" Cora said. "The MCU is still operating on a selective basis. That means you get to pick your own cases."

"I know," Virgil said. "But Lester Poole is an Indiana resident, a former state official, and is on file as a candidate for governor. If we turn down Agent Poole's request, it could lead to bigger problems down the line."

"In what way?"

"I'm surprised you have to ask," Virgil said. "You're the one who's always preaching optics to me. The man's family member is running for the office of governor. If we don't help Agent Poole figure out what happened to his brother, it makes the whole thing look like we're turning our backs on him and his father to serve our own agendas…both personal and professional."

Cora didn't like it, but she knew Virgil's thinking was correct. "Okay, get the rest of your squad on it. But right now I want all of your efforts—and Wheeler's—going into finding out who has the recording."

"We'll do that. And listen, you'll be hearing from Sandy at some point, probably sooner rather than later, but I spoke with her last night and wanted to let you know she isn't going to run for re-election. She wants to keep it quiet for as long as possible, but I told her I'd mention it to you because I know there are things you'll have to do to prepare. She'll finish her term if and when she's able—which seems unlikely at this point—but then she's out."

Cora's response surprised him. "How do you feel about it?"

Virgil did something he knew Cora wouldn't like, but he did it anyway. He gave her a hug. "Thank you for asking. To answer your question, I fully support any decision my wife makes with regard to her career choices. Plus, it'd be nice to be working for you again."

Cora laughed without humor. "Yeah, well let's hope it's not serving chow to the rest of the inmates. Keep me up. I want regular reports. This is one we can't let get past us, Jonesy."

"It won't. We'll figure it out. I—" Virgil was about to say promise, but cut himself off.

Cora gave him an odd look. "You…what?"

Virgil visibly swallowed, and because he couldn't think of anything else, simply repeated himself. "We'll figure it out."

If Cora noticed Virgil's eyes slide away when he spoke, she didn't say anything.

After Cora was gone, Virgil and Murton decided to go over to the bar and check on Becky's progress. They walked in through the kitchen, said hello to Robert, then as they were about to climb the stairs to the office over the bar, Virgil could hear Delroy speaking loudly with someone inside the walk-in cooler. Virgil tipped his head at Murton, and they both went that way.

When they stepped into the cooler, they discovered it was much warmer than it should have been, and Delroy—while not quite angry—was taking his frustrations out on the repairman.

"What's going on?" Virgil said.

Delroy turned from the technician and said, "What else, mon? Da caterpillars went out again."

"That'd be capacitors, sir," the technician said.

"I know dat, me." Then to Virgil: "It happen almost every month, like clockwork."

Virgil looked at the technician and said, "My bar manager is right. We've been battling this problem for quite some time."

The tech, a lean, middle-aged man with a crew cut and coke bottle glasses looked at Virgil and said, "I know, Detective. But I've been through the system every time I'm out here, and there simply isn't anything wrong. The compressor is fine, the coils are clear, the pressure is holding, and all the electronics test normal on the meter. But for some reason, the capacitors keep blowing out."

"What can you do about it?" Murton said.

"We're trying to find a new supplier, but it isn't easy. The supply chain is still backed up after the pandemic, and I know everyone is tired of hearing about that, but it's the truth. The only ones we can get right now are coming from China, and they don't seem to hold up very well. I've informed your bar manager that until we can find a new supplier our company is going to waive the call-out fees and repair time costs. You'll only be charged for the new capacitors."

"Appreciate it," Virgil said. "How long does it take to change them out?"

The tech bobbed his head around and it made his eyes look like they were swimming inside a fishbowl. "With the type of system you have here, I can usually get the panel off and have them swapped out in an hour or so."

"How about you just leave a box of caterpillars and Delroy swap them out himself? Every time I call it take long enough for you to get here dat our cooler turn to room temperature."

A look of mild shock crossed the technician's face. "I'm sorry, sir, but that's completely out of the question. The liability alone—"

Virgil understood. "Okay, all right, just get us going again, will you?"

"Yes, Detective. And I'll make sure our scheduling people know about the problem. That way I'll be able to get here much faster next time. Our company prides itself on…"

Virgil waved him off. He wasn't trying to disrespect the man, but he had more urgent matters to attend to. "Yeah, yeah. Just get it going, huh?" Then he and Murton went upstairs.

When Virgil opened the office door, he stopped so quickly Murton bumped into him, then had to quickly grab the handrail to keep from tumbling down the stairs.

"Hey, what gives, Jones-man? You damned near sent me ass backward down the steps."

Virgil apologized, then moved inside the office and the relief he felt must have been visible on his face. Becky was smiling, and when Murton finally made it through the door, he was as well.

"We are not from the federal government, but we are here to help Wu," Wu said.

"Man, I can't tell you how much we appreciate you guys being here," Murton said.

"It's our pleasure," Nicky said.

Virgil stepped further into the room, and said, "Listen I know you guys must have just gotten here, but—"

Nicky made a clicking noise with his tongue, then put his index finger to his lips. Everyone got the message. Then he tipped his head toward the office door and said, "It's getting a little stuffy in here. How about we step outside and get some fresh air?"

They all ended up sitting around a picnic table right outside the kitchen entrance. Virgil looked at Nicky and said, "You think the office is bugged?"

"We don't know yet. We brought our gear and were just getting ready to start a sweep. If there's a bug, we should be able to locate it."

"And if there isn't?" Murton said.

"Then Miss Becky's system has been compromised," Wu said. "What other explanation can there be?"

"None I can think of," Becky said.

"Is there anything we can do to help right now?" Virgil said.

Nicky shook his head. "Wu and I will do the sweep. Probably take about an hour if you guys want to wait."

Virgil checked the time. "Yeah, get started. I'd like to know right out of the gate if that's what we're dealing with. If it's not, then Murton and I will take off and head back to the shop."

Nicky and Wu stood, then went inside and back upstairs.

It didn't take quite a full hour, and when Nicky and Wu walked back downstairs they found Virgil and Murton and Becky sitting at a table tucked near the bar's bandstand.

"Anything?" Virgil said.

They sat down at the table with the others, and Nicky turned his palms up. "We've got the best gear money can buy. If there was a bug, we would have found it."

"So my system is compromised," Becky said.

"It would seem so," Wu said.

"What about the systems over at the Major Crimes Unit facility?" Murton said. "Would they be compromised as well?"

"It's much too early to know," Nicky said. "But if I had to venture a guess, I'd say the chances are fairly slim. I know Becky's work, and I also know why you're running two independent systems. So, my assumption is that you've all done everything you can to keep them isolated from each other."

"We have," Becky said.

Virgil looked at Becky and said, "I don't care how much it costs. Take the equipment apart right down to the last goddamned screw if need be. I'll have it all replaced. Both here and at the MCU if necessary." When no one said anything, Virgil looked around the table and said, "What?"

Nicky decided to do the heavy lifting for the group. "I'm afraid it doesn't work that way, Jonesy. This isn't a hardware problem. Hell, it isn't even a software problem."

"Then what kind of problem is it?" Virgil said.

"It is a data problem," Wu said. "A piece of code is buried somewhere in the data sets. It will not be easy, but do not worry. We will locate it."

Nicky finished his partner's thought. "Once we have, there's a good possibility we can trace it back to where it originated."

Becky knew what was coming next. She looked at Virgil and said, "Jonesy, don't."

Virgil couldn't help himself. "How long will it take?"

"I don't know why I bother," Becky said.

"It's a fair question," Virgil said. "We're under a lot of pressure here."

"It's impossible to give you a timeline," Nicky said. "Give us a day…probably two, and then we'll have a better idea."

Murton leaned over, gave Becky a kiss, then stood. "You guys get busy and do what you do. I don't look good in an orange jumpsuit."

Nicky looked at Wu and said, "You heard the man. C'mon, chop chop." Then he ran up the stairs before Wu could catch him. Becky shook her head and followed them up. There was a lot of work to do.

As they were walking outside, Virgil looked at his brother and said, "In case you didn't know, orange is for the county jail. In prison you get big fat horizontal stripes."

Murton, who was fond of his wardrobe, visibly shuddered. "I don't want to talk about it."

ON THE WAY BACK TO THE MAJOR CRIMES UNIT facility, Virgil and Murton talked about if and when they should bring the other MCU detectives in on the case. Virgil was leaning toward no, but Murton wasn't quite so sure.

"It's no different from what we talked about earlier

regarding Becky's involvement," Murton said. "At some point we may need them."

"And if we do, we'll be putting them right in the line of fire," Virgil said. "You said it yourself. Accessory after the fact is just as bad."

"I don't have a problem with holding off for now," Murton said. "But if we do need them, we can't spring the whole mess on everyone at the last minute."

They talked it back and forth all the way to the shop, but in the end, they hadn't come to any sort of conclusion, not that it mattered. When Virgil and Murton walked into the MCU, they found Ross and Rosencrantz, along with Mayo and Ortiz all huddled around Sarah's desk. None of them looked happy to have had the first half of the day to themselves. If anything, they looked upset.

Virgil didn't know what was happening, so he decided to ease into it. He tried on a smile and said, "How's it going, guys? Everyone enjoy their morning off?"

Ross, who was known for being rather blunt at times, looked at Virgil and said, "I think I speak for everyone when I say yes. Until we walked in here."

"What's going on?" Murton said.

"Remember Charlie Reed?" Rosencrantz said.

"MedCap CFO Charlie Reed?"

"That's the one."

"What about her?" Virgil said.

Rosencrantz looked over at his boss. "Apparently,

some time ago she got herself transferred out of the women's correctional facility and into a psych ward down in Madison."

Virgil was a bit underwhelmed, and said so. "Not our problem. Our job is to catch 'em. Afterwards, the lawyers get to decide what happens."

Rosencrantz barked out a laugh, but there was no humor in the sound. "Then we get to do our jobs all over again."

Murton caught Rosencrantz's eye. "What are you saying, Rosie?"

"Just this: She's disappeared from the hospital. The Jefferson County Sheriff's Department is asking for our help."

Virgil scratched at the back of his neck and said, "Well, we may be able to help, but it's going to come down to resources. Murt and I were briefed this morning by Cora and, uh, a family member of a missing person. They'd like all our efforts to go in that direction."

"We're letting distraught family members pick our cases now?" Ross said.

Virgil sighed and said, "Ross…"

"It seems like a valid question if you ask me," Rosencrantz said.

"I'm not," Virgil said.

"Okay," Rosencrantz said. "It's your call. Never mind the fact that we were purposefully excluded from this morning's briefing, which, by the way, has never once happened since I've been a part of this unit. But I guess that's a discussion for another time. Anyway, the Jefferson County cops have a working theory on how she got out. It seems she had some help from one of their newest security guards who hasn't shown up for work since Reed disappeared. He used to be a DNR officer until he got fired, by the way."

Virgil touched his chin to his chest. Then he looked up and said, "Roy Landry?"

"Yup," Rosencrantz said.

CHAPTER THIRTEEN

ONCE REED AND LANDRY HAD THE MONEY FROM THE offshore account, they had a little disagreement about their separate agendas. Reed wanted to go after Getz's money first, then they'd take care of Poole. But Landry wanted to do Poole first.

"We just cleaned out your account," Landry said. "We've got enough money for now."

"No, we don't. I want to do Getz, and then we can take our time and come up with a plan for your guy. What the hell is his name, anyway?"

"Lester. That's all you need to know."

"Whatever. I don't care. We still need to do Getz first."

Landry wasn't having it. "But don't you see, Charlie? Once we have the money from Getz, you won't need me anymore. That means I'll be on my own with my buddy Lester, and I'll still need your help."

"What's the matter, Roy? Afraid I'll run out on you?"

"That's exactly what I'm afraid of. I need you, and you need me. My way simply guarantees we both stay in the game until each of us get what we want."

Reed wasn't happy about it, but in the end she knew Landry was right. "Okay, your guy first, then Getz and the money."

THAT HAD BEEN OVER A WEEK AGO, AND THEY GOT Poole, but it didn't go the way they thought it might. The plan had been to simply kill the man, but when the time came, Landry discovered he was having more fun keeping Poole alive. They took him right from his home just after dark, bound and gagged, and tossed him into the trunk of the car for the drive down to the trailer in Kentucky.

Reed complained about it the entire way back. "This is stupid."

"No it's not. We'll chain him up in one of the bedrooms and leave his gag on. That way I'll be able to beat on him for a while. A bullet is too good for this guy."

"That leaves just one bedroom for you and me," Reed said.

"I'll take the couch. It'll be worth it."

"Is that how you get your kicks these days, Roy? Beating people to death?"

"You said you didn't have any problem with map wiping."

"I don't. What'd this guy do to you, anyway?"

"I told you…it's personal."

"And I told you…I'm the one who knows where Getz lives. If you want your half of the cash, start talking."

Landry let out a sigh and said, "He didn't back my play when I got hassled by a couple of state cops for doing my job. He fired me, then managed to get himself fired as well. That's how I ended up working security at the hospital. I'm sick of everyone using me as their punching bag. It's time to start hitting back…and that's exactly what I'm going to do."

"Sounds like you might be overreacting. It seems to me the guy got what he deserved."

Landry pointed a finger at her as he drove and let his teeth show. "I got canned for doing my job. He didn't. He got fired for *not* doing his job. There's a fucking difference."

They rode the rest of the way back to Kentucky in silence, the only sound an occasional moan coming from inside the trunk of the car.

From there, it only got worse. Once they got back to the trailer, Landry beat on Poole for a couple of days until the man finally lost consciousness and wouldn't wake up. But by then it didn't matter because it was time to go visit Getz and get their money.

That didn't go exactly as planned, either.

ROGER GETZ NEVER LET LUCK FACTOR INTO HIS LIFE. He likened it to a baseball game. In other words, as luck went, Getz knew sometimes you win, sometimes you lose, and sometimes you get rained out.

After he returned from his trip up to Indianapolis to collect his back pay, he grabbed his mail from the box and when he walked into his house he discovered a man he'd never seen before sitting on the living room sofa, his hand wrapped around the claw end of a crowbar, the bar resting casually in his lap.

When Landry spoke, he kept his voice light and full of cheer. "Hello, Mr. Getz. If you try to run, I'll bash your brains in. It's a miserable way to die. Do me a favor will you? Close the front door, if you don't mind."

For some reason, Getz thought the man's good-natured cheer made the crowbar seem much more dangerous. He swallowed, then said, "Who in the hell are you, and what are you doing in my house?"

"We'll get to all that in just a moment," Landry said. "But please…the door, if you will." He tapped the end of the bar on the floor like it was a gentleman's walking stick.

Getz tossed the envelope on the table like it was a piece of junk mail—if a piece of junk mail was worth almost two hundred grand—then did as he was instructed. When he turned back around, he repeated his question. "Who are you?"

"Who I am is not important. What you have is. We've already found the safe in the basement. Open it, and you'll live. Refuse, and you'll experience a death beyond your comprehension."

"Who's we?"

Reed came around the corner with a very large and very empty duffle bag slung over her shoulder. She looked at Getz and said, "Hello, Roger. Remember me?"

GETZ HAD TO THINK ABOUT IT FOR A MINUTE, BUT FINALLY the name came back to him. "You're Miss Reed. You stayed at the estate a while back. You were working for Mr. Said at the time."

"Well, not exactly, but close enough. We need to get into your safe, Roger."

"Why?"

Reed laughed like it was the funniest thing in the world. "Why? Because we want the money. Remember the conversation you and I had? You told me all about your cash in a bag. Said you were saving it for your kids. They won't be getting it now, I'm sorry to say, but that's the way these things go sometimes. C'mon, now. We don't have all day. Let's go down and open it up, and then me and my friend here will be on our way."

"There isn't any money in that safe," Getz said.

Reed tipped her head to the side and made a tsk tsk noise with her tongue. "Surely you can do better than that, Roger."

"I can't do better because it's the truth."

Reed looked at Landry. "Roy?"

Landry stood, walked over and stuck the claw end of the bar under Getz's chin. "It's time to go open the safe."

It didn't escape Getz that all the cheer had gone out of the man's voice. "Why? So you can kill me afterward?"

"No one is going to kill you, Roger," Reed said. "We simply want the money. We'll have to tie you up a little, but if you open the safe, I give you my word we will not hurt you. On the other hand, if you don't open it up, we won't just hurt you. I believe my friend made that very clear."

"I'm telling you the God's honest truth. There ain't no money in that safe."

"Okay, Roger," Reed said. "I'll play along. If there's no money in the safe, then you've got nothing to lose by showing us, right? What's the harm in that?"

Getz knew he was out of options. They'd kill him if he didn't open the safe, so he shrugged and said, "It's your ballgame. Let's go."

GETZ LED THEM TO THE BASEMENT, AND THE SAFE WAS right there at the bottom of the steps. "Quite the setup, Roger," Reed said. "Let me guess…bolted to the floor?"

"Yup. Back wall too. They had to dig up half the yard and take out a section of the foundation just to get it down here. Sorta looked like I was putting in a bomb shelter."

"Enough with the jibber jabber, old man," Landry said. "Open it up."

Getz stepped over to the safe and put his hand on the palm reader. When the light turned green, he spun the dial back and forth hitting each digit exactly right. Then he put his hand on the lever, twisted it downward, and began to pull the door open.

"Hold it," Landry said. "I might have been born at night, but it wasn't last night. You got a gun in there?"

Getz let his shoulders slump. The disappointment on his face was evident. He sighed, then said, "Yeah, I do. It's an Ithaca Model 37 12 gauge. It's for occasions just like this one here."

"Step aside," Landry said. "In fact, move all the way

over to the corner and get on your knees." Then to Reed: "Did you search for other weapons down here?"

"I did. The place is clean."

"It's dank, is what it is." Then Landry set the crowbar on top of the safe, pulled the door open, and discovered Getz had told the truth…on both counts. The shotgun was right there, leaning against the back corner. Other than that, the safe was completely empty.

Reed saw the empty safe and flew into a rage. She grabbed the crowbar and screamed at Getz. "You've got one chance to tell the truth. If you don't, this basement and my face are the last things you'll ever see in your miserable life." She raised the bar over her head like she was getting ready to split a log, and hissed at Getz. "Where's the fucking money?"

"Someone beat you to it," Getz said. "Why do you think I put the shotgun in there? Wasn't gonna let it happen again."

Landry walked over with the shotgun, and gently pulled Reed back away from Getz. "Who took it?"

"I don't have any idea. They came in the middle of the night…all masked up. Made me open the safe just like you done, took the cash and knocked me out cold."

"They should have killed you," Landry said. "It'd save

me the trouble. Charlie, step back here by me. You might want to cover your ears. This is going to be loud." He brought the gun up and tucked it against his shoulder, his face close to the stock, his eyes sighting right down the barrel and pointed it at Getz. "So long, asshole."

Getz, who was already on his knees, turned away and covered his ears as well.

ROGER GETZ HAD HATED TO DO IT, BECAUSE THE GUN really was a work of art. But a gun was only as good as the person using it, and since Getz knew he'd never actually fire the thing, he did what he had to do for his own protection.

Once the shotgun was clamped in the vise, Getz got his equipment out and began to work on the inside of the barrel. First, using a special boring tool, he began to thin the barrel from the inside. By the time he was finished, the barrel—from the chamber all the way down to the front bead sight—was little more than paper thin. Next, he welded the barrel shut about two inches down from the muzzle end, then after everything had cooled, he used a can of flat black spray paint and painted the inside to cover up the weld. If anyone looked down the barrel—and not many people would—it'd look perfectly normal.

Once that was done, he disassembled two shells, and

dumped the powder and shot into the barrel from the chamber end. He sealed it all up with a thin layer of glue, waited for the adhesive to set, loaded a clean shell, then put on a pair of gloves, took a rag and wiped every single inch of the gun down to remove his fingerprints. When that was done he placed the gun inside the safe, then closed and locked the door.

All that had been years ago, and it seemed like a fine idea at the time, but now it was about to be tested in a very big way…

CHAPTER FOURTEEN

EVERYONE WAS STILL STANDING NEXT TO SARAH'S DESK, and when Virgil heard Rosencrantz confirm his suspicions about Roy Landry, he looked at his other detectives and said, "Give us a minute." Then he pulled Murton aside and they walked down the hall, out of earshot of the others.

Murton looked at his brother and said, "If you're thinking what I think you're thinking, I'd think again. And don't give me any grief about using the same word multiple times in a single sentence."

"I won't," Virgil said. "And you're probably right about what's going through my head right now, but we have to go wherever this thing takes us."

"Chasing after a couple of idiots—that'd be Reed and Landry, by the way—doesn't get us any closer to finding out who is behind that recording."

"It might, though," Virgil said. "Look at it this way: Becky, Nicky, and Wu are doing everything they can on their end, and there's nothing we can do to help them. It's a waiting game for us as far as all that goes. And no matter how it played out between Lester Poole and Roy Landry, there is a connection between those two guys."

"You're saying Landry is after Poole?"

"He has the motivation, and the timing works, if nothing else. Landry helps Reed escape, and almost immediately after it happens, Poole goes missing."

Murton looked away in thought and Virgil let him. "What's in it for Reed?"

Virgil shook his head. "I don't know. Maybe nothing more than her freedom. I'm not sure it matters…at least right now. What does matter is finding out who holds that recording, and how they got it."

"And you're suggesting chasing after Landry is going to get us to whoever that is?"

"It's a place to start," Virgil said.

Murton crossed his arms and leaned against the wall. "I'll tell you where we should start, Jonesy. We need to have a chat with Poole's old man."

"Can't do it, Murt. The guy is a former United States Senator, he lives in Kentucky, and other than the fact that his son went missing after filing to run for governor, we've got no reason to look at him."

Murton didn't want to let it go. "He was hooked in

with the intelligence committee. I'll bet he's got friends in nearly every alphabet agency in the country. Think any of those guys—guys who probably owe the man a favor or two—are capable of getting a copy of that recording, because I sure do. His son is running for governor, Jonesy."

"I know the facts, Murt. I'm simply trying to pick a direction. All we have regarding the former senator and his sons is pure speculation on our part. But the one solid link in the chain is Lester Poole's connection to Landry. We've got to follow through with that. Maybe it will get us closer to the senator, somehow…I don't know."

Murton didn't agree. "It's a weak link, at best. What if we use the missing son…Lester, as our excuse to sit down with the senator?"

"To what end? Don't get me wrong. I know we'll have to speak with the man eventually, but whoever sent the recording to Cora knows two things: One, she has it, and two, we work for the woman. Given that, it's not much of a stretch for them to assume we know about it as well. That means—our suspicions aside—we can't confront the senator about the recording…at least not yet. Even if we did, he'd simply deny it all, then end up accusing us of foul play as a means to discredit his son's campaign…a son, I might add, who is currently missing. We've got to focus on Landry, and by extension, Reed."

Murton finally conceded the point. He tipped his head

down the hall, then said, "Like it or not, I think it's time we brought everyone else up to speed."

"We'd be putting them in harm's way," Virgil said.

"And not bringing them in will destroy the MCU no matter how this all shakes out. I trust every one of those guys with my life, and I know you do too. They know how to keep their mouths shut. They're not a bunch of idiots. In fact, they are the polar opposite. These are smart guys, Jones-man. They'll figure it out eventually, and when they do, if we haven't brought them in on it, that trust will evaporate."

Virgil knew his brother was right. "What about Cora? She not only wants this thing buried, she wants the circle kept small…for obvious reasons."

Murton shrugged it off. "What Cora doesn't know can't hurt her. Again, our guys know how to play ball."

"I hope you're right,"Virgil said. "This whole thing feels like it's spinning out of control. It's like we're trying to outsmart ourselves."

Murton rubbed his face with both hands. "Yeah, except I didn't realize it'd be so hard."

VIRGIL AND MURTON WALKED BACK OVER TO SARAH'S desk, looked directly at her, and said, "Call the women's correctional facility where Charlie Reed was being held.

Let the warden know Mayo and Ortiz will be there this afternoon to interview her regarding Reed's incarceration and why she was transferred down to the psych ward in Madison. Make sure she knows it's not a request."

"You got it, Jonesy," Sarah said.

"Also, find out who's running the DNR these days. Cora fired Lester Poole, but she didn't say who is in charge in his absence."

"Should I ask Cora?" Sarah said.

"No, don't do that," Virgil said, much too quickly.

Sarah gave Virgil a tentative smile and said, "Are you okay, Jonesy?"

"Yes, I'm fine. There's just a lot going on right now. Call the DNR office, let them know who you are, and simply ask who is in charge. Let them know Ross and Rosencrantz will be there this afternoon as well to speak with him…or her, as the case may be."

Then out of nowhere, Mayo said, "They have female fish dicks? That seems odd."

Mayo's comment helped break the tension in the room. Murton laughed and said, "These days, nothing surprises me."

Virgil looked at his men, then said, "Conference room. Right now. We've got a few things to talk about."

Virgil left the conference room door open, and once everyone was seated, he walked over to the window and stared out at the afternoon sky. He used the time to frame his speech, but in reality, he was stalling…trying to find a place to start. Ultimately he went with the advice Murton had offered Cora at the statehouse…he started from the beginning. Virgil turned, parked his butt against the window frame, looked at Ross, Rosencrantz, Mayo, and Ortiz, and said, "I have something to tell the four of you. Murton is already aware of everything, and you'll know why in just a minute. But before I go on, you guys need to know what I'm about to say has the potential to not only ruin your careers, but it could very well end up giving you legal trouble. Jail time wouldn't be out of the question, either. That's my way of saying if you don't want to know what's happening, neither Murton nor myself will hold it against you. I give you my word on that." Virgil tipped his chin at the conference room's open door and said, "All you have to do is get up and walk out. There'd be no pushback, no grief, and no one will think less of you for doing so."

The four detectives all looked at each other for a few seconds, then Rosencrantz, who'd been through his fair share of trauma lately over the loss of his fiancé and unborn child, slowly stood, walked over to Virgil, gave his shoulder a squeeze, and headed for the door.

Then he closed it, turned back around and said, "Not

long ago you told me any member of this squad would walk through the fire for me. You think we wouldn't do the same for you or Murt?" Then he sat down and said, "Fuck a bunch of legal trouble. Let's hear it."

So Virgil told them the whole story, right from the beginning…or so he thought.

Getz had never been much for prayer, but when he heard the man say, "So long, asshole," he covered his ears, opened his mouth to equalize the pressure, bent down into a ball and said a silent little prayer. What was the downside?

When Landry pulled the trigger the shotgun exploded in his face, killing him instantly. But Reed was quite a bit shorter than Landry, and had not only covered her ears, she'd turned her back as well and wasn't affected by the blast, other than it scared the living hell out of her. Her hair was covered with blood and gore and bits of things she didn't want to think about at the moment. When she screamed, the sound seemed contained to the inside of her own head.

Reed ran past Getz, gave him a quick kick in the side for no other reason than the fact that she was scared…and pissed. Then she took the steps as fast as she could, got the hell out of the house, and drove away in Landry's car.

Even though he had his ears covered, the blast was still deafening in the enclosed area, and all Getz could hear was a high-pitched whine…not that there was anything else to hear just then. He looked back at his attacker and saw him on the floor, half his head gone. He said another little prayer, this time as a thank you, then stood and opened and closed his mouth a few times to try to clear his ears. That's when he felt a stinging sensation in his right thigh and realized he'd taken a bit of shot that must have ricocheted off the basement's walls. It didn't hurt too bad, and the wound wasn't bleeding very much, so he ignored it for the moment.

He went upstairs and grabbed the envelope of cash, along with a box of his mother's old silverware from the top shelf of his bedroom closet, then went back to the basement. The silverware—which was actual pure silver—went into the safe, with the door left open.

The money went someplace else entirely.

Getz walked over to the far end of the basement, removed a piece of paneling that was tacked to a false wall and set it aside. Then he spun the dial on his old gun safe, opened it up and put the cash inside with the rest of his hard-earned money. After he had everything in its place, the safe got closed, the paneling went back up, then

Getz went out to his front porch, sat down, and sent a text to 911.

My name is Roger Getz. Can't hear right now. Gunfire. Need police and medical assistance at my home. One person dead and I've been shot. My address is…

Virgil and Murton took turns telling their fellow detectives what had happened and why. When they were finished, Virgil wrapped it all up by saying, "So, that's everything. But before we go any further, I want to restate something. So far, all you've heard is a couple of cops telling a tale. You're not involved in the story, and I know you can keep your mouths shut. That means my original offer still stands. Anyone who doesn't want to be even peripherally involved in this can walk away. I'll personally sign off on any vacation time even if you don't have it in the bank. It's up to you."

Mayo looked at Virgil and Murton and said, "I'm in."

"Same here," Ortiz said.

Virgil gave them both a sharp nod, then said, "Get with Sarah, and then do what I told you earlier. Go over to the women's correctional facility and get every piece of information you can on Reed. Reed gets us to Landry, and Landry, hopefully gets us to Lester Poole. If the guy isn't dead, we need to find him."

"We're on it, Boss," Ortiz said. Then he and Mayo left the room and got to work.

Virgil looked at Rosencrantz and said, "You okay, Tom?"

Rosencrantz gave him a smile. "I'm better than okay. You might have just given me the kick I needed to get out of my own head."

"How's that?" Virgil said.

Rosencrantz took his time answering, as if he wanted to formulate his response just right. "Carla isn't gone, you know? She's just…someplace else for a while. We'll all get there eventually. Why not help each other out if we can?" He was looking at Murton when he spoke.

"Good idea," Virgil said. "We could sure use it. You and Ross head over to the DNR office and get everything you can on Landry…and Poole, for that matter."

"You got it, Jonesy."

Ross looked at his partner and said, "I'll be right there."

Rosencrantz clapped him on the back and left the room. Once he was gone, Virgil looked at Ross and said, "What is it?"

"I've got a problem," Ross said. "And based on the way you guys laid everything out, I'm guessing you do too. Although, I'll admit I could be wrong about the last part."

"What is it?" Virgil said again.

"I don't keep secrets from Sarah. I'm going to have to tell her."

Virgil started to point his finger at Ross, but managed to catch himself in time. When he spoke, he made sure to keep his tone as friendly as possible. "Ross, I was hoping to keep the circle as small as possible."

"I know that. I also know what you, personally, did to not only save her, but how you essentially looked the other way when she made sure the man who killed her former lover went into the fire. We still talk about it… Sarah and I. She has her secret with you. Don't you dare think for one minute she wouldn't keep yours."

Virgil knew Ross was right, and for once he didn't try to fight him. "Fair enough. Just try to keep it…uh, you know—"

Ross gave him a dry look. "A secret?"

"I guess that's pretty much the word I was looking for."

"Ask you one more thing?"

"As long as it doesn't involve letting someone else know what this is all about," Virgil said.

"It sort of does," Ross said. "How much of all this does Sandy know?"

"You're starting to veer out of your lane, young man."

"Am I? Because if you don't tell her, it could destroy your relationship."

"And if I do, the stress of it could literally kill her."

Then Virgil saw something he didn't expect from Ross. He seemed to visibly soften. "Is there anything I can do to help?"

Virgil didn't know how to respond, so Murton picked up the slack and said, "We'll let you know. Thanks, kid."

"You bet," Ross said.

Then, just as he was moving out the door, Murton finished with, "Hey Ross?"

"Yeah?"

"Remember when you wrote Landry's name down in your little notebook? You called it your hit list."

"Yeah?"

"You might want to tear that page out…"

CHAPTER FIFTEEN

It took the county cops a bit longer to arrive than Getz thought it would. In fact, it took long enough he was beginning to wonder if they were going to show or not. Then he thought maybe the text didn't actually go through. He pulled his phone out and saw it had, the dispatcher's reply short and to the point.

En route. Wait outside your home.

Getz's leg was beginning to bleed a bit more, so instead of waiting, he went back into the house and retrieved his first-aid kit from the hall bathroom closet. The kit was buried behind a bunch of other things that always get stuffed into a bathroom closet, and since his hearing was still shot, he never heard the cops yelling at him to get on the ground, or to show them his hands. When he didn't respond to their commands, the cops tackled him, put him in cuffs and dragged him outside.

The county cops sat Getz down on the grass in the front yard, and when he tried to tell them what had happened it seemed like they were the ones who couldn't hear.

"Sir, you're going to have to calm down. Please stop shouting."

"I'm shouting because I can barely hear right now. Didn't your dispatcher tell you that?"

"I said stop shouting."

"Get these goddamned handcuffs off of me. This is my house. I'm the victim here. Two people tried to rob and kill me."

"Sir, stop shouting. You're only making things worse for yourself. Do you have any ID?"

"What?" Getz shouted.

"ID…do you have any?"

"What?"

The cop who was trying to communicate with Getz was now in full exasperation mode. He shook his head, then took out his own wallet and showed Getz his driver's license, then pointed at himself, then back at Getz. "ID, sir. I need to see your ID."

Getz got the message, rolled over on his side, and tapped his back pocket with his hands. The cop removed the wallet, opened it up, and examined the ID just as the other officers exited the house.

"That guy the homeowner?"

"Yeah."

"Better cut him loose. We've got a dead one in the basement with an open safe and a destroyed shotgun. Better get CAB on the way. Crime scene too."

The cop who'd been trying to communicate with Getz removed the cuffs, then gave him a sheepish look and said, "Sorry, sir. We didn't know if you were the victim, or one of the attackers."

Getz looked at the man and shouted, "What?"

The cop rubbed his own forehead with his thumb and index finger, then waved one of the medics over. "Take care of this guy, will you? Keep him here unless he needs immediate medical care at the hospital."

The medic said he would, then the cop went inside the house.

THE MEDIC DID A FULL FIELD EXAM ON GETZ AND determined he was not in need of emergency medical care. He gave him a shot in his leg to numb the pain, pulled three shotgun pellets from his thigh, covered it with antibiotic ointment and a large bandage, then gave him some medicine to help him calm down because his heart rate seemed a bit elevated. Then he took out a notepad and wrote a message to Getz, telling him his hearing would slowly start to return, but he should make an appointment with an ENT doctor to have his ears checked, and also one with his family physician to make sure the leg wound didn't get infected.

Getz told him he would, thanked him—much louder than necessary—then sat down on the back bumper of the EMS unit and simply waited.

Two hours later, Jack Grady, the lead detective with Kentucky's Criminal Apprehension Bureau showed up with one of the other detectives in his unit, Justin Cole. The county cops gave the details of what they knew to the CAB detectives, who took charge of the scene.

"Got an ID on the shooter in the basement?" Grady said.

The county cop nodded and handed Landry's wallet over. "Looks like he's out of Indiana. How he got here is still in question."

Getz, who'd managed to recover a fraction of his hearing, looked at Grady and said, "No it ain't." Still a little loud.

Grady turned and said, "You're the homeowner, sir?"

"That's right. But speak up a little, will you?"

"I remember you, sir. You're the caretaker of the Said estate. Roger Getz, if I'm not mistaken."

"That's right," Getz said. "I wish I could say it's nice to see you again, but it ain't, so I won't."

Grady had heard those sorts of comments before, so he wasn't offended and let it go. "What do you mean it's not in question how Mr. Landry got here?"

"You're talking about the dead fellow in my house?"

"I am."

"Because he didn't come alone. There were two of them. I never seen the one in the basement before in my entire life, so I don't know anything about him. The one that got away is named Charlie Reed."

"Can you give us a description of Reed?" Cole said.

"Yup. Short dark hair, about five foot four, good looking, and has a nice ass, if you want to know the truth."

Grady and Cole looked at each other, their expressions a mixture of amusement underlying their professional conduct regarding Getz's portrayal of Reed. Grady squinted an eye and said, "Anything else you'd like to add to your description? What was Reed wearing?"

Getz started at the bottom and worked his way up. "Sneakers…don't know what brand. Blue jeans, and a black, short sleeve T-shirt. Her arms were covered with scars. Some of them didn't look completely healed."

"And how do you know Reed?"

"I don't. We met once, is all…out at Said's estate. This was back when Rick was still alive. He had a bunch of people down to entertain them, and Reed was there. We had a nice friendly chat for about ten minutes, and I haven't seen her since."

Grady and Cole exchanged another glance and this time their expressions weren't a mixture of anything more than enlightenment. Cole looked at Getz and said, "So, Charlie Reed is a woman." It wasn't a question.

"Of course. I thought I made that clear when I was describing her fanny."

"I think we might have missed that part," Grady said.

Getz actually laughed. "Your faces said different."

"Can you tell us what happened here today, Mr. Getz?" Grady said.

"Most of it," Getz said. "Some of it I didn't actually see…like the part when the dead fellow was pointing his shotgun at me. Had my back turned for that. Damned near wet myself."

"Understandable, sir," Cole said. "How about you take it from the top?"

Getz sighed, then gave them the short version of what had happened. "Had to run up to Indy today to, uh, have a word with Mac." Getz didn't want to talk about the money.

"Who's Mac?" Cole said.

"The guy who runs Patty Stronghill's company."

Cole looked away for exactly one second, then turned back and said, "Who's Patty Stronghill?"

"Mr. Said's niece. The former governor of Indiana—that'd be Mac, if you're keeping up—now runs the company. I'm in charge of the company's estate down here, as you know."

"Yes, sir," Grady said. "We're aware. Why did you need to see Mac?"

"That matters about as much as the color of my socks," Getz said. Then before Grady or Cole could push him on his trip to Indianapolis: "When I walked in they were waiting with a shotgun and said they knew about my safe." Then he told them everything that happened, along with a few minor embellishments, because with the cops it was hard to tell where they might land on any given matter. He finished with, "When the gun blew apart, it killed that Landry asshole, scared the bejesus out of Reed, who gave me a kick and took off like her hair was on fire. I sent a text to 911, and here we are."

"Was the gun yours, or did they bring it with them?" Grady said.

Getz, nobody's fool, answered very carefully by saying, "I'm an old man. I don't like guns. Never have. Besides, weren't you listening? I just told you the guy was pointing his shotgun at me. Emphasis on 'his.'"

"Would you have any idea where we could find Charlie Reed?" Grady said.

"Don't have a clue," Getz said. "I've never done any

police work, but if you were looking for a place to start, I'd call Mac. If Reed was connected to Said—and she must have been—then Mac might be able to give you some useful information."

Grady, who didn't really have much to go on, thought Getz's suggestion was valid enough, so he excused himself to make a call. But it wasn't to Mac.

Instead, he called Virgil.

When Mayo and Ortiz returned from their interview with the warden of the women's correctional facility, they sat down with Virgil and Murton and told them what they'd learned.

"It's not much," Ortiz said. "But it's not nothing, either."

"Let's hear it," Murton said.

Mayo took out his notes and said, "The general consensus among the administrative personnel within the system—according to the warden, anyway—was Reed faked her way out."

"How?" Virgil said.

"She started hurting herself. Grew her nails out and started scratching her arms up. It got so bad they ended up putting her in hard restraints. But apparently Reed isn't a quitter because even after they trimmed her nails right down to the quick, she started using her teeth. They said it looked like she was trying to chew her own arms off."

"Why do they think she was faking?" Murton said. "It sounds like classic nut job behavior to me."

Mayo gave them a half shrug. "She stopped talking except for one single phrase. Any time someone tried to speak to her, all she'd ever say was 'cash in a bag.'"

"What the hell does that mean?" Virgil said.

"No one knew. But they had one of the docs come in, and after a series of evaluations, the doc thought it best if she went to the psych ward. That's how she got transferred."

"Does the doc check out?" Murton said. "Any chance they worked it together?"

"Haven't gotten that far yet," Ortiz said. "But we did learn one little nugget that pretty much confirms what we already know about how Reed escaped the hospital."

Virgil was pretty sure he knew what Ortiz was going to say, so he filled in the blank. "Let me guess. Landry was a guard at the prison at the same time Reed was there."

"You got it," Mayo said. "He was fired for, mm, servicing some of the inmates."

"Okay," Virgil said. "Write it up, then check out the doctor who approved the transfer and see if there's anything to look at in that regard. There probably isn't, but we'll want to cover every angle."

"You got it, boss," Mayo said. "I've got an idea, if you're interested."

"Always," Virgil said. "Let's hear it."

"Let me and Ortiz run over to the DNR office, find out where his fellow officers are working and see if Landry was friendly with any of the guys he worked with…you know, like drinking buddies, or whatever. Might be a waste of time, but you never know."

"You're right on both counts, Mayo," Virgil said. "It might be a waste of time, but it's still a good idea. If Landry took Poole and we can find someone he was close to, that person might get us going in the right direction."

"We're on it," Ortiz said, then he and Mayo got back to work.

After they'd left his office, Virgil looked at Murton and said, "Quite a coincidence Landry ended up working at the same hospital where Reed was being held."

Murton waved it off. "Maybe, but like I told Cora, coincidences…they do happen."

"I guess so," Virgil said. "We should probably look into the hospital down in Jeff County. I don't think there's much to learn, but at least we'd be putting on a show of support."

"I don't think we've got that kind of time, Jonesy."

Virgil knew Murton was right. "Yeah, I know. Tell you what, get Cool on the line and have him head this way.

Once Ross and Rosencrantz get back, he can run them down there."

"And what are we going to do?" Murton said.

"Hell if I know."

And that's when Virgil's phone buzzed at him.

CHAPTER SIXTEEN

Sandy wasn't exactly feeling sorry for herself, but she knew what Virgil had told her was true. There was an emotional element to the healing process, and that part of the entire affair seemed to be taking the longest. The one bright spot? She was starting to feel better since making her decision not to run for re-election. It felt like an actual physical weight had been lifted from her person. As much as she enjoyed the work, it had never entirely defined her. Did it add to her sense of self? She used to think it did, and maybe in some small way it had. But after speaking with Virgil and telling him she was going to let Cora take the reins, the amount of relief she felt surprised her more than she thought it would.

Except when the alarm on her phone went off letting her know it was time for another round of meds, the sound made her want to scream…her emotional see-saw tipping back the other way. Then she had a thought: The pain pills were in the gun safe. Was she in such pain a Percocet was necessary? Maybe yes, maybe no, but Sandy knew one thing for certain: The pills did more than numb the physical condition…they helped with other types of pain as well. She'd been very careful with them, and was, in fact, taking much less than what had been prescribed. Given that, she thought, what was the harm?

She took her anti-rejection medication first, then opened the safe, grabbed the bottle of Percocet, shook out a pill, and chased it with a full glass of water. When Sandy put the pill bottle back in the safe, she noticed something she'd not seen before. She reached for the object and discovered it was a small handheld digital recorder. She knew the recorder must belong to either Virgil or Murton because they were the only other people who had the combination to the gun safe. It was, Sandy thought, probably recorded notes on one of her husband's cases. She considered listening to what was on it—if anything—but the euphoric effects of the pain pill were hitting her system already, so she decided it was none of her concern and put the recording device back where it had been, then locked the safe.

Twenty minutes later she had another thought, and it wasn't an original one, either. In fact, it had been on her mind for quite some time. She picked up the phone, and made a call.

Becky, Nicky and Wu were hard at work, tearing into the underlying code of the computer system over the bar. It was slow and laborious work. There were tens of thousands of lines of computer code to look through, and Becky felt like her eyes were about to start bleeding. When her cell phone rang, she answered without bothering to look at the screen. "Becky Taylor."

"Hey, Becks, it's me."

"Hi, Sandy. How are you? Is everything okay? You sound a little fuzzy."

"Oh, I'm fine," Sandy said. "All these different meds make me a little loopy. The doctors said I'd eventually get used to them and the feeling would go away. I'm still trusting them—the docs—but I also have my doubts."

"Hang in there. You're doing great, and it won't be long before you're back in the saddle."

"Well, you might be right about the first part, but my saddle days, as you called them, are all but over. I thought you would have heard by now."

"Heard what?" Becky said.

"I'm not going run for re-election. Cora will run in my place."

Becky's reaction to the news was—much like Virgil's—one of relief. "You know what? I think that's great.

You've done your part and life's too short. Let Cora take the heat for a while."

"That is exactly what I intend to do."

"Listen, I hate to cut you off, but I'm sort of in the middle of something here. Can we talk later?"

"Sure, but I just have one quick question before you go."

"Fire away," Becky said.

When Sandy told her what she wanted, the only thought that went through Becky's head was, *Oh, no…*

When Virgil glanced at his phone and saw who was calling, he put it on speaker so Murton could hear the conversation. His greeting got right to the point. "Hey, Becks. Please tell me you've found something."

"I've found something all right, but you're not going to like it."

Virgil touched eyes with Murton, then said, "What is it?"

"I guess I should say I've found something out, and it doesn't have anything to do with what our Jamaican friends and I are looking for."

Virgil thought he could get away with it since Becky couldn't actually see him, so he rolled his wrist and said, "I'm all ears."

"Don't do that," Murton said. "It's impolite."

"Did he just roll his wrist at me?" Becky said.

"He did indeed, m'love."

"Guys, please," Virgil said. Then into the phone. "What have you got, Becks?"

"I just got off the phone with your lovely wife. She's asked me to do something for her."

"She's on leave from her office," Virgil said. "You don't have to do it, whatever it is."

"This was a personal request, Jonesy. She asked me if I could get into the UNOS records and find out who donated their kidneys to her."

And while he didn't know it, Virgil's initial thought was the same as Becky's: *Oh, no…*

"What'd you tell her?" Murton said into the phone.

Becky let out a little sigh and said, "I told her the truth…or as close to the truth that I could get without crossing a line."

"Any chance you could be a bit more specific?" Virgil said.

"Well, I did make it very clear that the UNOS records are sealed…and for good reason. But you guys know Sandy. She didn't really want to let it go, and she knows what I'm capable of. So I told her we were having system troubles, and they were bad enough that Nicky and Wu were up here helping me, and even if I agreed to take a peek at the records, it wouldn't be anytime soon."

"How'd she take it?" Virgil said.

Becky shrugged into the phone. "Okay, I guess. There might have been some disappointment, but she also sounded a little fuzzy…like maybe the request was nothing more than a whim."

"When you say fuzzy…" Murton said. He let his statement hang, his eyes locked on Virgil.

"Yeah," Becky said. "Like that."

Virgil and Murton didn't see the situation the same. How could they? The pills had almost killed his brother years ago, and now it felt to Murton like they were about to go down the same road.

But Virgil—who knew his wife better than anyone—didn't quite agree, and said so. "She's a strong woman, Murt. After everything I went through…after everything I put her through when I was on the pills…she knows better. I don't see Sandy doing what I did."

But Murton wasn't the type of man to sit idly by and wait to see if things went bad. "And you're one of the strongest guys I know, Virgil. This isn't me blowing smoke up your butt, either. In fact, you better than anyone should recognize all that strength goes away once you cross a certain line."

Virgil nodded. "I'm not disagreeing with you, Murt. But I've been watching her…and the pills. In fact, the other day while she was sleeping I opened the bottle and did a quick count. If anything, she's way behind on what they've prescribed."

Murton let his eyes slide to half-mast. "So were you at one point, as I recall."

Virgil knew it was a debate he couldn't win, so he simply acknowledged his brother's concerns, and said, "I'm watching her, Murt. I'm on it. You've got my word. If I'm being honest with you, I'm more concerned about her curiosity regarding the donor."

Murton didn't get a chance to respond because Virgil's phone buzzed yet again. He hit the Answer button and said, "Hey, Jack. How are things with the Criminal Apprehension Bureau? You're on speaker with Murt, by the way."

Grady said hello to both men, then said, "To answer your question, things are always sort of interesting down here. They seem to get even more interesting every time you and I have a conversation."

Virgil found it hard to disagree with Grady's statement. The MCU and Kentucky's CAB unit had worked together on any number of occasions, and while they didn't always go as smoothly as either Virgil or Grady would have liked, both men had a deep level of respect for each other.

"Is this one of those times?" Murton said.

"I'll let you tell me," Grady said. "Remember Roger Getz, the caretaker of Said's estate?"

"Sure," Virgil said. "I only met him once." Then with just a whiff of sarcasm: "That would have been the time you thought Ross was a professional hitman."

"Are you ever going to stop poking me with that particular stick, Jonesy?"

Virgil let out a little chuckle. "Only when it stops bothering you, buddy. So, what's up with Getz? Did he find another body in the lake?"

"No, but you're not too far off the mark. It wasn't in the lake. This time it was in his own basement."

Virgil was mildly surprised. "Getz killed someone?"

"I'm still trying to figure that part out. He says it was a home invasion, and it probably was, but my crime scene people are giving me an alternate version of events."

"Like what?" Murton said.

"I'll explain everything when you get here."

Virgil was suddenly suspicious. The last time he went down to Kentucky to take a look at a crime scene with Grady, it didn't go well. "Why would we want to come down there?"

"Because as a fellow detective, I thought I'd help you out with one of your cases, even if it is across state lines."

"What case are you talking about?" Murton said.

"The one that's being driven by an ex-senator from my home state. I'm just guessing, but I'd wager you've heard of the man by now. His name is John Poole. It seems his son is missing—you know, the one who recently filed with your state's board of electors—to run for governor."

"We're familiar with the senator, and his missing son," Virgil said. "It's one of our top priorities. Please tell me the body in Getz's basement isn't Lester Poole."

"It's not," Grady said. "But let me ask you this: Are you looking for a woman named Charlie Reed, and a guy named Roy Landry?"

"Yeah," Virgil said. "How'd you know?"

Grady sidestepped Virgil's question by saying, "Because I've found one of them…or rather, Getz did."

"Which one?" Virgil said.

"Roy Landry. Either Getz is lying to me, or Landry managed to blow his own head off with a shotgun. Charlie Reed is in the wind, by the way. Anyway, how's that helicopter treating you these days?"

"It's en route as we speak," Murton said.

"Good. I'll text you guys the coordinates of our location. Try not to keep me waiting too long, huh?"

Ross and Rosencrantz arrived back at the MCU facility just as Cool touched down on the rooftop. Virgil said he'd get with them later, but Murton had a different idea. "Give me two minutes, Jonesy." Then he ran upstairs and told Cool what he wanted.

"That's not a problem," Cool said. "We'll be flying almost right over the place anyway."

"Good enough. Keep her running. We'll be right up."

When Murton got back downstairs, he pulled Virgil aside and said, "Cool told me we'd be flying right past the hospital where they were holding Reed…you know, the one where Landry worked."

Virgil picked up on the idea right away. "You're saying we drop Ross and Rosencrantz there while we go talk to Grady?"

"We'll save a little on the fuel bill if nothing else. We'd have to go down there eventually. Why not kill two birds with one stone?"

"That's a bad cliché to use right before climbing aboard a helicopter," Virgil said. "But it is a good idea."

Five minutes later, they were all on board and headed south. But as Virgil was about to discover, sometimes good ideas don't turn out quite the way he thought they would.

CHAPTER SEVENTEEN

ONCE THEY WERE ALL ONBOARD THE HELICOPTER, Ross and Rosencrantz gave Virgil a verbal report regarding their visit to the state's DNR office.

"So the bottom line is this," Rosencrantz said. "Poole didn't like Landry, and it seems he was a mediocre director at best. And by all accounts, Landry didn't care for Poole, although based on the information we got, Landry didn't really care for anyone, so I guess you have to factor that in as well. Anyway, the whole thing came to a head during the meeting they had with Cora."

"That's not exactly new information, Rosie."

"I'm aware. But unless you want me to make something up—and I know I've said this before—it is what it is. One guy got fired for not doing his job, and the other got fired because he did. To tell you the truth, I'm a little surprised with the way Cora handled it."

"What do you mean?" Virgil said.

"Poole fired Landry right on the spot. She could have stopped it, or even reversed it, but didn't. Kind of makes you wonder why."

Virgil turned and looked out the helicopter's window and watched the scenery pass by below. Rosencrantz's statement had merit. Why did Cora let Poole fire Landry? She had the power to stop it, but didn't. Was she already aware Poole had intentions to run for office? Even if she did, Landry wouldn't have factored into that, and Virgil couldn't make the math work. Another thing to look into…maybe.

They rode in silence for a while, then Ross looked at Virgil and said, "What, exactly, should Rosie and I be looking for at the hospital down here?"

Virgil was still thinking about what Rosencrantz had said. "I'm not sure there'll be much information that can help us, but it might benefit Cora down the line if it ever comes out that she didn't block the firing of Landry when she could have. It's probable—but not yet certain—that Landry helped Reed escape custody."

"So what?" Ross said, in his usual direct manner. "The guy is dead and Reed is still on the loose. What difference does it make at this point if he helped her or not?"

Cool interrupted their conversation. "Two minutes, guys."

"Thanks, Rich," Virgil said. Then back to Ross: "I

know all that. But if you can get definitive proof showing Landry helped Reed, it takes one minor problem off the table. And though I'm not yet sure, it could help us figure out where Lester Poole is, or even if he's alive or not. Get with their security chief, see what you can see, and get a record of everything."

Ross said they would, and ninety seconds later Cool touched down outside the hospital's gate. Twenty minutes after that, he landed in an open field next to Getz's property, then Virgil and Murton climbed out and went in search of Jack Grady.

They didn't find Grady right away, but they did see James Poole hovering just outside the crime scene tape strung around Getz's property.

When he saw them, Poole walked over and said, "Detectives. I'm surprised to see you here. A little out of our jurisdictional boundaries, aren't we?"

"In a manner of speaking," Virgil said.

"What manner would that be, sir?"

Virgil didn't want to waste time by getting into a verbal sparring match, so he simply told the truth. "We were invited down here by Detective Grady to take a look at a crime scene and offer our perspective as it relates to our ongoing investigation."

"I see," Poole said. "I'm wondering if your efforts might better serve my family by focusing on the case within your own state's borders."

"What are you hiding, Poole?" Murton said.

Poole spun on his heels and faced Murton. "It's Agent Poole, sir, and I've nothing to hide. I'm simply doing everything in my power to locate my brother."

Murton leaned forward a fraction. "As are we. How is it that you came to be here today, Agent Poole?"

"I go where I please. As a federal agent, no area is off limits to me."

"Oh, I don't know," Murton said. "I could think of a few. How did you described yourself? Something about being an accountant with a badge?" When Poole didn't answer, Murton pressed on. "Your response, not to mention your attitude, is a bit different from the one you presented last time we spoke. In any event, I'm afraid you've misinterpreted my question."

"In what way?" Poole said.

Virgil stepped into the middle of the conversation, tipped his head at Getz's house and said, "I think what Detective Wheeler was asking is how did you know about this particular crime scene?"

Poole lifted his chin slightly. "My family has a close working relationship with law enforcement in this state."

"Is that right?" Virgil asked.

"If it wasn't, I wouldn't have said so."

"Who notified you of this crime scene, Agent Poole?" Murton said.

Poole shook his head like he was disappointed with the nature and direction of the conversation. He reached into his pocket and pulled out a business card, then wrote an address on the back before handing it to Virgil. "My father would like a word with you both when you're done here. He doesn't like to wait." Then he turned and walked away as if anything else left to say was of little importance to him.

Once he was out of earshot, Virgil looked at Murton and said, "He's lying about something."

Murton, who was still watching Poole, turned back toward his brother and said, "You think?"

"Yeah, I do. C'mon, let's go find Grady."

VIRGIL AND MURTON ASKED ONE OF THE COUNTY officers if he knew where Detective Grady was.

"Last I saw him, he was down in the basement with the crime scene folks."

"Mind if we go in?" Murton said.

The deputy gave them a shrug. "It ain't my show, so it makes me no never mind at all." Then he pointed over Virgil's shoulder and said, "Might want to check with that fellow first, though."

Virgil and Murton turned and saw Justin Cole standing next to the front door. Murton looked back at the deputy, said, "Thanks," then they both headed that way.

Cole saw them coming and said, "Hey, Jonesy, Murt. How's it hanging?"

"Slightly right of center," Virgil said, then laughed at his own joke.

Murton simply shook his head.

Cole gave Virgil a friendly punch on the shoulder. "Keep after it. One of these days you'll have them rolling on the ground and wetting their pants."

"Please don't encourage him, Justin," Murton said. "There's still quite a bit of work to do." Then, right down to business: "Did you happen to see the guy we were just talking to?"

Cole nodded. "Yeah. Who is he?"

"That seems to be the question of late," Murton said. "You didn't speak with him?"

"Nope, just seen him hanging around. Anyway, Jack said you all would be coming down. He's in the basement. Follow me, and try not to touch anything."

"We know the drill, Justin," Virgil said.

"Yeah, yeah. Force of habit."

"I hear ya," Murton said. He was looking at Virgil when he spoke.

Virgil and Murton slipped into shoe coverings and gloves, then went down to the basement where they found Jack Grady having a little debate with one of the crime scene techs.

Virgil cleared his throat, then said, "Hey, Jack. What have you got?"

"Depends on who you ask," Grady said. "I'm leaning toward manslaughter, as is my tech here, but Mr. Getz is trying to sell it to me as a home invasion gone bad."

"Getz is the homeowner," Murton said. "He has every right to defend himself and his property. How do you get to manslaughter?"

Grady turned to the crime scene tech, pointed at a piece of the shotgun barrel on the floor and said, "May I?"

The tech nodded. "Yep. It's been photographed and printed, so have at it."

Grady picked up the section of barrel, then said, "Let's go outside, huh?"

Once they were out of the house, Grady handed Virgil the shotgun's section of barrel and said, "Take a close look and tell me what you see."

Virgil examined the barrel without comment, then handed it over to Murton, who did the same.

"I have some thoughts, but you called us down here, Jack," Virgil said. "I'd like to know your thinking before I offer my own opinion."

"Okay," Grady said. "We'll do it your way. For

starters, the barrel is so thin I don't think it'd handle a firecracker, much less a 12 gauge shell. If you look closely you can see the tool marks on the inside. Someone used a boring tool and thinned it down to almost nothing. I'll tell you something else: That Getz fellow is one lucky son of a bitch. He could have ended up with this entire muzzle end buried in his back."

Murton looked at Virgil and said, "It is awfully thin."

Virgil turned his palms up, looked at Grady and said, "What else?"

"Either of you guys ever do any welding?"

"I haven't," Murton said. "But Virgil does like to try to weld chickens together on the grill. As a point of fact, he's pretty good at it."

Grady wasn't aware of Virgil's grilling problems, so he didn't respond to Murton's statement. Instead, he pulled a penlight from his pocket and pointed it down what was left of the muzzle end. "I happen to know a little bit about welding…mainly because I like to restore old trucks when I have the time, which lately, I don't. Anyway, if you look about three inches down inside this piece of barrel, you'll see a nice clean weld…one that completely blocks off the muzzle end."

"You're saying Getz rigged the gun so it would blowback?"

"I'm having a hard time coming up with an alternative," Grady said. "Who works over a shotgun to blow up in their own face, then takes the same gun and tries to use it in a robbery?"

"Maybe Landry never intended to fire it," Murton said.

"Then why load it?"

Virgil didn't have an answer to that, so he said, "What did Getz have to say about it?"

"That's sort of my problem," Grady said. "He told me he's never seen the gun before in his life. So, either Landry is the dumbest guy on the planet, or Getz is lying to me regarding a crime where a life was taken."

"Based on what we know about the guy, I wouldn't rule out your comment regarding Landry and the planet," Murton said.

"Maybe not, Murt. But if Getz rigged the gun with foreknowledge that someone would use it, then lies to me about it, I won't have any trouble charging him with manslaughter. Pretty sure the prosecutor would back my play."

"Any prints on the stock?" Virgil said.

"Just Landry's."

Virgil looked down at his shoes for a few seconds, then said, "I gotta tell you, Jack, I don't see it."

Grady laughed without humor. "What's not to see? The guy set a trap, baited it with intent, and now he's lying about it. Even if you take everything else out of the equation, the lie alone is enough to charge him."

"Where is he?" Virgil said. "Getz."

Grady pointed over Virgil's shoulder. "Sitting in the back of my squad car…unrestrained, by the way."

"Mind if I have a chat with him?"

"Be my guest," Grady said. Then, before Virgil could get away: "I'm not the hard ass everyone thinks I am, Jonesy. But I do follow the rules. Get the man to change his story and we might be able work something out. If he doesn't, he'll be going into the system."

"Let me see what I can do," Virgil said. "Murt? I'll be right back."

CHAPTER EIGHTEEN

Ross and Rosencrantz met with the hospital's security chief, a young man by the name of Jimmy Warren. He had too much gel in his hair, and wore a uniform that made him look like a school crossing guard.

After the introductions were made, Rosencrantz looked at the man, and said, "Mr. Warren, we'd like to speak with you about one of your patients, Charlie Reed, as well as one of your security personnel, Roy Landry."

"You find them yet? Couple of dipshits, you ask me. Landry took me over the hurdles and I damned near lost my job because of it. I can't say much about Reed because of patient confidentiality, but I'll tell you this: She wasn't as crazy as she let on."

"We've already sort of pieced that part together, Mr. Warren," Rosencrantz said. "About Reed."

Ross leaned forward and looked at the monitors

behind Warren. "What we're looking for is definitive proof showing Landry helped Reed escape. I assume you keep copies of your security footage."

Warren nodded with enthusiasm. "We do, but it's not going to help you much."

"Why not?" Rosencrantz said.

Warren pointed at one of the monitors. "Because the night they took off, the cameras covering the south exit door malfunctioned. Wait, wait, that ain't even right. They didn't malfunction. I'm pretty sure they simply got turned off."

"Why do you say that?" Rosencrantz said.

"Because Landry was covering for me the same night. I had a hot date, so he worked a double. He was the one who was on duty when Reed escaped, the cameras were conveniently out of operation, and Landry hasn't been back since. When I showed up the next morning and checked the logs, I discovered he'd made a note about a malfunction, but when I checked the system, everything was fine. I entered my code, hit the switch, and the cameras came right back online."

"Tell me about that," Rosencrantz said. "The code."

Warren turned the corners of his mouth down. "Not much to tell, really. If you want to turn any of the cameras on or off, you have to enter a code on the keyboard. Like this: Watch the monitor on the top left." Warren typed in a short series of letters and numbers, then said, "There, I just entered my personal code. All I have to do now is hit the Enter key and the camera for that particular monitor shuts down…along with the recording, obviously." He hit the button and the screen went dark. Then he quickly reversed the process and brought everything back online. "When I checked the logs I discovered Landry's code was used to kill the cameras. It ain't exactly rocket science. I don't know what the guy was thinking. He might as well have left them turned on."

"Well, I don't know what he was thinking either," Ross said. "But I can tell you what he's thinking right now."

"What's that?" Warren said.

"Nothing. He's dead."

Virgil walked over to Grady's squad car, opened the back door, then tipped his head…an indication for Getz to get out. Then he parked his butt against the trunk of the car, crossed his arms, rested a heel on the bumper and waited.

Getz climbed out, joined Virgil at the back of the vehicle and said, "I know we've met…it was back when they pulled the Novak woman out of the lake, but I can't remember your name."

Virgil stuck out his hand and introduced himself.

Getz shook Virgil's hand and said, "Ah, that's right. You're from up north, aren't you? Across the river?"

"That's correct, Mr. Getz. I'd like to speak with you about what happened here today."

"Name's Roger, and I hate to disappoint you, Detective, but based on the way that Grady fellow is acting, I'm beginning to think I should call a lawyer."

"That's certainly your right, Roger, but I'm hoping before everyone goes down that road you'd be willing to let me make a little speech."

Getz wrinkled his nose and said, "I guess that would be all right."

"Thank you." Then Virgil looked away for almost a full minute before he spoke, and Getz let him. "I don't think you'd have any reason to know this, but other than my family, Rick Said was one of the best friends I ever had. His death hit me hard, and if I'm being honest with you, in many ways, it still hurts. I guess it always will."

"He was a damned fine man, that's for sure," Getz said.

"Yes, he was. But more than that, he didn't trust easily. You had to earn it."

"How'd you manage that?"

Virgil didn't want to get sidetracked, so he simply said, "The way I earned Rick's trust is a story for another time."

Getz snapped his fingers, then pointed at Virgil in a

friendly way. "No it ain't. I just now put it together. You're the fella who saved Patty from them kidnappers, aren't you?"

"I got lucky, but yes. Out of that one incident a bond was formed between myself and Rick, and through Patty, I believe, still lives on to this day. What I'd like to know is this: How did you earn Rick's trust?"

Getz took ten minutes and told Virgil the story of how he met Said years ago, and how that had led to the job as caretaker of the company estate. He even told Virgil of the payment arrangement he and Said had worked out. "Rick called it cash in a bag. Wasn't really a bag, though. It was an envelope. Either way, the man kept his promise and came down here once a month and paid me ten grand in cash. Never missed one single payment until he died."

"Then what happened?" Virgil said.

"Not sure I follow."

"I mean, did you quit, or…what?"

Getz let out a chuckle. "Nope. Just kept on doing the work. Somebody had to, and I wasn't about to get mixed up in all the infighting with the board. Figured if I tried to get the same arrangement with any of them like I had with Rick, they'd tell me to urinate up a string and toss me out on my butt. Besides, you gotta remember, by the time Rick died, I'd already been doing the job for over ten years. I hardly ever touched a nickel of the money, so I thought, what the hell, I'll just keep the place up. I enjoy the job anyway."

"So you're still working for free?"

Getz let his eyes slide over to Virgil without turning his head. "Patty Stronghill is one hell of a young woman, ain't she?"

Virgil answered without thinking. "Yes, she certainly —" Then his brain kicked into gear and he smiled. "Patty got you back on the payroll, didn't she?"

Getz smiled right back. "Not only that, but she got Mac to agree to the same arrangement, and pay me for all the money I missed out on while I was working for free. The only difference is Mac don't come down here. I have to go to him. That's where I was today. When I got back home, the dead fellow in my basement and Miss Reed was waiting for me."

Virgil found he liked Getz, his feelings based not only on the conversation they were having, but also because Said had trusted the man. "Roger, I'm going to tell you something, and what you do with the information is entirely up to you, but I strongly suggest you listen very carefully and do as I say."

"Can't make any promises, but I'm willing to listen."

"Fair enough," Virgil said. "First, as you know, I'm a detective with the State of Indiana…not Kentucky. That means unless Detective Grady says so, I don't have any authority down here at all. I give you my word he has not done that, so whatever you tell me stays between us, but I need to know about the shotgun."

"Why?"

"Because I'm trying to help. You've managed to paint yourself into a corner by telling Detective Grady you don't know anything about the weapon. Lying to a police officer is a crime. And if the lie is even remotely connected to the death of another individual, you could be in real trouble. Now, if you'll let me, I think I can make it all go away, but you have to trust me."

Getz stared at Virgil for a few seconds, then said, "Can I borrow your phone? Mine's in the house and they won't let me in."

"You going to call a lawyer?" Virgil said.

"Nope."

Virgil reached into his pocket and handed Getz his phone.

"I'm going to step over by that tree yonder, and make a quick call. I'll be right back. Appreciate the privacy."

Virgil told him to go ahead and then waited while Getz made his call. It didn't take long.

Getz walked back over, handed Virgil his phone, and without preamble or hesitation said, "I rigged the shotgun to blow in case anyone ever tried to use it against me. Those sons a bitches come into my own home and they were going to rob and kill me. Think you could convince Detective Grady to let me amend my statement?"

"Sit tight," Virgil said. "I'll see what I can do."

Virgil walked back up toward Getz's house, looked at Grady and said, "I understand your position, Jack, I really do—"

Grady looked at Murton and said, "Here comes the 'but.'"

Virgil held out his hands, palms forward. "There is no but, Jack." Then, like a dope: "But, I'm wondering if maybe a little diplomacy wouldn't serve everyone's interest in the long run."

"How exactly would that work?" Grady said.

"I'm speaking hypothetically here, okay?"

"I'm listening."

"The man was defending himself. Was there forethought? Maybe. But that forethought doesn't rise to the level of premeditation. If an individual in the same situation as Mr. Getz were to amend his statement, could we chalk the whole thing up to a homeowner defending himself during a robbery gone bad?"

"What sort of amendment are we talking about?" Grady said.

"Well, hypothetically speaking, how about admitting to ownership of the shotgun as a means to let the bad guys take themselves off the map."

"Why does everything have to be so complicated with you, Jonesy?"

"What's complicated? The guy made a dumb choice. He could say he was in shock while being questioned, or his hearing was still off, or anything along those lines. A jury would take one look at him and think, 'Grandpa,' and the whole thing would get tossed before the judge's coffee got cold. What do you say?"

Grady sighed and said, "Bring him over."

"I can, and I will," Virgil said. "But I gotta hear you say the words, Jack."

"Yeah, yeah, if he amends his statement, he's off the hook. I wouldn't be offended if he managed to work in an apology as well."

Virgil went and got Getz, gave him the particulars, then they headed over to talk to Grady. Along the way Virgil said, "Stick to the facts, use as few words as possible, and apologize. You might want to start with the apology."

Getz looked at Virgil and said, "You ever notice how sensitive everyone is these days?"

Grady kept his word, and Getz was in the clear. When it was all wrapped up, Getz looked at Grady and said, "Any idea when I can have my house back?"

"Probably tomorrow," Grady said. "My department will put you up in a hotel for as long as it takes us to clear out."

"Appreciate the offer, but that won't be necessary," Getz said. "I've got a standing invitation to use the Said estate if no guests are present. Since there's nothing on the schedule at the moment, I'll just stay there. I assume I'm free to go?"

"You are," Grady said. "Word of advice?"

"Sure," Getz said.

"Don't ever lie to a police officer. You have the right to remain silent, but you can't lie. It only leads to trouble down the line."

"Lesson learned," Getz said, then turned and walked away.

But Virgil wasn't quite done with the man. He chased him down, and said, "Hey, Roger. Hold up a second."

Getz stopped and turned, his face a question. "Yes?"

"If you don't mind me asking, who did you call when you used my phone?"

"We were speaking of trust, weren't we?"

"Yes," Virgil said.

"I called someone I trusted to see if you were worthy of mine. I was pretty sure you were, but it never hurts to check. Anyway, turns out I was right."

"Good to know," Virgil said. "But it doesn't exactly answer my question."

Getz gave Virgil a kind smile. "Check your recents, Detective. I didn't erase the number. Thank you for your help." Then Getz turned and was gone.

Virgil pulled out his phone, brought up the recent calls list, then smiled. The last outgoing call had been to Patty Stronghill. And Virgil thought, *Thank you, Rick.*

Virgil made a quick call to Rosencrantz and asked if they were finished at the hospital.

"Yeah, we are. There's no question, Jonesy. Landry helped Reed escape. He essentially walked her right out the door."

"Okay, I'll let you fill me in on the particulars later. I'm going to send Cool to pick you guys up. We've got another stop to make down here, and I wouldn't mind a show of force."

Rosencrantz said they'd be ready, and after Virgil got Cool headed back across the Ohio River, he and Murton spent the wait time bringing Grady up to speed on what they knew about Lester Poole's disappearance…which, admittedly, wasn't much. They talked it around without coming to any sort of meaningful conclusion, then Virgil asked Grady a question.

"Do you know, or have you ever met James Poole? He's the senator's other son."

"I know who he is," Grady said. "But I've never met the man. Heard he was with the feds in some capacity. Wouldn't recognize him if I passed him on the street."

"He was here earlier," Murton said. "You were still inside. Cole saw him."

Grady was a little confused. "What's his role in all this?"

"Good question, Jack," Virgil said. "Without telling you how to run your side of the investigation, maybe you should look into that. When we asked him how he heard about what happened here today, his response was less than forthcoming."

"What, exactly, did he say?"

"That his family has a close working relationship with law enforcement in this state. When we pressed him about his knowledge of this particular crime scene he refused to answer, then left. That was right before he summoned us to his father's house. It's your state, Jack. Care to ride along?"

CHAPTER NINETEEN

GRADY'S ANSWER SURPRISED VIRGIL. "THE MAN IS A political powder keg. I'll let you guys take the point. You'll want to watch your yourselves. He keeps a bit of security around him."

"I've never known you to back away from a fight, Jack. What's going on?"

"I'm not backing away. I'm being careful. Weren't you listening? I just told you the man is connected at levels that are way over my head. My position is political, Jonesy, just like yours. One misstep on my part and the next job I'll have will be working as the assistant manager at the Cineplex. Besides, you said the family reached out to you. Why do you think that is?"

"We have our suspicions," Murton said.

"Care to share them?"

Virgil stepped back into the conversation before they

ended up in the ditch. "I'm pretty sure James Poole reached out because his brother, Lester, is from Indiana. They probably left your department out of the loop because they consider it an Indiana matter."

"That's because it is," Grady said. "Why do you think I told you guys to take the point? The ex-senator doesn't live in Kentucky anymore. He's a resident of Indiana now."

"What?" Virgil said. Then he reached into his pocket and pulled out the business card James Poole had given him. The address was listed in Peru, Indiana, up in Miami County, which was near the Grissom Air Force Base. He showed the card to Murton, who simply shook his head in disbelief.

Virgil looked at Grady and said, "Ask you something?"

"Sure."

"Anything out of the ordinary going on in your department these days?"

"Care to be more specific?"

"I'm afraid I can't," Virgil said. "Let me ask it this way: Has any information come to light from your department that shouldn't have? Confidential information."

"None I'm aware of. We run a pretty tight system."

"Word of advice?"

"Always," Grady said.

"Run a sweep of your offices, and check your system for leaks."

"What's going on, Jonesy?"

Off in the distance they could hear the beat of the helicopter's rotor blades. "I wish I knew, Jack. But someone is running a game on us. I intend to put a stop to it…any way I can."

Then Grady said something else that surprised Virgil…not because of the question itself, but the timing. "How's Sandy doing, by the way?"

Grady went back to work at the Getz crime scene, and Virgil and Murton headed over to the field where the helicopter had just landed. Virgil looked at his brother and said, "Better call Becky." He didn't have to explain why.

When Becky answered, Murton didn't waste any time. "How long to get out of CAB's system and erase any tracks of our presence?"

"I've got an emergency escape set up," Becky said. "All I'd have to do is pull the plug, so to speak, and it'd be like we were never there. I'd hate to use it unless we absolutely have to though, because it'd be a lot of work to get back in."

Murton didn't hesitate. "Pull it. I'll explain tonight. Gotta run. Our ride is here."

Once the call had ended, Virgil looked at his brother and said, "How long?"

"She said two minutes."

"Good enough. C'mon, let's go meet the man behind the curtain."

Murton looked at the helicopter as they walked over. "Cool's going to be pissed."

Except Cool didn't really care. He looked at Virgil and said, "We're going to have to stop and refuel in Indy, though."

"That's fine," Virgil said. "If I'd have known the guy lived up by the base, I would have kept you down here."

"You like your job?" Cool said.

"Of course."

"Me too. I'm always up for the stick time. Ready when you are."

Virgil handed Cool the business card Poole had given him and said, "This is our destination. Might want to check it out on the map and see if there's a place to land on his property. I'm hoping there is…for more than one reason."

"You want an entrance?"

"Like you wouldn't believe," Virgil said. "Life's too short. Why not have some fun?"

Once they were in the air, Virgil asked Ross and Rosencrantz about the details of their interview at the hospital.

"I know I keep saying this," Rosencrantz said. "But there isn't much to tell. The security chief, who looked almost old enough to drive, by the way, took us through their system and showed us the logs. It's clear Landry and Reed worked her escape together. While there was no actual footage of the escape itself, he did have quite a bit that showed Landry and Reed interacting with each other on more than one occasion. Even got video of him passing her a set of scrubs. I've already emailed everything to Sarah back at the shop."

"Anything else?"

"Nothing to help us find Reed, or Lester Poole, but Landry told his boss he'd forgotten his keycard at home and had him code another. There's also footage of him passing the card to Reed."

"Okay, listen: When we get back to Indy—Cool has to refuel the helicopter—I want you and Ross to go back to the MCU and dig up the case notes on MedCap and Freedom Pharm. I want every scrap of information we have on the woman. Sarah is getting pretty good with the computers, so maybe she can do a little digging. Becky's tied up, for obvious reasons."

Rosencrantz said they'd do just that, and while Virgil was fairly certain it wouldn't amount to much, it was a place to start. What he didn't realize at the time was the information he needed went back further than Reed and MedCap. Much further.

When they were less than two minutes away from Senator Poole's property, Cool came over the intercom and said, "If you guys want an entrance, you're about to get one. Use the shoulder harnesses and buckle up tight now. This is going to be a blast."

Virgil and Murton did what Cool asked and tightened their seat belts. Thirty seconds later Cool put the helicopter into a spiraling dive until he was less than fifty feet off the ground. Then he poured the power to it, went screaming over the top of Poole's house, dropped even lower once he'd cleared the roof, then spun the chopper on its tail and set down right in the backyard, as close to the house as possible. The rotor wash upended most of Poole's outdoor patio furniture, and one of the chairs hit the rear French doors hard enough to shatter the glass.

Once they were down, Murton looked at Virgil and said, "He's going to be pissed."

Virgil let out a snort. "Yeah, this time you're probably right. I hope he is. I want this guy off balance from the start. You with me?"

"Like you wouldn't believe," Murton said. Then he

pointed out the window of the helicopter and finished with, "Look, here comes the cavalry."

Virgil slid the door open and said, "Fuck 'em. We were invited."

Neither Virgil nor Murton knew how many security personnel Senator Poole had, but they knew he had at least two, because they ran through the opening of where the French doors used to be only moments ago. The men were dressed in black from head to toe, had military buzz cuts, and short-barreled automatic rifles with suppressors slung from shoulder harnesses.

Virgil and Murton got their badges out, then stepped from the helicopter like they didn't have a care in the world. The security men kicked a few pieces of broken furniture out of their way, their anger evident, then raised their guns at Virgil and Murton and began screaming at them.

"This is private property. Down on the ground right now. We are authorized to use deadly force if necessary. On the ground, on the ground."

Virgil never took his eyes off the men running at them, but he did speak quietly to his brother. "I've got the one on the left."

"Roger that," Murton said. It sounded like he was about to ask someone to pass the salt.

Virgil and Murton both had their hands out, away from their bodies, their guns still holstered. Virgil knew there wouldn't be a gunfight. The helicopter was clearly marked with both the state seal, and the ISP emblem. Still, the men kept coming and shouting the entire time.

"Amateurs," Murton said. "If they meant business, they wouldn't be shouting, they'd be working. Whoops, here we go."

The man directly in front of Murton lowered his rifle and let it swing from its harness. He pulled out a tactical baton, flicked his wrist to extend the weapon, then took a vicious swing at Murton. But Murton was ready. Instead of backing away or trying to duck under the baton, he stepped into the swing, dropped his shoulder beneath the man's armpit, used his attacker's momentum against him, then spun the man around, the impetus of his movements more like a dance than a fight. Murton swept the man's legs out from beneath him, grabbed the baton, and hit him in the throat just hard enough to take him out of play. When he turned to assist Virgil, he discovered it wasn't necessary.

While Murton's movements had been graceful and calculated, Virgil's were more direct and to the point. He waited until his attacker was within arm's reach, then simply punched him—hard—right in the nose. The man staggered back, and Virgil matched him step for step. When the man set his feet to try to stay in the fight, Virgil kicked him in the groin. The man bent forward in shock and pain, and Virgil landed an uppercut to his nose yet again, and then it was over. Fifteen seconds later both security men were handcuffed in the grass, and disarmed.

Murton looked at his brother and said, "Told ya. Couple of amateurs. I bet they bought their clothing at the Halloween store."

When Virgil looked back at the helicopter, he saw Cool leaning against the side of the aircraft, pretending to examine the fingernails of his left hand.

"You guys good?" Cool said. When he saw the looks Virgil and Murton gave him he said, "What? I'm a lover, not a fighter." Then he pulled his right hand from behind his back, holstered his weapon, and finished with, "I'll be out here whenever you're ready to go."

Then Virgil saw something so surprising he wondered if maybe his brain was playing tricks on him.

A well-dressed man walked out through the same shattered patio door, looked around at all the broken furniture and the handcuffed security men in the grass. When he finally let his eyes settle on Virgil and Murton in the backyard, he smiled and said, "Good afternoon, Detectives. If you've had your fill of mayhem for the day, step inside won't you?"

The man wasn't Senator Poole, or his son, James.

It was Mac.

CHAPTER TWENTY

Virgil and Murton walked over to where Mac stood, both men somewhat at a loss for words. Finally, Virgil said, "Mac, what the hell are you doing here?"

"It's good to see you too, Jonesy. That's a question I'll be happy to answer, but I'm afraid it will have to be in a different setting…and at a different time. I was just on my way out. Nice entrance, by the way."

"I don't like being summoned," Virgil said.

Mac ran his tongue across his perfect teeth and said, "I know the feeling."

"Where's Senator Poole?" Murton said.

Mac looked at the broken patio furniture and the busted French doors. "Based on what I know about the man, if I were to venture a guess I'd say he's inside trying to contact his attorney. Was all this really necessary?"

"Probably not," Virgil said. "But you've got to get

your kicks when you can." Then he jerked his thumb over his shoulder. "What's with the goon squad?"

Mac raised his eyebrows, his expression flat. "The man's an ex-senator. He's accustomed to having people he can order around."

"Does he need them?" Murton said.

Mac glanced out at the two men in the backyard. "No…I'd say he probably needs someone better. This whole situation with his son has him spooked. He doesn't want to be next. Any leads on that, by the way?"

"We can't officially comment about an ongoing investigation," Virgil said. "You know that, Mac."

"Indeed I do. Maybe next time we speak—unofficially, of course—I can answer your question and you can answer mine."

Virgil squinted an eye at his friend and former boss. "Maybe. Why not come over for dinner this evening? I know the boys would love to see you, as would Sandy. Seven o'clock work for you?"

"I believe it will," Mac said. "Mind if Nichole comes along?"

"Absolutely not," Virgil said. "She is welcome any time, Mac…as are you."

"Thank you." Then Mac tipped his head toward the inside of the house. "Go easy on the man, Jonesy. His son is God knows where, and it's tearing him up."

Virgil said they would, then he and Murton walked

into Senator Poole's house like they owned it, Mac's request already drifting away like a dream caught in the sweet evening breeze.

THEY FOUND POOLE INSIDE THE KITCHEN, HIS BACK turned away as he poured himself three fingers of bourbon. His hair was a combination of silver and gray, and he was dressed casually, like he might have just returned home from an afternoon at the tennis club. When he spoke, he didn't bother to turn around. "Was it absolutely necessary to damage my home and property upon arrival, Detectives?"

Virgil had many talents—his issues with grilling chicken notwithstanding—and among them was the ability to verbally spar with those who thought their station in life was above his own. He didn't answer until Poole turned to face him and Murton.

"I asked you a question, Detective."

"I heard you, sir. Absolutely is an interesting word, isn't it? As an adverb, it means without restriction or limitation. You'll find I have very few of either as they relate to my job, or how I do it. The state will cover any damage done here today. They'll also most likely bring charges against your two poodles out in the backyard. Threatening police officers with violence in any setting is a serious offense."

"Those men are no longer employed by me. They'll be replaced before the evening is out, I assure you."

"Might want to go for the upgraded model next time," Murton said. "Excuse me for a moment. I need to make a quick call."

After Murton had stepped aside, Virgil looked at Poole and said, "I'm surprised to see you drinking, Senator."

"Why?"

"Because recipients of a liver transplant generally aren't allowed to consume alcohol."

"No one tells me what I'm allowed, Detective Jones. That's something you should keep in mind. In any event, I don't know where you're getting your information, but I've never had a transplant of any kind."

Murton had just stepped back within earshot and caught the tail end of Poole's statement. "That's not what we were told."

"Then you were misinformed."

"That's not outside the scope of possibility," Virgil said. "But I don't yet have reason to doubt the authenticity of any statements made regarding the matter."

"Then you'll have to take my word for it," Poole said.

"Your word doesn't carry much weight with myself or my partner," Murton said. "Why not simply prove us wrong?"

"Because you can't prove a negative."

"In this case you can," Virgil said. "Remove your shirt, sir."

"I will do no such thing, Detective."

Murton stepped close to Poole, gave him a nasty smile, and said, "Take off your shirt or I'll rip it from your body."

"Step back, Detective. I'm not intimidated by either your threats, or your antics upon arrival at my home. And make no mistake, if you put your hands on my person it will be the end of both your careers."

"Hasn't that been your goal all along, sir?" Virgil said.

Poole frowned, his expression one of genuine surprise. "Excuse me? I'm afraid I don't understand."

"I think you do," Murton said. "And, as a point of fact I no longer wonder where your son learned his acting skills. Now take off your goddamned shirt. You can do it here, or over at the Miami County jail. I'll let you decide. I've already got two deputies en route to take out your backyard trash. You're welcome to join them."

Poole took a long drink of his bourbon, draining the entire contents of the glass. Then he set it gently on the counter and removed his shirt. His chest was covered with white hair, his stomach surprisingly flat for a man of his age.

"Raise your arms and turn around," Virgil said.

Poole turned a full circle, his arms out and away from

his body. When he finished his turn, he was smiling, but there was no light in his eyes. He looked at Virgil and said, "As you can see, I have no scars on my body." Then he turned and faced Murton. "Perhaps you'd like me to remove my pants as well. Once you're on your knees you might discover you've found a new calling in life."

"Vulgarity doesn't suit you, sir," Virgil said. "My wife is not going to run for re-election. Your family has all but won. Why are you trying to destroy us?"

"That's the second time you've accused me of something. I don't know what you're referring to, or why you think I'm involved in whatever you're speaking about. Either be more specific, or drop it."

"We'll drop it for now," Murton said quickly, his eyes on Virgil. "Put your shirt back on."

Poole pulled his shirt over his head, and when he spoke next, his voice was softer, almost kind, and his eyes were filled with moisture. He focused on Virgil and said, "I'm aware of your wife's difficulties, Detective. I know it's not my business, but I do wish her well. I'm hoping her recovery continues to go as expected." Then before Virgil could wrap his head around the dramatic change in the senator's attitude and tone, Poole placed his hand gently on Murton's shoulder and said, "It has always been my experience that when words become weapons, nobody wins. Your partner is right. Vulgarity is not my style, and it has never served me well. I apologize for my remarks.

Please…tell me. Do you have any idea where my son, Lester, is?"

Charlie Reed had a problem, but she had always been a problem solver. Her current dilemma? She was stuck in a shit box single wide in the middle of Humpville, Kentucky with a prisoner she knew very little about. When she checked on the man chained in the back bedroom, she discovered he was no longer unconscious, but his injuries weren't exactly minor. His face looked like a Yokohama squash that might have been pulled from the garden well past its use-by date, his right arm appeared to be broken, and his eyes were mere slits.

Reed looked at him and said. "Can you hear me? Nod if you can."

Poole nodded and moaned at the same time.

"Okay, there are some things you should know, and chief among them is this: I don't give two genuine shits about you. I don't care if you live or die. Are you hearing me on this? Exactly zero shits given. That's number one. Number two—and this is just to prove I'm not a complete monster—the man who took you from your home and beat you half to death is now dead himself. If nothing else, that should give you some sense of satisfaction."

Poole moaned again.

"We were in it together, you see," Reed said. "I was supposed to help him—which I did—and he was going to help me. That last part went bad so fast it was almost comical. It actually would have been pretty amusing, except I was going to get my hands on over a million in cash…cash that was going to get me out of this country for good. My current thinking is you can help me with that. What do you say? Want to buy yourself out of this little dilemma you currently find yourself in?"

Poole's legs and hands were chained together and attached to the bed frame. But since his hands were bound in front of him, he still had some movement. When he tried to reach up and pull the gag from his mouth, his broken arm flared and he passed out again.

Reed shook her head, and thought, *pussy.* Then she rolled him, dug his wallet out of his back pocket and looked at the ID. After that, she turned on her computer and went to work. When she finally discovered who she had locked up in the trailer, she laughed like a crazy woman, which, of course, she was.

ONCE BACK AT THE MCU FACILITY, MURTON PULLED Virgil into his office and said, "We might have overplayed our hand with Senator Poole."

"Maybe," Virgil said. "But only if he's the one who

managed to get his hands on the recording. I'm not so sure it's him."

"You're thinking the son, James?"

Virgil nodded at his brother. "I am. I'm not one hundred percent, but you have to ask yourself, why make up a lie about a transplant his father never had?"

Murton gave him a half shrug. "Some people lie just because they can. Maybe it was nothing more than a way to try to gain our cooperation in looking for his brother. He gives you some false sympathy for Small, and does so by tossing a little empathic manure around the room."

"To what end, though?" Virgil said. "We'd have done it anyway. We are doing it."

Murton looked away in thought for a few seconds. "I don't know. None of this makes any sense."

They talked it back and forth for a while, then Virgil said, "We need more help. I want Becky down here working our system at the shop. Let Nicky and Wu chase down the computer code at the bar."

"She's not going to like that, Jonesy."

"Probably not, but we need hard intel on each of the Pooles…for more than one reason. She's the only one who can get it. Give her a call?"

Murton made a rude noise with his lips. "So much for brotherly love." Then, "Hey, where are you going?"

"I don't want to witness the telephonic carnage. I'm going to check in with Ross and Rosencrantz and see if they've come up with anything out of the MedCap and Freedom Pharm files."

After Virgil left the office, Murton took out his phone and stared at it for a long time. Then he finally made the call. "Hello, love of my life. Listen, there's been a slight change of operational plans…"

VIRGIL WALKED INTO THE CONFERENCE ROOM WHERE HE found Ross and Rosencrantz going through stacks of notes and reports regarding the MedCap case. "Anything?"

"Three paper cuts and enough whining that I'm beginning to think we should order a cheese tray," Ross said.

Rosencrantz let his shoulders sag. "I'm not whining. I'm simply stating paper cuts hurt like a mother."

"I'm looking for more of a professional answer, guys."

"Nothing yet," Rosencrantz said. "We're still sorting. Tell me again what we're hoping to find, because I gotta tell you, Jonesy, I'm not seeing it…whatever it is."

"It's a place to start, Rosie. Reed was in the MedCap mess up to her neck, and then she got involved with Landry, who we believe took Poole. If we can find Reed, we can probably get to Poole, assuming he's still alive. Once that's cleared, I'm hoping it will lead us down a path that helps solve our other problem."

"Sounds like quite the long shot," Rosencrantz said.

"That's why Ross is helping you. Find me something, guys. We need it."

"Care to join us?" Ross said.

"I can't."

"Why not? What are you doing?"

Virgil started backing out of the room. "I, uh, have dinner plans. Keep after it, huh? See you in the morning." Then he hurried from the building.

He only looked over his shoulder twice along the way.

CHAPTER TWENTY-ONE

During the drive home, Virgil asked Murton about Becky. "How'd she take it?"

"Surprisingly well. I think it had something to do with my skill set of never-ending charm and good-natured cheer."

Virgil laughed through his nose. "More like your never-ending line of bull—"

Murton cut him off. "Better watch it, Jones-man. We're almost home. You gotta get in the groove, or Jonas will have you for dessert."

"Yeah, you're probably right." Then as they turned into Virgil's driveway: "Mac and Nichole are already here."

"How do you want to play this, Jonesy?"

"Carefully. But I do think—mainly because Mac is a friend more than anything—that we can do what he suggested. We can unofficially let him answer our question as to why he was with Senator Poole."

"And his question to us?" Murton said.

"That's where we need to be careful."

"You know what? Something just occurred to me. If Nicky and Wu know what's going on regarding our little problem, then Nichole probably does as well. If that's the case…"

Virgil picked up the thread for his brother. "Then so does Mac."

"Well, let's go say hello and see what happens."

Mac and Nichole were sitting on the front porch with Sandy. When Virgil and Murton walked up, Mac stood, shook hands with both men, and Nichole gave them each a hug. "It's good to see you again, guys," Nichole said. "Although I do wish it was on the island."

Virgil gave her a wink and said, "Next time…I hope." Then he bent down and gave Sandy a kiss. "How are you feeling?"

"I'm okay, Virg. A little tired of that question though, if I'm being honest with you."

Virgil knew the feeling, so he gave his wife another kiss, then parked his butt against the porch railing. He looked at Mac and said, "I hope we haven't kept you waiting too long."

"Not at all," Mac said. "As a point of fact, we're a little early. You're, uh, not planning on doing any grilling are you?"

Virgil gave Mac a dull stare. "No." He drew the word out into as many syllables as possible. "Delroy is bringing home some of Robert's specialty pizzas. I'm sure he'll be here any minute. Take a walk with me and Murt? There's something I want to run by you."

Nichole laughed. "Jonesy, you're about as subtle as a stump sometimes. How about if Sandy and I go inside and catch up on all things women related?"

Virgil glanced at his wife, her expression a mixture of confusion, and something else. Virgil thought it might be annoyance. But then Sandy stood, gave her husband a hug and said, "I love you, Virgil Jones. Maybe one of these days you'll fill me in regarding whatever is going on lately. I am still the governor…at least for now." Then Sandy and Nichole went into the house, the front door closing a fraction harder than necessary.

Murton looked at his brother and said, "Smooth."

Virgil waved him off. "Yeah, yeah. C'mon, let's all take a walk."

The three men ended up sitting down by the pond, their chairs tucked into a tight little triangle near the water, next to Mason's cross. After Mason had died, Murton, Delroy, Sandy, and Virgil had planted a willow tree on top of Mason's blood-soaked shirt. The tree was later destroyed by a freak summer storm that popped up out of nowhere, and Virgil, though heartbroken at the time, had carved the stump into a cross to honor his father. His life hadn't been the same since.

Virgil decided to ease into the conversation. He looked at Mac and said, "Did you hear about Roger Getz?"

"No. I did meet with him not long ago down at the estate. It was Patty's idea. What's going on?"

"Jack Grady with CAB called me and asked us to come down." Virgil hit the highlights of their trip and explained why they went, then finished with, "So, Getz will be okay, but Reed is still out there, and we believe she and Landry have—or had—Lester Poole."

"When you say had…"

"The truth is, Mac, we don't know if the man is alive or not."

Mac looked out across the pond for a few seconds, then said, "I'd like to make a casual observation, if I may. There's a good chance you won't like it."

"Let's hear it," Virgil said.

"I have the impression the Major Crimes Unit is moving a little slower than normal when it comes to finding Senator Poole's son. Is that a fair or accurate statement?"

Instead of answering Mac's question, Virgil asked one of his own. "Did Nichole happen to mention why Nicky and Wu are up here?"

When Mac answered Virgil, he had his eyes on Murton. "She mentioned something to the effect of a major computer glitch of some kind that Becky needed help with."

"That's accurate enough," Virgil said. "I wouldn't say we're moving slower than normal, but we are up against some obstacles right now, and you just mentioned one of them. I know you're aware that a great deal of the work we do is technical in nature. Without our systems up and running, our resources are limited."

"I can understand that," Mac said. "What kind of support are you getting from the county?"

"I've seen the Marion County report," Murton said. "They've done everything right. They took Lester Poole's house apart, practically right down to the studs. His car keys, vehicle, and phone were all still at his residence. They never did find his wallet. They also didn't find one single thing on paper or on his computer that provided any actionable intelligence. His bank accounts are sitting dormant."

Mac didn't have anything to say about that, so he changed directions. "Sandy informed me—although I already knew through Cora—that she has decided not to run for re-election."

"That's right," Virgil said. "And to tell you the truth, I'm glad."

"Believe it or not, I am as well," Mac said. "She saved my life that night by pushing me out of harm's way. There's nothing I wouldn't do for your wife, Jonesy. Nothing. Are you hearing me on this?"

"I believe I am," Virgil said. "Let me ask you something: Why do you think Senator Poole waited an entire week before reaching out to us about his son, and by extension, why didn't he do it himself instead of using his other son as his proxy?"

"Good questions, both," Mac said. "The delay in making the request to the MCU was a political decision. His son is going to run for the office of the governor…an office Sandy still holds even though she's on sabbatical. And, as both her husband and the lead detective of the Major Crimes Unit, I'm guessing the Pooles didn't think they would get the sort of results they were looking for from the MCU. Cora is going to run. That's a foregone conclusion. She's also your boss. Based on what I've been able to gather, they came to you as a last resort because they were out of options."

Murton wasn't buying it. "But they weren't, Mac. They could have gone to the FBI, but they didn't, otherwise we would have known. Why hasn't that happened?"

"That's…complicated," Mac said. "Now ask me the right question. I'll answer to the best of my ability."

Virgil knew what Mac was driving at, so he came right out with it. "Why were you at Senator Poole's house today?"

Mac took some time to formulate his response. Finally, he looked at Virgil and Murton and said, "I have to be very careful about what I disclose here, so you'll have to bear with me in that regard. Have either of you ever been up to the HUMVEE manufacturing plant in Mishawaka?"

Both men said they hadn't, so Mac pressed on. "It's quite an operation. They build all the armored vehicles that eventually end up in other parts of the world as a means to help U.S. troops ensure our national security."

"Mac, Murton and I have both been to war. We know what HUMVEEs are, top to bottom. What do they have to do with anything?"

"I've toured the place on more than one occasion when I was in office," Mac said. "It's basically an automobile assembly line, no different from what you'd find in Detroit. But the main difference is this: Because they contract with the Department of Defense, the entire facility is considered a military base."

Murton—without meaning to—did a passable imitation of Ross. "So what?"

"Senator Poole, though no longer in office, has—because he used to chair the Senate Intelligence Committee—any number of valuable contacts within the DoD. Contacts, I might add, that largely deal with procurement. One of the companies under the umbrella of Said, Inc. has developed a new technology and the military wants it. Bottom line? I'm moving forward with contract negotiations, and the senator is helping make it happen."

"What kind of technology?" Murton said.

Mac shook his head. "I can't talk about that. It's classified information. I've been sworn to secrecy with the threat of prison if I disclose proprietary information to unauthorized persons."

Virgil thought for a few seconds, then said, "You're saying Poole doesn't want the FBI looking into his son's disappearance because once the feds are involved…at any level, it could jeopardize his dealings with the Department of Defense?"

Mac shook his head. "No, but you're close. Poole isn't the one who wanted the FBI kept out of the picture."

"Then who was it?" Virgil said.

"It was me."

"Why?" Murton said.

"Because A leads to B, then C, and so on."

"Care to be a little more specific?" Virgil said.

"You're operating from a presumption that Poole's kidnapping was nothing more than Landry seeking revenge over being fired. Do I have that right?"

"Essentially," Murton said. "Everything we've discovered so far points in that direction."

"Then you're probably right. But if it becomes known at the federal level that Senator Poole's son, Lester, is missing, the FBI will come bulldozing through here like a steamroller on speed. And they won't be operating from your perspective. They'll have their own playbook…one that probably looks something like this: Lester Poole wasn't taken by Landry over an employment dispute. He was taken by someone else as a way to leverage the senator—and by extension myself—to keep us from moving forward with the DoD contract. And if that happens, we're talking about billions of dollars disappearing like piss in the river.

"I know that both of you are under some sort of pressure, and I'm guessing it is connected with something you've done to protect one of our own." He glanced over at Virgil's house before continuing. "Let me be clear: I don't want to know what it is, but I'll help in any way I can."

"Appreciate it, Mac," Virgil said. "We might take you up on your offer if and when it becomes necessary."

"Bit of advice from your old boss?" Mac said.

Virgil nodded. "Always."

"I appointed Poole as director of the DNR as a favor to his father, the man who I am now partnered with in the DoD contract. But Lester Poole wouldn't win the governor's chair if he ran unopposed. He simply doesn't have what it takes. If you're being…mm, pressured by someone, I can guarantee you it isn't the senator. Find his son and you might also discover your other problem goes away."

Virgil was suddenly a little irritated. "I've always known you to be a master politician, Mac. But it feels like you're playing both sides of the fence here, and you might know a bit more about our predicament than you're willing to say."

Mac leaned forward slightly. "Meaning?"

Virgil pointed a finger at his friend and said, "If you're not willing to say it, I'll say it for you. There's a recording of—"

Murton reached out and grabbed his brother's arm. "Virgil."

Mac sat back in his chair. "I'm aware that there is a recording. I give you my word I do not know what's on it. But I do know that it must be incriminating enough that you two are risking just about everything to keep it under wraps. All I'm suggesting is that if you do your jobs and find Lester Poole, other evidence may come to light to help you with your own problem."

Virgil took a deep breath and forced himself to relax. "Where are you getting your information, Mac?"

"You're using the wrong adverb, Jonesy. It's not where. It's when." Then with no segue at all: "Did either of you know Senator Poole was one of the original investors in MedCap?"

"No, we didn't," Murton said.

"That's something you should think about."

"So Poole would know Charlie Reed?" Virgil said.

Mac let a slight grin tug at the corner of his mouth. "Oh yes, I'm sure of it. Why?"

"We can't tell you…at least not yet," Murton said.

"Fair enough," Mac said. "At least I've got your thinking moving along the right track."

"Have you, though?" Virgil said.

"I believe I have," Mac said. "Okay, last question: Have either of you ever found yourself in a position where you felt you couldn't trust me?"

Virgil was almost offended by the question. "Of course not. You know better than that."

"Then trust me now. Think about MedCap and everything that happened…and I mean everything, right down to the smallest detail. Do that and you'll not only help the senator save his son's life if he's still alive, you'll probably catch Reed in the process. When that happens, I think you'll find all will be right with our little section of the world."

Virgil looked at Mac and said, "A moment ago you acknowledged that you knew about the recording."

"I did."

"You also gave us your word that you don't know what's on it."

"That's right."

"Who has the original, Mac?"

"I don't know, Jonesy. That's the God's honest truth. But I'd be willing to bet my last nickel it's not who you think it is." Then Mac loosened his tie, looked up at the house and said, "Let's go eat, huh? I've heard Robert's pizza is delicious."

CHAPTER TWENTY-TWO

Despite the kaleidoscopic nature of the conversation Virgil and Murton had with Mac, everyone ended up having a fine casual dinner. Virgil noticed Sandy seemed to be enjoying herself, but was moving a little slower than normal. After everyone had eaten, Mac and Nichole said goodnight, and Murton took Ellie Rae home to wait for Becky. Virgil played with Jonas, Wyatt, and Larry the Dog in the backyard for a while until Huma came out and put her foot down, letting the boys know it was time for bed.

Virgil followed his sons inside, told them both he'd be in to say goodnight in a few minutes, then went to check on Sandy. When he walked into the bedroom, he found her examining her scars in their full-length admiration mirror. "Everything okay?"

Sandy wrapped her robe up and said, "Yes. I'm still trying to get used to my new look, though."

"Up on your meds?"

"Of course," Sandy said. "I think I must be getting used to them because I'm not quite as nauseous as before."

Virgil felt like he had to do a little dance, and he didn't like it. "That's good. The docs said you'd adjust." Then, with a whisper of trepidation, "What about the pain meds?"

"What about them?"

Virgil visibly swallowed and thought, *That sounds like an answer I would have given.*

"What was that?" Sandy said.

Virgil walked over to his wife and wrapped his arms around her. "You're my whole world. There isn't one single thing I wouldn't do for you, no matter the cost."

"I had one pill today, Virg. One. You don't have anything to worry about."

"Believe it or not, I can remember saying the same thing to you at one point. Is it just me, or do you sound a little defensive?"

Sandy untangled herself from Virgil's hug. "I'm not defensive. I'm tired. I'm also sorry for worrying you. I'll toss the pain meds right now if it makes you feel better."

"This isn't about me, sweetheart. It's about you."

"The pain pills are in the gun safe, Virgil. You can count them again if you want to."

"I don't have to. I never should have in the first place. I only did it because I'm scared. I do trust you…I just don't want to lose you."

Sandy finally smiled. "Fat chance, Mister. You're stuck with me until the end of time." Then: "What did you and Murton and Mac talk about?"

Virgil matched his wife's smile with one of his own. "That's a good question."

"It's also not much of an answer," Sandy said.

"Ah, it was nothing really. We're looking for a guy who went missing—he's the son of an ex-senator who is in business with Mac. Remember Charlie Reed and the whole MedCap mess?"

"Yeah, I do. That one is a little hard to forget."

"She escaped from a mental hospital and is mixed up in it somehow. Murt and I just had a few things to ask Mac…mainly because he was at the senator's house when we arrived there today."

"Is the guy still alive? The senator's son?"

Virgil shrugged. "I don't know. It's possible, but you know how these things go. The longer it takes, the less chance he has. Mind if I ask you something?"

"Of course not. What is it? Virg?"

Virgil held out his hands in a peaceful gesture. "Okay, look, I'm not trying to betray a trust or anything, but…"

"But what?"

Then Virgil thought better of asking the question and tried to let it go. "Ah, never mind. It's not important."

Sandy knew better, and said so. "Becky told you what I asked her to do, didn't she?"

"Yeah. Except our system is all jacked up, and it is sort of dangerous…poking around in the UNOS database for personal reasons. Why do you want to know?"

"I'm not sure. I thought if the person who donated their kidneys to me had family…maybe kids or something, we could set up a trust for their education."

"And that is why I love you," Virgil said. "Let me get some things worked out, and I'll get with Becky to see if we can figure out how to go about it. That sound okay?"

Sandy said it did, then tried to hide a yawn, but Virgil caught it. He gave his wife a lingering kiss, then said, "Get some sleep, baby. I'm going to go say goodnight to the boys, and I'll be in after a bit. I've got a few things to think about."

"Don't be too long."

"I won't," Virgil said. But he was.

Virgil spent some time with his sons, then got them tucked in for the night. As he was getting ready to leave their room, Wyatt called out to him.

"Hey, Dad?"

"Yeah, buddy?"

"Is mom okay?"

Virgil walked back over to Wyatt's bed and sat down next to him. How do you explain the complex nature of survival to a young boy? Virgil wasn't sure, but he knew his son well enough to know he couldn't sugarcoat the answer. "It's a hard thing to go through, Wyatt. She was hurt very badly, but the doctors and other people in her life did everything they needed to do to make sure she remains healthy and strong."

"She doesn't seem to be either of those things right now."

"That's because she's still healing. It takes time, Son. But the thing to remember is this: She's going to be okay."

Then Jonas—who had been listening quietly—looked at Virgil and said, "Are *you* okay, Dad?"

Virgil felt his jaw quiver, and discovered he wasn't quite sure how to answer.

AFTER HE GOT THE BOYS SETTLED IN, VIRGIL WALKED outside and sat down on the back deck and once again did the thing Delroy had asked him not to do. He stared at the spot in the backyard where Sandy had been shot. But this time he wasn't staring because he was reliving what had happened. He was thinking about what Mac had said to him and Murton about MedCap.

He thought it through—from the time they were called out to Connor Shaw's residence and found him and his wife brutally murdered and mutilated—and all the way to the end when he'd had the chance to kill Reed, but didn't. He would have, but Murton stopped him.

Virgil took out his phone and gave his brother a quick call. "Becky back yet?"

"Yeah, and before you ask, Nicky and Wu haven't made much progress tracking down the system leak. They do seem to be going as fast as they can, though."

"That wasn't what I was going to ask," Virgil said.

"What is it? Small okay?"

"Yeah, she's fine. I wanted to get your impressions regarding the conversation we had with Mac this evening before dinner."

"Care to be a little more specific?"

"I'm surprised I need to be. Didn't it strike you as odd that he seemed to be holding his cards pretty close?"

Murton thought for a few seconds, then said, "I don't really see it that way, Jonesy. Is he withholding information? I'd say almost certainly. But I don't think he's working against us. I was left with the impression he's trying to help us."

"Then why not come right out and tell us what we need to know?"

"You're looking for a false flag, Jones-man. Mac has always had our backs. He admitted he knew of a recording. The information probably came from Cora."

"What makes you say that?"

"Because he said he didn't know what was on it, and I believe him. I can see Cora giving him enough rope to let him know we're in trouble, but not enough to hang himself with. If this thing goes back to MedCap and we don't figure it out, he'd be swinging in the wind with the rest of us."

"Yeah, I guess you're right. Think about it, will you?"

"It is one of those top-of-mind situations. Catch you in the morning, huh?"

Virgil said goodnight, then ended the call. He was still thinking about the whole mess when the pole barn's exterior light clicked on. The light was on a timer, and it was just bright enough to illuminate not only the area around the shed, but the corner of the pond as well…the same corner where Mason's cross sat. Virgil looked over that way, then got up from his chair and headed toward the water.

When he reached the pond, Virgil pulled a chair close to his father's cross, looked up, and said, "Hey, Dad. How are you?"

Mason was shirtless as usual, a bar towel thrown over his shoulder. The scar from the bullet wound that had taken his life looked every bit as fresh and new as the ones Sandy now had. "I'm doing well, Son. Better than you, I'd say." Then Mason reached down in the grass and picked up a caterpillar that was inching its way along and set it on top of the cross.

"What makes you say that?" Virgil said.

"I'm surprised you have to ask. Delroy is right, you know."

"Right about what?"

"Pretty much everything he says, including the fact that staring at a spot in the backyard isn't good for you. It doesn't change what happened, Virg. It never will."

"I'm not trying to change anything, Dad."

"Aren't you?"

"No, I'm not. I'm simply trying to come to grips with what seems to be the new normal."

"New is a relative term, Virg. So is normal, for that matter." Then Mason laughed and said, "Relative. I've always liked that word."

Virgil was confused. "Why?"

"You mean besides the fact that it has nine different meanings?"

"Or a simple answer will do," Virgil said. Then before Mason could respond: "I'm in trouble, Dad. Murt and Becky are too."

"I'm aware," Mason said. "But it's all relative, Son. You should keep that in mind."

"To what end?"

Mason reached over and tickled the caterpillar, then watched it continue to explore the top of the cross. "Murton and Becky did what they had to do to ensure Sandy's survival. I'd have done the same."

"As would I," Virgil said. "But now we're all mixed up in something and there doesn't seem to be a way out."

"Mind if I ask you a question?" Mason said.

"Sure."

"Sure, you mind? Or, sure, go ahead."

Sometimes the conversations Virgil had with his father frustrated him to no end. "Dad…I'm in no mood."

"Well, it seems you're in no mood for levity, that's for sure." Mason picked up the caterpillar and held it in his palm. "I'm simply trying to lighten your load, Virg."

"What's the question?"

"Did you listen carefully to what Mac told you?"

"Of course I did."

"Do you trust the man?"

"With my life," Virgil said.

"Then you'll do what he asked? You'll look back at MedCap?"

"We already are. I've got Ross and Rosencrantz working it."

Mason nudged the caterpillar around in his palm, then said, "You and Murt need to do the same."

Virgil knew he was missing something that his father was trying to tell him, but he couldn't put his finger on it. "Why?"

"Because it's your job, if nothing else. You know how I keep trying to teach you that everything is connected?"

"I seem to recall you mentioning it once or twice."

"Good. Now pay attention," Mason said. Then he closed his hand around the caterpillar he held and tightened his grip. "You're getting squeezed. Murton is too. So is this bug. It's time for my boys to start doing something about it."

Virgil watched as his father continued to squeeze his hand tighter and tighter until he saw a green goo start to ooze between Mason's fingers.

"We're doing everything we can, Dad. And why did you just kill that caterpillar?"

"Hopefully to teach you a lesson…one that might keep you and Murt from going to jail." Then he opened his hand and the caterpillar was gone, replaced by a giant butterfly. It flapped its wings a few times, then fluttered around Mason's head. "Remember what I said, Son. Everything is relative, and everything is connected."

"I don't understand, Dad."

"Then keep replaying this conversation over in your head until you do. You don't have all the answers you need, Virg, but you have people in your life who have all but painted the solution to your problem on the ceiling. You should listen to them." Then Mason held out his hand and the butterfly settled gently into his palm. "All you have to do is keep looking up." Then he raised his hand and the butterfly flew off, higher and higher.

Virgil tipped his head back and watched until the butterfly was out of sight. "What are you saying?"

But when Virgil lowered his gaze, like the butterfly, his father was gone.

CHAPTER TWENTY-THREE

The next morning Virgil walked into the MCU facility and asked Sarah for an update.

"Ross and Rosencrantz are in the conference room going through the MedCap files. I'm doing everything I can to help them. Becky is in the computer lab gathering as much intel as she can on the Pooles…including the senator. I'm not sure how far along she is with the process."

"What about Mayo and Ortiz?" Virgil said.

"They're in the field chasing APOs around and trying to find out if any of them were buddies with Roy Landry during his time with the DNR."

"What about Murt? Is he in?"

"Not yet," Sarah said. "But he did call. He asked me to let you know he had a thought about something—he didn't say what—and wanted to run it by Nicky and Wu over at the bar. He should be in shortly."

"Good enough. Thanks, Sarah." Virgil turned to head toward the conference room, but Sarah stopped him.

"Hey, Jonesy?"

Virgil turned back and said, "Yes?"

Sarah stood from behind her desk and walked over toward Virgil. She placed her hand in the crook of his elbow and led him out of the main area and over to the supply room. Once they were inside, she closed the door, turned, then faced Virgil.

"I guess you already know this, but Ross has told me everything you guys are up against. I'm good at my job, and I can also keep a secret, as you well know. That's my way of saying if there is anything you need from me, all you have to do is ask." She gently poked Virgil in the chest with her finger, and said, "Anything."

Virgil gave her a fatherly hug. "I appreciate it, Sarah. I know I can count on you. Just keep doing what you're doing and we'll find our way out of this mess."

"I hope you're right."

"Speaking of out, what's with the cloak and dagger meeting in the supply room?"

Sarah gave her boss a warm smile. "I had to come in here anyway. Ross and Rosencrantz asked for more paper for the printer. Hand me one of those boxes from the top shelf?"

"Sure." Virgil turned and grabbed the box. "I'll take it in. I'm headed to the conference room anyway. Get the door?"

Sarah opened the door, and Ross was standing right there. He gave Sarah a wink, then looked at Virgil, his face as flat and blank as river rock.

"What?" Virgil said. "I'm bringing the paper you asked for."

"With the door closed?" Ross said.

"Sarah wanted a word in private."

Ross nodded like it was the most natural thing in the world. Then he reached into his pocket and pulled out his notebook and pen. He flipped through a few pages, wrote something down, then put the notebook away and started down the hall.

Virgil followed him in a hurry, the whole time saying, "Hey, Ross, is that your hit list? Ross? C'mon man, we were just talking…"

AFTER VIRGIL DROPPED THE PAPER OFF IN THE conference room he told Ross and Rosencrantz he'd be right back. "There are some things I want to go over with both of you, but I need to make a quick phone call first."

"No problem," Rosencrantz said. "I get the feeling we'll be pushing paper all day."

Virgil ran upstairs to his office, then sat down behind his desk and dialed Franklin Franklin, the field agent for Indiana with the Department of Homeland Security.

"Franklin, it's Jonesy. How are you?"

"I'm well. And you?"

"I've been better if I'm being honest with you. Listen, have you heard about Charlie Reed's escape from the psych ward down in Madison?"

"I did see a memo to that effect," Franklin said. "Heard she had some help from one of their own security guards, if I'm not mistaken."

"She did," Virgil said. "I was hoping you could do me a favor."

"What do you need?"

"Could you email your files on Reed, MedCap, and Freedom Pharm over to Sarah Palmer, our operations manager?"

Franklin didn't answer right away, and Virgil thought maybe he'd lost the connection.

"You still there, Franklin?"

"Yes, I am. I'm trying to figure out how to make that happen, is all."

"What do you mean?"

Franklin made a funny noise with his lips. "In case you've forgotten, that whole mess—including anything of evidentiary value—was sealed by the federal government after the closed-door hearings regarding the efficacy of the medication Freedom Pharm was trying to produce."

"I haven't forgotten. That's why I'm calling. You are the federal government. I need to see those files."

"May I ask why?"

"You can ask," Virgil said. "But I don't think I can answer you."

"Is Reed really that important? Because if she is, why not put the U.S. Marshals on the case and let them hunt her down? I'm not sure the files are going to help you find her."

"I do need to find her," Virgil said. "There's no question about that, but she's only part of what we're dealing with over here. She's a thread we need to pull…but I want the whole spool."

Franklin thought about it for a minute before saying, "Let me make a few calls. The guy who chaired the closed-door committee has since retired, but as I understand it, he still has a fair amount of influence within certain circles."

Virgil suddenly had a sick feeling in his stomach. "What was the name of the man who chaired the committee?"

"Senator John Poole. Why do you ask? Hey, Jonesy, are you still there?"

Murton stepped into Virgil's office shortly after the call with Franklin had ended.

"You look a little green around the gills, Jones-man. What's going on?"

"I'll tell you in a minute," Virgil said. "Sarah said you had a thought about something and needed to speak with Nicky and Wu?"

"Yeah. I needed to confirm my thinking was right about something. As it turns out, it was. Now we need to go have a chat with my lovely wife."

They found Becky in the computer lab working behind three different monitors. She looked at the gap between the screens and said, "Please don't ask me what I've come up with yet, Jonesy, because I only started a couple of hours ago. I've got three Pooles to look at, and two of them are connected with the feds in one way or another. It won't be quick, and it won't be easy."

"That's not why we're here," Virgil said. "Although I appreciate the update. And, not to put any pressure on you, but the quicker the better."

"Like I haven't heard that before," Becky said. "So why are you here?"

"I have no idea. Murt said he needed to ask you something."

"Oh, okay…then I'm all ears."

Virgil put his hands on his hips, then quickly dropped them. It was a habit he was trying to break. "If you're all ears when Murton wants to ask you something, what are you when I do?"

"All aggravated," Becky said with a fake smile. Then to her husband: "What's up?"

"I just came from the bar," Murton said. "I wanted to check my thought process with Nicky and Wu regarding the conversation we had in the office prior to our departure to Toronto."

Becky slid her chair out from behind the desk so she could get a better view of Virgil and Murton. "Your thought process about what?"

"I was so paranoid about the whole thing that when I talked to those guys I took the battery out of my phone, and they did the same. After that I thought we were good, but Wu stopped me from speaking. He went over to your system and flipped a few switches and shut everything down. Then he said it was safe to talk."

Virgil didn't understand. "That's the same thing you told me, Murt."

"I know. But I needed to make sure I was right. That's why I went and checked with them this morning."

Becky slowly lowered her head and let it rest on the desktop. She didn't even bother to look up when she spoke. "I can't believe that got past me."

"What got past you, Becks?" Virgil said.

"Probably about the most obvious thing in the world if

you know my system top to bottom, and I'm the only one who does."

"Lay it out for us," Murton said.

"Wu didn't shut the whole system down. He couldn't have. It takes a special access code to do that. Neither he nor Nicky knew that, and even if they did, they wouldn't have been able to do it because of the code."

"So your system was running the entire time we had our little chat about Lisa Young?" Murton said.

Becky lifted her head from the table. "Yes, but not the entire system. I've got some of it partitioned off. That means we can narrow our search parameters, which means we could have what we're looking for by the end of the day."

Becky stood and grabbed her purse.

"Where are you going?" Virgil said.

"Where else? I'm headed to the bar to get those guys pointed in the right direction. I'll be back as soon as I can."

"What about the research on the Pooles?" Virgil said.

"It will have to wait."

Virgil didn't want to hear that. "Becky, we really need the information on those guys."

"I know, Jonesy, but we also need this. If I don't get Nicky and Wu pointed at the right portion of the system those guys are doing nothing but wasting their time. They'll be looking for something that isn't there."

Virgil tried to hold his ground, but Murton convinced him to change course.

"Listen, Jones-man, I think Becky is right. We'll get the information on the Pooles soon enough, but if Nicky and Wu can get us to the recording—and who has it—that takes a big monkey off our backs."

"How much time will you need at the bar?" Virgil said.

Becky thought about it for a few seconds, then said, "Not counting drive time, no more than twenty minutes."

Virgil didn't like it, but he also knew it was the right way to go. "Do it. Just get back here as soon as you can."

"Can I take Murton's squad car?"

Virgil put his hands on his hips again. "Becky…"

"Well, can I?"

Murton laughed without humor. "Might as well say yes, Jones-man. What's one more offense in the big picture of things?" When Virgil didn't respond, Murton tossed Becky his keys and said, "Keep it under eighty, will you?"

Becky smiled and said, "Excellent."

AFTER BECKY LEFT, VIRGIL AND MURTON WENT UPSTAIRS to speak in private. Virgil looked at his brother and said, "I had an interesting conversation last night."

Murton knew what Virgil's statement meant. "Did you get anything out of it?"

"I'm not sure. I went inside and wrote everything down so I wouldn't forget. I'd like to go over it with you."

"Sure," Murton said. "But you never did answer my question when I walked in here earlier…before we went to speak with Becky. Who was on the phone, and why did you look so unsettled?"

"I was speaking with Franklin. I asked him for his MedCap files."

"Because of what Mac said?"

"Among others," Virgil said. "Remember the closed-door meeting after Freedom Pharm was shut down?"

"Yeah. What of it?"

"Just this: The guy in charge of the meeting was Senator John Poole."

Murton shook his head. "What in the hell are we mixed up in, Jonesy?"

CHAPTER TWENTY-FOUR

"TELL ME ABOUT YOUR INTERESTING CONVERSATION LAST night," Murton said.

Virgil spent nearly fifteen minutes telling his brother about the talk he had with his father. He finished with: "I understand what he was saying about everything being connected. I even think I know what he means when he said it's all relative. But I'll tell you what I don't understand is the part with the butterfly."

"Maybe it doesn't mean anything," Murton said.

"But it must. He wanted me to see it. In fact, he was adamant about the whole thing. He actually made me watch."

"It might have been a metaphorical demonstration," Murton said. "You know, the circle of life, or whatever."

Virgil wasn't convinced. "I don't think so. I mean, that could be part of it, but it feels like there's more."

"Well, if it's any consolation, there usually is. We'll figure it out. In the meantime, I suggest we do what the man said. Let's get busy and pour through those MedCap files."

"That's a good idea," Virgil said. "Go ahead and get started. I'm going to do something first."

"What?"

"I'm going to set a new land speed record from here up to Miami County."

"You're going to go speak with our favorite ex-senator again?"

"Yeah, I am. And this time, I'm going to get some answers."

CHARLIE REED KNEW ALL ABOUT SENATOR POOLE FROM their previous dealings when she was still working for MedCap and Connor Shaw. She couldn't remember every last detail, but it didn't matter because Reed had always been ready for the worst case scenario. Was it paranoia? Probably. Except Reed knew, given the types of people she worked with over the years, it was never a bad thing to be prepared.

She signed into her cloud account—the account had been set up under a completely different name before Reed had gotten herself caught at MedCap's production facility—and pulled up everything she had about the senator. She studied the files well into the night, took a little break to sleep, then got back up and continued to read until she had all the information she needed.

Once that was done, she hopped into Landry's car and drove to the nearest Walmart where she bought a shotgun, a box of shells, earplugs…and from the machine outside the store, a USA Today newspaper.

When she got back to the trailer she put the gun on the kitchen counter, loaded it, then filled a pitcher of water from the tap and carried it to the back bedroom where Lester Poole was still chained to the bed. After Reed ripped the gag from Poole's mouth, she took the pitcher of water and dumped it over his head and walked out. Two minutes later she was back with the newspaper, shotgun, and her laptop.

Poole had finally come around, and she looked at him, and said, "Don't worry, Lester. It won't be long and I'll be out of your life forever."

Poole, who was nearly dead from lack of food and water—not to mention his injuries—looked at her and said, "Why are you doing this to me?"

Reed laughed. "You're a tool, Lester…in every sense of the word. But strictly speaking, in this sense, you're a tool I intend to use to get what I want. Look sharp because I'm going to make a little movie of your condition. I'm guessing there's someone who'd like to see you right about now. Oh, one more thing: I know you're hurting… that you're in pain, but if you say one word during your short cinematic debut, you won't be getting your Screen Actors Guild card. You also won't get another beating. You'll get a belly full of buckshot. Understood?"

Poole nodded and kept his mouth shut.

Reed tossed the newspaper on his lap and made sure the date was visible. After that, she grabbed the laptop, turned on the video capture App and took a few shots of Poole from different angles. It wasn't as easy as she thought it might be because the laptop didn't have a front-facing camera. Even so, the whole thing took less than two minutes. Once she was finished she took the computer back to the front of the trailer and reviewed the footage she'd captured. It wasn't great, but it'd get the message across.

Proof of life…at least for now.

Virgil called James Poole as he was turning out of the MCU parking lot. "I'm on my way up to speak with you and your father. I'm hoping he's home."

"Have you ever heard of making an appointment, Detective?"

"I don't make appointments when I'm investigating a crime. Is he there or not?"

"As it happens, yes. I am as well. Do you have any new information regarding the disappearance of my brother?"

"Stay put. And tell your security people if they try to hassle me in any way whatsoever they'll end up like the last two."

"Answer my question, Detective."

Virgil hung up without responding.

HE MAY OR MAY NOT HAVE SET THE LAND SPEED RECORD for travel time from Indy to Peru, but Virgil knew even if he didn't win the trophy, he'd made the podium. He turned into Poole's drive, dumped the Range Rover right in front of the house, and climbed the porch steps.

The door opened as he approached, and Virgil fully expected to see one of Poole's security personnel, but he didn't. Instead, the senator himself stood in the entryway, his expression at once one of apprehension and hopefulness. "Have you found him?"

Virgil shook his head. "No, sir. Not yet. I need to have a word with you, and your son, James."

Poole turned away and stepped back inside, the door hanging open as if it mattered little if Virgil entered or not.

He followed Poole through the house without speaking, and they eventually ended up in what Virgil thought was probably the senator's home office, a richly appointed room with polished hardwood floors and uncomfortable looking furniture.

Poole pointed at a chair, poured himself a drink, then sat down across from Virgil. "My son will be along any moment, Detective. What brings you back here today?"

"I'll wait for your son, if you don't mind," Virgil said.

"Then you don't have to wait to answer my father's question," James Poole said as he walked into the room. "I'm right here. How may we help you Detective?"

"For starters? You can stop lying to me."

James Poole looked at his father, then turned his attention back to Virgil. "I wasn't present the last time you were here, Detective, so I'm not aware of anything my father may or may not have said to you. However, I did come to learn you put on quite the show. But all that aside, I do know the man. He is tough, tenacious, and very shrewd in his political and business dealings. But he is not a liar or deceiver of any kind."

"That might be the first honest thing that's come out of your mouth since our paths crossed," Virgil said. "I wasn't speaking of your father, his honesty, or lack of it. I was speaking of you."

"I resent that, Detective. In fact, I'm beginning to resent you, personally."

"That's an interesting attitude to take with the man

who is doing everything in his power to find your brother."

"Are you, though? Doing everything you can? If I didn't know better, and I'm not sure I don't, it feels like you're doing the exact opposite. It doesn't escape me why that might be."

"And why is that?" Virgil said, his tone full of sarcasm.

"Because you're married to the woman my brother is going to unseat."

Virgil laughed. "You're wrong, Agent Poole. My wife isn't going to run for re-election. So how about we all drop the charade and talk about what is really going on around here."

"And what would that be?"

"Your lies and manipulation of information, if nothing else. Every time you tell a lie, it hinders our ability to locate your brother. It almost feels like you don't actually want him found, Agent Poole."

Poole stood from his chair and said, "I will not stand for this."

Virgil let his eyes do a little half-roll. "It looks to me like you just did."

CHAPTER TWENTY-FIVE

Virgil pointed a finger at Agent Poole and said, "Sit down."

"I will not be told what to do inside this house."

Virgil stood, got right in Poole's face and said, "Sit down right now, or I'll put you in restraints and physically seat you in that chair myself."

One of Senator Poole's security men stuck his head into the room. "Is everything okay in here?"

Virgil pulled his gun and pointed it at the doorway without ever taking his eyes from Agent Poole. "Senator, tell your dog to get out."

The senator walked over to the door and told the security guard everything was under control.

"No disrespect, sir, but it doesn't seem like it. The man has a gun pointed at me."

The senator turned to Virgil and said, "Detective,

there's no need for showmanship here. I'm asking as a gentleman. Please holster your weapon. Mac speaks very highly of you. I trust him, which means I trust you to do the right thing."

Virgil holstered his Sig, Poole sat down, and the guard went away.

Once the door was closed, the senator returned to his seat, took a deep breath and said, "How about we start over? No one in this room means you any harm, nor are we trying to complicate your life. We're all on the same side here."

Virgil laughed without humor. "Are we? Because it sure doesn't feel like it."

"To what are you referring, Detective?"

"Your son's lies and manipulation of facts surrounding his brother's disappearance," Virgil said.

"I have not lied to you," Agent Poole said.

Virgil couldn't believe Agent Poole was sticking to his story. "But you have." He pointed at the senator and said, "You told me your father had a liver transplant. I know for a fact he has not. I don't know what purpose it serves to lie about something like that, but the next words out of your mouth better be the truth or I'll arrest you on charges of interfering with an on-going investigation…federal agent or not. Now why are you lying?"

"I have not lied to you, Detective. Not once."

Virgil pressed on. "But you have. You showed up in

Kentucky and told me your family has a close working relationship with law enforcement in the state."

"That's because we do," the senator said. "My son was not lying."

"Then how is it the state's top law enforcement official hasn't met either of you?"

Agent Poole let a sad grin form on his face. "I know who Detective Grady is. He works directly for the governor, just as you do in our state. Do I have that right?"

"Yes," Virgil said.

"My family's relationship isn't with Detective Grady. It's with the state's attorney general. That was my point of reference. He informed me what was happening at Mr. Getz's house."

Virgil was starting to relax. "Why would he do that?"

"Because once it became known who attempted to rob and murder Mr. Getz, we got a call from the man."

"Why would he tell you?" Virgil said.

"Because of me," Senator Poole said. "I've had dealings with Miss Reed before she went to prison."

"I'm aware," Virgil said. "As I understand it, you were one of the original investors in MedCap."

"That's right. Harlan Shaw and I worked closely together in certain circles. He informed me of an investment opportunity and I took advantage of it. Miss Reed handled the transaction."

"You also chaired the closed-door hearing regarding

the efficacy of the medication MedCap was backing. Wouldn't that be considered a conflict of interest on your part?"

The senator nodded. "Undoubtedly. But…politics, Detective. Sometimes you have to move whichever way the wind happens to blow. I wanted to make sure my name stayed out of the entire affair. That meant I needed to make sure those records were sealed."

"Was your son involved?"

"I most certainly was not," Agent Poole said.

"I was referring to Lester."

"Only in a peripheral way," the senator said. "I informed him of the opportunity and he invested a small sum which we lumped together with my own contribution. Why do you ask?"

"Because asking questions is generally how we get to the truth," Virgil said. He turned his attention back to Agent Poole. "And speaking of questions, now is the time to answer my original one. Why did you lie about your father's transplant?"

"He didn't lie," the senator said.

Virgil turned back to the elder Poole. "Then how is it you don't have any scars on your body, sir?"

"I don't have any scars because I've never had surgery in my entire life. Mac told me you're one of the smartest men he's ever had the pleasure to know or work with. I'm hoping you can validate that statement right here and now."

Virgil looked away in thought for less than five seconds before he finally got it. He looked at Agent Poole and said, "You're adopted?"

Poole nodded, a vacant look in his eyes. "It was such a long time ago. I was a very young boy, but old enough to remember the drinking and abuse I suffered at the hands of that man. Child Protective Services took me from that little house of horrors—and believe me, that's what it was— where I bounced around in the foster care system until the man I consider my real father, Senator Poole, came along."

Virgil remained quiet, his thoughts turning to his own brother and everything Murton had to endure as a child. After a few minutes he looked Agent Poole in the eye and said, "You told me you were aware of your biological father's liver transplant, that he's doing well, and spends his days watching the news. How would you know all that?"

Poole stood from his chair and walked over to where his adoptive father was seated and stood behind him, both of his hands resting on the senator's shoulders. "This man saved my life, Detective. I'd be dead if he hadn't come along when he did. Make no mistake, I consider him my real father through and through. But nobody is perfect. I'm speaking of myself. A number of years ago I got curious about my family and decided it was time to take a look at my past."

"And you found your biological father?" Virgil said.

"Yes, and my biological brother as well. Sadly, my brother passed a few years ago. Regarding my father, we've only spoken a few times, and I'm certain he's sorry for what he put me through as a young boy. He's aged, and with age sometimes you find wisdom…or at the very least, sorrow and regret. I think he might have found two out of three."

"You've reconciled?"

Agent Poole seemed to consider the question carefully. "Not exactly. My biological brother and I became quite close over the years until he died."

"If you don't mind me asking…how did he die?" Virgil said.

"He was murdered. It's not something I like to dwell on. As for my father and the lack of a meaningful relationship…I suppose it might be mostly my fault. The house of horrors I spoke of? I still have dreams about it, but nevertheless, I check in with the man from time to time. In some odd way it helps me…lets me know how I might have turned out. The truth is, I'm not sure if I'm rooting for his life, or praying for his death. Usually it's an odd combination of both. I wasn't trying to deceive you in any way during our initial conversation when I mentioned him while referencing your wife's recovery. I was simply trying to offer you my support."

And Virgil thought, *Way to go, Jonesy.*

All three men sat in silence for a few minutes before Virgil finally said, "I'd like to ask each of you a few questions, but I need to do it in private. The questions will be similar, and you'll be free to talk about them afterward if you like, but I'm hoping you'll cooperate."

"Will it get you closer to finding my son?" Poole said.

"The honest answer is this: I don't know. But I can tell you it certainly won't get us any further away from our objective."

"We're at your disposal, Detective," Agent Poole said. "Who goes first?"

"It doesn't really matter," Virgil said. "But since you're asking, how about we start with you?"

Agent Poole turned to the senator and said, "Father?"

"Fine with me. I need to fetch my laptop and check on a few things anyway. How long will you need, Detective?"

"No more than two minutes," Virgil said.

Senator Poole stood from his chair and headed for the door. "I'd better hurry, then."

Once they were alone, Virgil looked at Agent Poole

and asked him a few questions. Poole's answers didn't seem calculated, and he never once broke eye contact with Virgil. Bottom line? For the first time since they'd met, Virgil believed him.

"Ask your father to step in? Please don't mention what we've talked about until I can speak with him myself."

Poole said he would, and less than a minute later the senator walked back into the room, set his laptop on the desk with the lid still open, and took a seat. "Fire away."

"I will," Virgil said. "But first I'm going to share something with you, and I'm asking you for your word that what I say stays between you, me, and your son, James. He agreed, I believe him, and that brings me to you."

"I don't know what you're going to say or ask, but I give you my word any statements made in this room stay in this room." Then, as men from older generations often do when placed in a particular situation, the senator offered Virgil his hand.

Virgil shook hands with the senator and said, "Certain people—I won't say who, so please don't ask—are being leveraged. These are good people who did a difficult thing, and in doing so, right or wrong, they've made the world a better place. You're not going to want to hear this, but our initial thinking was that the leverage originated from within your family."

"You're speaking of the things you mentioned last time you were here."

"I am," Virgil said. "And while I no longer think that's true, I need to also let you know that I'm aware of your involvement with Mac, the technology one of his companies has, and the military contracts that go along with it."

"The details of those contracts and what they represent are highly classified material, Detective."

"I'm aware. I also know how to stay in my own lane. Rest assured, Mac hasn't divulged any proprietary information. I know absolutely nothing about it, and as a point of fact, I don't want to. What I do want to know is this: Is there anyone within your sphere of influence—and I mean anyone at all—who could use the leverage I spoke of to derail your contracts with the military, and by extension, Mac and his company?"

"Those people do exist. Washington is rife with them. Are they within my sphere of influence as you called it? Absolutely not. You have my word, Detective."

Virgil stared at the senator for a full minute, and the man never blinked. Finally, he said, "Okay, I believe you."

"Thank you. If I may, how bad is it?"

"Again, I can't get into the details, but it's bad enough that if the information became public knowledge, some very good people will be hurt in ways I don't want to think about. Mac could be one of them. If that happens, your military contract goes right out the window."

"How can I help?" Senator Poole said.

"You just have," Virgil said.

"In what way?"

"You've all but eliminated yourself as a suspect, as has your son."

"And how does that get you any closer to finding Lester?"

"I'm afraid it doesn't, but as I mentioned, it doesn't get us any further away. Does anyone have anything on you, sir?"

"You're speaking as a means to influence me by holding my son captive?"

"Yes," Virgil said. "He was either taken as revenge over nothing more than an employment dispute, or as a way to take you and Mac out of the bidding process."

"Then it must be an employment dispute. The contract negotiations were complete before he ever went missing."

"That's been our thinking all along," Virgil said. "The employment dispute. You've not received any ransom demands?"

"None. I'd have told you the moment it happened."

"Okay." Virgil stood and said, "Let me get back to work."

Senator Poole stood as well, then grabbed Virgil's arm to steady himself.

"Are you all right, sir?"

"Lester is dead, isn't he?"

Virgil thought in all honesty he probably was, but he didn't want the senator to lose faith. He was about to respond in the most neutral way possible, but right then in the moment it didn't matter because the senator's laptop dinged and answered for him…a message that offered nothing more than false hope.

CHAPTER TWENTY-SIX

Virgil's phone buzzed at him at almost the same time the senator's laptop notified him of an incoming email. He glanced at his screen, saw it was Mayo, and answered by saying, "Find anything?"

"Nothing," Mayo said. "But Ortiz had a thought."

"Let's hear it."

"We couldn't find anyone with the DNR who had one good thing to say about Landry. Ortiz thinks we should go back further and take a look at the prison guards he worked with. You know how those guys are. Most of them are cut from the same cloth. We might find someone there."

Virgil was watching the senator as he listened to Mayo's report. Poole seemed to be vibrating with either rage or fear. Virgil wasn't sure which. He told Mayo to go ahead and follow through with Ortiz's idea, then ended the call.

"Senator? What is it, sir?"

Poole pointed at the screen of his laptop, his hand quivering, his index finger shaking so badly it was beginning to curl in on itself. His lips were moving, but no words came from his mouth.

Virgil ran around to the other side of the desk, and when he saw the image on the screen he immediately understood why the senator was so upset.

"Is that your son, sir?"

Virgil noticed that the movie clip was playing over and over on a constant loop. "Answer me, sir. Is that your son?"

Poole nodded, swallowed, then spat on his own floor. "It is."

"Move aside please."

Poole slid away from his computer, and Virgil looked at the underlying email. The message was direct and to the point.

Five million wired to the account of my choosing within twenty-four hours. Details to follow. Lester is counting on you, John.

Virgil had to physically pull the senator away from his desk. "Listen to me, sir. This is the first real break we've had. I need to leave right now, and I need to take your computer with me."

When Poole spoke, his voice sounded hollow, like he was speaking from the other end of a tunnel. "You can't. It's full of classified information. The only time it's ever out of my sight is when it's locked up in my safe."

"I have people who might be able to trace the email, sir. We have no interest in your classified information."

"I will go to jail if I surrender this computer to you."

"Your son will die if you don't."

Poole grabbed Virgil by his shirt with both hands. "You and your people will go to jail as well if I turn that thing over to you."

We probably will anyway, Virgil thought. He untangled himself from Poole's grasp and took out his phone. When it was answered on the other end, Virgil got right to the point.

"Where are you?"

"On 465 headed back to the shop."

"Where specifically?"

"Top of the loop, coming up on 31."

"Take the exit north. You're coming up to Peru. I'll text you the address."

"What's going on, Jonesy?"

"I'll explain when you get here. Do you have your gear with you?"

"Yeah."

"Fast as you can," Virgil said. And even though he was loath to do it, he finished with, "Lights and siren all the way, Becks."

Becky said, "Excellent," then killed the call.

Virgil saw Poole drifting back toward his desk. "Please, Senator, do not touch the computer. I've got someone on the way who can help us right now. But we've got to wait."

"I'm not going to touch anything. I just want to see my son."

Virgil kept an eye on him as he texted the address to Becky. Once that was done, he called Cora.

"I've got an unmarked unit headed hard from Indy to Peru. I don't have time to explain, but I need a path cleared. Can you get with the superintendent of the Indiana State Police and make it happen?"

Cora knew better than to ask any questions in the moment, but Virgil knew she'd be asking later. Nevertheless, her response was what Virgil had hoped for.

"Consider it done," Cora said.

Virgil ended the call, then walked over to where Poole

stood, both men simply watching and waiting. Becky would work her magic or not. It felt like it was their only hope.

VIRGIL WAS WAITING OUTSIDE WHEN BECKY PULLED UP. She'd covered the seventy mile distance and arrived at the Poole residence within forty minutes. Virgil did some quick math in his head and determined she'd averaged a little over one hundred miles an hour. She walked up with her laptop bag slung over her shoulder and said, "Whew, what a rush. I'd have been here sooner but the front end started to shimmy at about one-twenty so I had to back off a bit." After that—and before Virgil could give her any grief—she got right down to business. "What have you got?"

"A problem…and maybe an opportunity."

"Whose place is this, anyway?"

"Senator Poole's."

"Oh boy."

"You don't know the half of it," Virgil said. He quickly explained the situation and finished with, "We need a trace on where the email came from. Can it be done?"

"That's the kind of thing you ask before you have me come flying up here like a screaming eagle."

"I'm looking for a yes or no, Becks."

"It depends on any number of factors, none of which you'd understand, so please don't make me try to explain. Let's go take a look."

"Hang on a second. I need you to do something else."

"What is it?"

When Virgil told her what he wanted, Becky squinted at him and said, "Yeah, it can be done. The question is, do you really want me to do it?"

"I don't think we have a choice," Virgil said. "I've got a pretty good read on the man, but one way or another I need a definitive answer."

Becky gave Virgil a frown and said, "If we get caught, is it treason or espionage? I always get those things mixed up."

"Probably both."

"Then you'll have to buy me a new computer when this is over."

"Why?"

Becky patted her laptop bag. "Because this baby is going to end up in the river. Let's go, huh?"

Virgil led Becky inside, introduced her to both Poole men, explained in very broad strokes what Becky did for the Major Crimes Unit, and what she was going to do regarding the email. When he was finished with his little speech, he looked at Senator Poole, and said, "Do we have your permission, sir?"

"Yes, yes, let's get on with it already." He turned his attention to Becky and said, "My computer has some highly classified information on it."

Becky answered very carefully. "I'm aware, sir. I won't be examining anything here today other than this one single email."

Virgil watched the senator's expression as Becky spoke. If the man caught her careful wording, he gave no indication. "Could I have a quick word, senator?"

"I'd like to stay close if you don't mind," Poole said. "Why is she hooking my computer to her own?"

"There is no cause for concern, Senator. She has special programs which will allow her to trace the email. I have that right, don't I, Becks?"

Becky nodded and answered without looking up. "Yes. I don't want to do the trace from your machine. I don't know who sent the email or how smart they are, but there may be a trap set up. If so, I don't want to lose any information. Don't worry, sir. I know what I'm doing, and Detective Jones has made it very clear what I am allowed to do, and what I'm not. I won't do anything other than what he's asked. You're in good hands."

Virgil walked the senator to the far end of the room. "I

know what you're thinking, sir, and I strongly suggest you reconsider."

"You're speaking of the wire transfer." It wasn't a question.

"I am. It's widely known in law enforcement circles that paying a ransom rarely works out."

"It's a risk I'm willing to take."

"I understand, sir. I really do. But if you send the wire, not only will it be the end of your son, you'll lose the money as well."

"I don't care about the money, Detective. I care about my boy."

Virgil felt like he wasn't getting through to the man. "Senator, earlier you mentioned Mac told you I'm one of the smartest men he's ever had the pleasure to know or work with. And while that's a fine compliment from a good friend, the truth of the matter is this: I look smart because I surround myself with people who are smarter than I am." He tipped his head toward Becky and said, "She's one of them."

"What are you suggesting, Detective?"

"Let her do her work. We have twenty-four hours. There is a very good chance we'll get a location from the email well before that time has expired."

"And if we don't?"

It was a good question, and Virgil knew it. "Let me ask you something, if I may."

"What is it?" Poole said.

"I'm not trying to get in your business, but do you have that kind of money readily available?"

"Of course I do. What are you thinking?"

Virgil bit into his lower lip. "I was going to suggest we stall. It's a common tactic in situations like these. We can tell Reed—and I promise you, that's who sent the message—that you need time to gather those kinds of funds together."

Poole shook his head. "I believe you about Reed sending the message. Who else could it be? But that creates a problem all in itself."

"What sort of problem?" Virgil said.

"When Harlan Shaw approached me about an investment opportunity with MedCap, I was very interested. He introduced me to his son, Connor, who, in turn, sat me down with Charlie Reed. After I reviewed their prospectus, I wrote a check for the exact same amount she's asking for now."

"And that means what, exactly?"

"Just this: She asked me if it was necessary to hold off on making the deposit until I had time to transfer the funds." Poole shook his head and laughed without humor. "I let my ego get the best of me right there in her office. Told her that she could walk it down to the bank over her lunch hour if she wanted to."

"So she is aware of the fact you have the means to

access at least that much without any trouble at all."

"Yes, and it also means your idea of stalling the woman is off the table. I'll let your people do what they do best, but no matter the risk or the possible consequences of my actions, I'm going to prepare the wire. Once we know where it's supposed to go, if you and your people haven't figured anything out, I'm going to send it before the deadline."

"Senator…"

"I will not be swayed on the issue, Detective. You and your people do whatever it is that you do. I'll stay out of your way, and help where I can, but this is my son, and that means it's my decision. End of discussion."

BECKY SPENT AN HOUR WORKING ON THE SENATOR'S computer, but she didn't try to trace the email. She did a massive data dump to her own machine, got everything disconnected, shut her laptop down and stuck it back into her bag. She looked at Virgil and Poole and said, "That's all I can do from here. Wait, that's not exactly accurate. I could do more from here, but the truth is, it's safer if I do it from the lab back at the Major Crimes Unit facility."

"Why?" Poole asked.

Becky didn't miss a beat. "We know Reed and her capabilities, sir. Once the email was sent, she can monitor what happens in any number of ways. She can tell how many times it has been opened or viewed, and all sorts of things. I've copied it onto my computer and by taking it back to the lab, I can set up…well, it's all very technical, but she won't be able to see what I'm doing. If I do it from here, she might."

The senator seemed to be losing his patience. "Yes, yes. Get to it already."

Virgil said they'd be in touch, and asked the senator to call him immediately when the next email came through.

"I will," Poole said.

"And Senator, please…don't make the wire transfer. We still have time."

Poole looked at Virgil without responding, so he and Becky turned and walked out of the house. Once they were outside, Virgil looked at Becky and said, "You get it all?"

"Every last byte."

"Good work. Nice speech too."

Becky smiled and said, "Thanks."

"Will you be able to trace the email?"

"I can try, but it came from a Gmail account, so it's going to take some time."

"Well, you know the clock we're working against. Let's get back as quick as we can." He glanced at Murton's squad car and said, "Be careful…but drive it like you stole it."

CHAPTER TWENTY-SEVEN

As it turned out, Becky didn't have to try to trace the email. By the time she and Virgil made it back to the Major Crimes Unit facility, all the other detectives were there and waiting for Virgil.

Murton looked at his brother and said, "We think we've got her."

"Reed?" Virgil said.

"Yep. We're not one hundred percent, but we're damned close. Mayo and Ortiz figured it out."

Virgil turned to his two newest detectives and simply said, "Tell me."

"My partner's idea panned out," Mayo said. "We weren't getting anywhere with the fish dicks who knew Landry because everyone pretty much hated the guy, so—"

Virgil interrupted him. "Mayo?"

"Yeah?"

"Jump ahead to the part I don't already know about."

"Right, right. Okay, so we went to the women's correctional facility to speak with the guards Landry used to work with. We got lucky because the first guy didn't know much, but he pointed us at another guard, who, he said, was pretty tight with Landry."

"How tight?" Virgil said.

"Tight enough that even though they hadn't spoken to each other in nearly a year, when Landry called him up and asked if he could borrow something the guy said yes."

"What'd he borrow?"

"A single-wide trailer in Eminence, Kentucky," Ortiz said.

"You're kidding."

"I kid you not, boss. The guard told us the same thing he told Landry…he only uses it for hunting and drinking. Says Landry called and asked if it was available. The guard told him it was, and he could use it for as long as he wanted."

Virgil looked at Mayo and Ortiz. "That's some great work, guys. Tell me about this guard."

"What do you mean?" Mayo said.

"I'm hoping you mentioned that Landry is dead."

Mayo let his eyes rest at half-mast. "Not our first day, Jonesy."

"I know, I know. Just making sure. I don't want this guy trying to call and warn Reed."

"He won't," Ortiz said.

"How do you know?"

"Because we made up a little story and told him the people who killed Landry were after anyone who helped Reed escape from the psych ward, and that included him."

"He buy it? The story?"

"Yeah, he bought it," Mayo said. "But he also told us he was going to go down and check the place out and make sure it was still in one piece."

"Did you talk him out of it?" Virgil said.

"We tried," Ortiz said, "but he didn't want to hear it. So we did the only other thing we could think of."

"Which was what?"

"We arrested him for planning to attempt to interfere with a multi-state criminal investigation."

"I'm not a legal scholar, but I don't think that's an actual crime," Virgil said.

Mayo shrugged. "Who cares? Central Booking told us they'd lose the guy's paperwork for twenty fours hours, then kick him. Bottom line? He's out of our way."

Virgil ran his fingers through his hair. "Well, maybe not how I would have done it, but it sounds good enough for government work."

Mayo slapped Ortiz on the back and said, "Told ya."

Virgil looked at Murton. "Cool?"

"He's on his way as we speak. Should be here any minute."

"Grady?" Virgil said.

Murton gave his brother a half grin. "Thought I'd let you make that call."

"All right," Virgil said. "I'll do that now. Somebody get me a map of Kentucky. I don't know where Eminence is located."

"I don't want to speak out of turn here," Rosencrantz said. "But I'm pretty sure your phone has a map function."

Virgil gave him a frown. "Yeah, I guess it does."

Ross took out his phone and said, "I'll look it up and get you a print."

Virgil thanked him before heading to his office to call Grady, and Murton followed.

Once they were upstairs, Murton said, "Listen, I've got the feeling Grady isn't going to want our whole unit dropping in like it's the reenactment of Normandy Beach, if you know what I mean."

"You're saying just you and me?"

"And a couple of Grady's guys, obviously. We're going after one woman. How hard is it going to be?"

"Okay, you're probably right. Let everyone know, and have them keep digging into the MedCap files. We're still missing a big piece of the puzzle. Once we have Reed in the bag—and hopefully get Lester Poole home—all our attention can go toward our other problem."

Murton said he'd handle it, and walked out of the room.

Ross walked into Virgil's office at the same time Grady came on the line. "Jack, it's Jonesy. Can you hang on for just a second?"

"You called to ask me to hold?" Grady said dryly.

"Two seconds, Jack."

Virgil punched the Hold button on his desk phone, then looked at Ross. "What?"

Ross handed Virgil a printout of a map that indicated where Eminence, Kentucky was, along with marks showing where the trailer was located.

He pointed to two other spots on the printout and said, "Looks like you can stage here…or here. Probably far enough away that the chopper won't be heard."

"Thanks, Ross. Send Becky in, will you?"

Ross said he would, then went back downstairs.

Virgil looked at the map for a few minutes and decided Ross had picked good spots for them to stage with Grady's men. Then he remembered he still had Grady on hold.

He snatched the receiver from the cradle, punched the phone's button and said, "Sorry, Jack. You still there?"

"I'm not the keeper of all things time, but that wasn't two seconds."

"I know. That's why I apologized. Are you up for a little multi-state operation?"

"Yours or mine?"

"My op, your state."

"Why am I not surprised?" Grady said.

"Beats me. Maybe because all the criminals think they're safe from the clutches of law enforcement while hiding in Kentucky. Anyway, we've got a line on Reed, who we think is holding Lester Poole. Proof of life was sent today, and we'd like to fly down and grab them."

"Where are they?"

"Near a place called Eminence. I've already got a spot picked out to get staged, so if you're up for it, the State of Indiana would be forever in your debt."

"What's your timeline?" Grady said.

"Two hours, tops. Cool is on the way over here right now."

Grady dropped a little sarcasm in his voice. "Are your two hours anything like your two seconds?"

"I said I was sorry, Jack. Are we doing this or not?"

"Okay, send me the coordinates of the staging area and we'll meet you there. Please don't make me wait."

Virgil said he'd do his best, then ended the call.

Becky walked in a minute later. "You wanted to see me?"

"Yes. First, I know I put you in a difficult position at the senator's house, but you handled it like a pro. That's my way of saying nice job."

Back gave him a warm smile. "Thank you."

"You're welcome. Now, forget everything I asked you to do regarding the Pooles. We don't need deep backgrounds on them anymore. And obviously, we don't need to trace the email. I'd like to see if you can find anything on the senator's laptop that will help us with our other problem. I doubt you will, but it's still worth looking at."

"I'm on it," Becky said. "Do you want me to monitor his email account for another message from Reed?"

"You can do that?"

"A few seconds ago you gave me a very thoughtful and genuine compliment. Now you're insulting me?"

Cool touched down outside of Eminence, and right as they landed Virgil's phone buzzed at him. He glanced at the screen and saw it was Becky. He opened the helicopter's door, hopped out, hit the Answer button and said, "Hey, Becks. We just landed. What's up?"

"How long until you and Murt get to Reed?"

Grady and Cole had just walked over to the helicopter, so Virgil asked Becky to hold for a few seconds while he found out.

"Hey, Jack," Virgil said. He handed him the map, pointed at the area where the trailer was located, and said, "How long to get there from here?"

"That where Reed is?"

"Should be," Virgil said.

"Probably fifteen minutes. Ten if we push it."

Virgil went back to Becky and the phone. "Grady says ten to fifteen minutes. Why?"

"Because Senator Poole got another email with instructions on where to wire the money."

Virgil wasn't overly concerned. "It's okay, Becks. We'll have Reed in custody well before her deadline. Hell, we could spend the night and still have enough time."

"No you can't, Jonesy. Reed changed the play. She wants the money right now."

"Shit. Okay, we're rolling. Call the senator and tell him we're practically right on top of Reed. Don't let him wire the funds. If he does, his son is going to die."

"Then he's already dead. The wire was sent before I called you. There wasn't any way for me to stop it."

When Reed checked her account she saw the wire transfer had come through. She immediately transferred it to a different account so the funds couldn't be pulled back out, then decided it was time for a bit of housekeeping. What Reed had told Landry was true. She didn't have any problem with map wiping. But that didn't mean she necessarily liked it, either.

She got the key to unlock Poole's legs from the bed, then made her way to the back of the trailer, the shotgun tucked neatly under her arm.

"Here's the deal, Lester: I'm going to leave you chained up, but I'm taking you outside."

Poole glanced at the gun and said, "Why?"

"Because this place stunk before you got here, and it's getting worse by the second. If you try to run—though that's not likely—or if you try to fight me in any way, I'll blow your brains out. Got it?"

Poole swallowed, then nodded.

Reed very carefully approached Poole, bent down and without ever taking her eyes from his, she unlocked the section of chain that held Poole to the bed frame. With that done, she quickly backed away, grabbed the gun from the bed and said, "Get up."

"I'm not sure I can," Poole said.

"Try, or I'll drag you out on your ass."

Poole did try, but he was far too weak, and because he had a broken arm he simply couldn't do it.

Reed shook her head. "All right, we'll do it the hard way." She bent down and grabbed the chain that held Poole's legs together and began dragging him down the hall. It wasn't easy, but Poole didn't have any fight in him, so eventually she got him out the door, the back of his head banging down the steps as they went.

Once she had him far enough from the trailer and out in the weeds, she rolled him on his side, and gave him a hard kick in the butt. "Stay put."

Poole cried out in pain from the kick, then after he'd managed to catch his breath, he said, "Does it look like I can move?"

Reed went inside, stuck her earplugs in, then came back out with the shotgun. Poole was trying to slither away like a snake wrapped in chain, but he hadn't made any significant progress.

Reed shook her head at the sight, pointed the gun at Poole, and said, "Hey, dipshit. Guess what? Your old man just paid me five mil. That means I don't need you anymore. Any last words?"

When Poole saw the gun and the look on Reed's face he knew he had arrived at his own end, and any grand plans he had…plans that had been in the works for a very long time were about to die right along with him.

"Yeah, I do. I was going to be the next governor of Indiana. Fuck off, you twisted bitch."

"Just what we need," Reed said. "Another crooked

politician with the intelligence of a Cane Toad." When she pulled the trigger, Lester Poole's dreams died in a spray of blood that looked like someone had dropped a bucket of barn paint on his chest.

Reed removed her earplugs, and for a moment she was slightly concerned about the noise she'd just made. But the more she thought about it, she knew hearing a shotgun blast in Nowhere, Kentucky was about as alarming as hearing a car horn in New York City.

She started back toward the trailer and was almost to the door when everything changed in a hurry.

CHAPTER TWENTY-EIGHT

COOL STAYED WITH THE HELICOPTER, AND SINCE GRADY and Cole had arrived together in an SUV, Virgil and Murton rode with them. Grady pushed it hard all the way to the trailer, and they arrived just in time to see Reed making her way up the steps, carrying the shotgun in her hand like she might be holding a leaf rake.

WHEN REED HEARD THE SUV COMING UP THE PATH, SHE turned, saw it was the cops and froze for about one second, maybe two. She watched as the vehicle skidded to a stop, all four doors opening at once. Her choices? Give up, stand and fight, or let the fight come to her. Now that she had five million tucked offshore, giving up was out of the question, and the box of shells was still in the trailer.

Together, those thoughts made the decision as if it was already a foregone conclusion that had been chiseled into stone. Reed hurried inside, slammed the door behind her and ran toward the kitchen where she'd left her ammunition.

Grady stopped his vehicle nose-on to the trailer, but kept back far enough to give them some cover. All four men opened their doors and stayed low, close to the SUV. Cole yelled, "State Police. Drop your weapon and freeze." But it was already much too late because Reed was through the door before he ever finished shouting at her.

Grady turned, looked at Virgil and said, "She's your fugitive. How do you want to play this?"

"It's your state, Jack. That means it's your call."

Grady gave Virgil a look. "Why is it always my call when things are about to go to shit?"

That's when Reed started firing through the window.

"Maybe we should talk about it some other time," Virgil said between blasts. "I don't know how much ammo she has in there, anyone who tries the front door will be blown out of their socks, and it's too far to circle around to the back."

Reed fired again, and all four men scrambled to the rear of the SUV. Virgil took out his phone and called Cool. "Rich? Wind it up and get airborne. You've got our location?"

"Close enough," Cool said. "I'll be there in two minutes."

"Keep it high. She's got a shotgun for sure, but we don't know about other weapons."

"Roger that," Cool said.

Virgil could hear the helicopter's turbines winding up through the phone. "Get overhead and watch the rear for us. I don't want to lose her out the back. If she makes it to the woods, we'll have to go in after her."

"I'm on my way. Let's keep the line open."

Reed fired again and the front of Grady's vehicle canted down as one of the tires went flat. Two seconds later she let off another blast, and the SUV's radiator started blowing steam through the grill.

"This woman is starting to piss me off," Grady said. "I've only had this truck for six months."

"Cool is on the way, Jack. He'll be here any minute. Stay loose and we'll figure it out."

"Based on the condition of my squad, we'll also be walking out."

A minute later they heard the sound of the helicopter's

rotor blades overhead. Cool was high enough that the shotgun wouldn't be a threat, but the weapon was still a major concern for everyone on the ground.

Virgil put his phone up to his ear. "You've got the back?"

"I do," Cool said. "There's no rear door, so if she's going to try to make the woods she'll have to go out through a window. No movement yet."

"Got it," Virgil said just as another round hit the SUV and took out the other front tire.

Grady crawled forward to the front of the vehicle, grabbed the microphone, and switched over to the PA system. "Charlie Reed. This is the State Police. You are completely surrounded. Drop your weapon and come out with your hands above your head."

Reed fired again, then screamed, "Fuck you. You want me, come and get me. I've got enough ammo to last all night." It was a lie, but no one knew it.

Murton looked at Cole and said, "What kind of toys do you have in this thing?"

"Two Colt M16A4s with extended mags."

"Mind if I borrow one?"

Reed fired again, taking out the front windshield. Cole opened the back door of the SUV, unlocked the gun case, and said, "Help yourself. What do you have in mind?"

"Putting a stop to this before any of us get hurt. How thick do you think those trailer walls are?"

Cole handed him the rifle and said, "About the same as a coffee can, but with this baby it doesn't matter."

Murton touched eyes with Virgil, who said, "It'd be nice if we could take her alive. She might have information that could help us figure out—"

Reed fired again, and this time the shot went through the SUV's nonexistent front windshield and blew bits of the interior back at them.

Virgil was done. "Fuck it. She made the play."

And that was all Murton needed. "Get low. I'm about to make some noise." The other three men got down on the ground, and as soon as Reed let off another shot, Murton stood and with the Colt set to full auto, he sprayed the entire front half of the trailer where Reed was shooting from.

After that, Reed didn't fire again.

BUT THEY STILL HAD A PROBLEM. JUST BECAUSE REED had stopped shooting didn't necessarily mean she was dead, or even injured. Everyone knew she could simply be lying in wait. Virgil got back on the line with Cool.

"Anything at the back?"

"Negative."

"Okay, hold in position."

"I'm Cool," Cool said.

Virgil looked at Grady. "You want the left or the right?"

"What's the plan?"

"Cole can cover the front from here. Cool's got the back from the air. I say we let Murton hose the trailer one more time while we swing wide to the corners."

"Good enough," Grady said. "I'll take the right."

Virgil told him to get ready, looked at Murton and said, "Keep it tight, Murt. We'll be running wide, but I don't want a face full of aluminum."

"I've got it, Jones-man. Whenever you're ready."

Virgil gave Grady a nod, and said, "Go. Murt? Hit it."

Murton stepped up and laid down the cover fire in three round bursts as Virgil and Grady ran in an arc that would place them at opposite corners of the trailer. As soon as they got close, Murton stopped firing.

Virgil hated making an entry on a trailer of any kind. Nearly every single one had the same setup. Three short side steps and a tiny little porch. If someone was right behind the entryway on the inside, all they had to do was wait until the door was kicked, then start shooting.

Everyone held in position for ten minutes, and finally Virgil started duckwalking his way toward the front stoop. He stayed low, moved past the side steps, then got down in front of the porch. He waited another thirty seconds before he stood and emptied his entire clip through the trailer's front door.

As Virgil was swapping out his clip, Grady ran over, took all three steps in one giant leap and crashed through the front door.

Then it was over, except for the paperwork…and a few minor lies.

REED WAS DEAD, HER BODY RIDDLED WITH BULLET HOLES from the automatic fire. Once all four men were in the trailer—and after a quick search—they discovered Reed was nearly out of ammunition. Only one shell remained in the shotgun. Cole ejected the round to make the gun safe. Off in the distance they heard the sound of sirens.

Grady looked at Virgil and said, "I'm about to do you and your brother a big favor."

Virgil didn't understand. "What do you mean?"

"I'll explain in a minute. You're lucky we carry the same sidearm." Grady took his Sig and began stripping the gun. "C'mon, Jonesy, get with the program because this whole incident is already going to require about two reams of paperwork. If you don't want it to be four, swap out your barrel with mine. Give me your clips as well." The sirens were getting closer, so Virgil did what Grady asked.

Once they'd swapped their gun parts, Grady looked at

Virgil and Murton and said, "I took the front door. Cole handled the Colt. You guys good with that?"

Murton shrugged and said, "Sure, as long as it doesn't cause you any grief down the line."

"It won't, but the county sheriffs down here don't like it when the state comes charging into their territory without knowing about it ahead of time. I think it's mostly because they don't want to get left out of the action."

"Works for us, Jack," Virgil said. "Appreciate it."

"Don't mention it…ever," Grady said. "If anyone asks, you guys alerted us to an imminent threat at this location based on intelligence you gathered on your end. I requested your presence here to observe and make sure we had the right suspect. Clear?"

"Absolutely," Murton said. "Maybe we should go look for Poole…or his body."

"Not a bad idea," Grady said. "Make sure your badges are visible, and keep your weapons holstered at all times. Cole and I will handle the county guys."

AS IT TURNED OUT THE COUNTY GUYS WEREN'T A problem because most of them had been present at Getz's house after Reed and Landry had tried to rob and kill him. The senior deputy walked over to where Virgil and

Murton stood, looked at the body in the weeds, and said, "Lord Almighty. That woman done this?"

"Probably not the beatings," Virgil said as he looked at Lester Poole's body. "But she killed him for sure. Happened right before we got here. He's still warm, and we saw her walking back to the trailer carrying the murder weapon."

"Her and that other idiot who blew his own noggin off the ones who kidnapped this poor fella?"

"Yeah," Virgil said. "We got a tip they were hiding out down here. We weren't sure where until the victim's father paid the ransom."

"That don't never work out," the deputy said. "I hope you done told him so."

Virgil ignored the deputy's use of a double negative. "I did, but he didn't listen."

"That's the job anymore, ain't it? You can talk to people all day long but half the time they don't hear a word you say."

"I can't argue that, but the father had his back against the wall and the Reed woman changed the timeline on him."

"How much did she ding him for?"

Virgil didn't want to get dragged into an endless conversation with the man, so he said, "I'm not sure yet. I wasn't really involved in that part of it."

The deputy looked over at the single-wide and said,

"Don't surprise me none. Looks like you was more involved with the operational end of the situation. I've seen tornados ain't done as much damage to a trailer as you boys did today."

"Take a look at the vehicle we arrived in," Murton said. "The woman didn't leave anyone much choice."

The county cop made a snick noise with his tongue and cheek, then hitched up his gun belt. "I wasn't being critical, just making a casual observation. Kinda sorry I missed it. Grady and them seem to get all the fun."

CHAPTER TWENTY-NINE

It took Virgil and Murton nearly three hours to untangle themselves from the Kentucky crime scene. They both gave statements to the county's sheriff's deputies, then stood idly by while the crime scene technicians did their work. The technicians had a few questions of their own, and Virgil let Grady and Cole answer those. Once the coroner arrived, Virgil asked how long the autopsy would take.

"Don't need one," the coroner said. "I'll make a report stating cause of death was a shotgun blast to the chest at close range. Manner of death will be listed as Homicide, obviously."

"Can your local funeral home prep him for transport back to Indiana?"

"Yup. They don't deliver, though. The man's family will have to make those arrangements. There are services for these types of situations. I'm sure the family's funeral home can provide all the details."

"I'll let them know," Virgil said.

"You want our local mortician to fix him up before they let him go?"

Virgil glanced at Lester Poole's body. "As much as they can." He thanked the coroner, then went in search of Grady and found him on the back side of the trailer.

"If there's nothing else, Murt and I are going to head out."

"We've got it from here, Jonesy," Grady said. "Good working with you again."

"You too, Jack. Think one of these county guys could give us a lift back to our staging area?"

"Yeah, I'll get someone for you."

"Appreciate it. And listen, I can't say for sure, but it's highly likely that sometime within the next day or two the owner of this trailer is going to come down here to have a look. He isn't going to be very happy."

Grady turned his palms up. "Can't say I blame him."

"Well, there's a little more to it. You see, we needed him out of our way for a little while, so a couple of my guys arrested him for planning to attempt to interfere with a multi-state criminal investigation."

"I don't think that's an actual crime," Grady said.

Virgil nodded. "Yeah, I'm just saying…the guy is going to be pretty mad when he shows up."

Virgil had Cool fly them up to Peru, Indiana, from Eminence, Kentucky. This time when they landed in the senator's backyard, it was done with care and as far away from the house as possible.

"This is the part of the job I hate," Murton said.

Virgil knew the feeling. Informing a family member of their loved one's death was never easy. "Me too."

The senator stepped out in the backyard and met Virgil and Murton halfway between the house and the helicopter. When he saw the looks on their faces he stopped, and simply said, "I killed him, didn't I?"

Murton stepped up and gently placed his hand on the senator's shoulder. "No sir, you did not. Don't take on a weight that isn't yours to carry."

The senator's jaw quivered as he spoke. "I didn't have a choice. Don't you see? I was out of options. Reed said she'd kill him instantly if I didn't send the money."

"You were placed in an impossible position, sir," Virgil said. "I don't think there was anything else you could have done."

Senator Poole sat down in the grass, and since Virgil and Murton didn't want to stare down at the man, they did the same.

No one spoke for a few minutes, and to Virgil, the

silence felt deafening. Finally, Poole looked at both men and said, "Will there be some sort of autopsy?"

"Not unless you request it, Senator," Virgil said. "The coroner in Kentucky made it clear it wasn't necessary due to…uh, the cause of death."

"Which was what, exactly?"

Virgil knew some things couldn't be said with delicacy so he came right out with it. "Your son was gunned down at close range by a single shotgun blast. His death was instantaneous. As bad as that is, I don't believe he suffered, sir. "

"No, but that's the legacy he's left me to bear, isn't it? The suffering…it's mine now. He had plans, you know? He was going to run for governor of this state, and I'll tell you something: He knew he was going to win."

Virgil touched eyes with Murton. "I'm sure he would have made a fine candidate, sir."

Poole shook his head. "No, I don't think so. I'm not speaking ill of my son, but I know what his strengths and weaknesses were. Running for office and being in office are two entirely different things. He would have been able to hold the seat once he got there, but I've always known the race itself would be a challenge."

Murton waited until he had the senator's attention. "Yet you said he knew he was going to win. Those two statements don't exactly line up with each other, sir."

"My son was many things, Detective, and I would

have liked to see him in the governor's chair, but not the way he had planned. Any character deficits he may have had probably came from my side of the family."

"What do you mean?"

"He told me he had a plan to ensure his success but refused to tell me what it was. Said it was the kind of thing he didn't want me mixed up in. It doesn't take much imagination to connect the dots, does it?"

"No sir, it doesn't," Virgil said. "But we'd like to hear you say the words."

The senator tried to stand but seemed incapable in the moment. "Help me up if you would, please."

Virgil and Murton each took hold of the senator's hands and pulled him to his feet. When he spoke, it was at a point about six inches in front of his own face. "I don't know for certain, but if you're being leveraged, as you say, I believe there's a chance my son might have been involved somehow. That's all I know."

Virgil shook his head. "I wish you would have said something sooner."

"Could it have saved him?" Poole said.

Virgil thought carefully before he answered. "I don't see how."

"Then what purpose would it serve? I'm sorry if either of you feel I've deceived you in any way. It was never my intent."

Virgil took out one of his cards and handed it to Poole.

"Sarah Palmer, our operations manager, will be in touch with you regarding the transportation of your son's remains back to Indiana. If you have any questions, she can be reached at the number on my card."

Poole took the card and said, "So much loss. So much death. My son, James, will be heartbroken." Then turned and walked back toward his house without another word. Virgil and Murton watched him walk away, and it didn't escape either man that the senator dropped Virgil's card in the grass where it fluttered away like a fallen leaf caught in the clutches of a brutal winter wind.

Virgil looked at Murton and said, "What do you make of that?"

Murton was still looking at the senator as he disappeared inside his own home. "Which part?"

"The man all but admitted his son, Lester, was at the very center of our other problem."

"That's not what worries me," Murton said. "Did you notice he didn't ask about the money?"

"Yeah, I did. But I don't think he cared about it. All he wanted was his son back."

Murton had always had a keen intuitive sense regarding other people's thoughts and the actions that usually followed. He finally looked away from the house and turned toward his brother. "He dropped your card in the grass like it didn't matter what happened to his son's remains."

"What are you saying, Murt?"

"I've seen the look before. Do you think it's possible to stop a suicide?"

Virgil didn't get a chance to respond, because Senator Poole answered for him. When he heard the shot from inside the house, Virgil sat back down in the grass even though he didn't mean to.

THE MIAMI COUNTY DETECTIVE WHO QUESTIONED VIRGIL and Murton went over their statements three times to make sure he had all the facts. "Just so I'm clear, you're saying you arrived here by helicopter, informed the man his son had been murdered down in Kentucky, offered him assistance in coordinating the transportation of said victim, then while you were still standing out here he went inside and blew his brains out."

"That's the gist of it," Murton said.

"It feels like you're leaving something out."

"You're allowed to feel whatever you like, Detective," Virgil said. "But that's all there is to it."

The detective looked at nothing for a few seconds, then said, "It was common knowledge up here that Lester Poole was going to make a run at the governor's spot."

"Good to know," Virgil said. "We were also aware of that fact."

"And if I'm not mistaken, your wife is the current governor."

"Yes, although she is on sabbatical at the moment."

"So the man who was going to run against her is dead, the father of the same man is as well, and your department is running the investigation?"

"What are you implying?" Murton said.

"I'm not implying anything," the detective said. "I'm simply gathering facts…a few of which you seem to be withholding for reasons I don't yet understand."

Virgil had had enough. "The case we are working is a state case, Detective. The notification was part of it. The suicide isn't. Have a nice evening."

"I'm not done yet," the Miami County detective said.

Murton shook his head. "Maybe not, but we are."

Cool dropped Virgil and Murton at the Major Crimes Unit facility, then headed back to the airport. The hour was late and everyone had gone home for the evening except for Becky, who was still working and waiting for Murton to return.

"How was it?" Becky said. She'd already spoken with Murton regarding the events with Charlie Reed and Lester Poole. She was speaking of the senator's death by his own hand.

"About like you'd imagine. The county guys were trying to throw their weight around. They accused us of withholding information, if you can believe that."

"I can," Becky said. "Because we are."

"Did anyone get what we were looking for out of the MedCap files?" Virgil said.

Becky shook her head. "No…and here's why: It's because none of us really know what the heck we're looking for. We all have the case practically tattooed on our brains. We know who the major players were, what their level of involvement was, and how everything happened…right down to the last detail. If the answer is there, we're missing it. Franklin sent his files over, by the way."

"Did you get anything out of them?"

"Nope," Becky said. "His files had less information than ours."

Murton turned to his brother and said, "Did you believe what Poole told us?"

"That he didn't know what his son was up to?"

"Yeah."

"Hell, Murt, I don't know. My gut says yes, but now the man is dead and we'll never know for sure."

"What if I do what you asked me to do before?" Becky said. "I could do a deep dive on Lester Poole, gather every scrap of information there is to get, then cross-check it against the MedCap file. If I can convince

Nicky and Wu to help—they're up here anyway—I'll bet we could have all the information we need in a day or less."

Virgil tipped a finger at her and said,"Do that. But let me ask you this: Where are you on Senator Poole's computer data?"

"I've got a sequence running right now that's looking through the data sets. Some of it is encrypted, which means we'll never get that information. Based on what we know, I don't think we should be looking at it anyway. As for the other files, if anything is there I'll be able to tell you tomorrow. Oh, and speaking of Nicky and Wu…they finished the system sweep at the bar."

"And?"

"Well, you're not going to want to hear this, but they didn't find one single bit of code out of place. Everything is normal as it's ever been."

Virgil clenched his jaw. "How is that possible? The recording didn't just pop up out of nowhere. Christ, was someone hiding in the room when Murt made his request?"

"Take it easy, Jones-man," Murton said. "We'll figure it out. Lester Poole might have been in this thing up to his neck, but since he's out of the picture I'm guessing we've bought ourselves some time."

"Have we, though?" Virgil said. "Just because Poole is

dead doesn't mean we're out of the woods. That recording is out there, and we need to find it."

"What about the brother?" Becky said. "James."

"Ah, he's not part of the equation, Becks. He lives in DC, and the only reason he was here was to help his father locate his brother."

"So what do we do now?" Murton asked.

Virgil looked at Becky and said, "Has anyone put together a summary report on everything? And I mean everything…this case, MedCap, Freedom Pharm, all of it?"

"You've met Sarah, right?" Becky said. "The summary is in your office. There's a copy in Murt's office as well. What are you going to do?"

"Go home," Virgil said. "I'm going to take the summary, go home, and think. Someone got ahold of that recording somehow—probably at Lester Poole's request if what his father said is true—and someone sent it to Cora. I'm going to find out who they are and where the recording is. The answers are there, we're just not seeing them."

And Virgil was right. The answers were there. But they weren't the answers he expected to find.

CHAPTER THIRTY

THE FOLLOWING MORNING VIRGIL WAS OUT ON HIS DECK, the summary report open in front of him. Sandy came out with two cups of coffee, gave her husband a kiss, and said, "What time did you get in last night? I never heard you."

"It was late, and you never heard me because I'm a loving husband who tried extremely hard to be very quiet."

"And your loving wife appreciates it. How was your day?"

Virgil thought about everything that had happened the day before and when he answered, it was with one word. "Sad."

"Want to talk about it?" Sandy said.

Virgil hit the highlights for his wife and finished with, "So Reed and Landry are dead, as are Senator Poole and his son, Lester. I think the saddest part is we almost saved him. I'm speaking of Lester. I don't think he'd been dead for more than two minutes by the time we arrived at the trailer. I keep looking for those two minutes but I can't find them. That's the sad part. Two minutes and we could have saved two lives."

"You can't be all things to all people, Virgil. If you did the best you could, then there's nothing to feel guilty about. I know you right down to your core. That means I'm aware of the fact you'd do everything in your power to save someone if you could. So would Murton. If the two minutes weren't there, then they weren't there."

"Simple as that, huh?"

"Not everything has to be so complicated," Sandy said.

Then why is it? Virgil thought.

"So you've got it wrapped up?" Sandy asked.

"For the most part. There are a few things we still need to take care of."

"Like what?"

Virgil tapped his index finger on the summary report. "Paperwork, mainly."

"Did you talk to Becky about the UNOS search?"

Virgil shook his head. "No, not yet. We've all been so busy she wouldn't have had time to look anyway."

"But you will speak with her about it?"

"Yes, as long as you're sure you want to know."

"Why wouldn't I?"

Virgil shrugged it off. "Well, what if the kidneys came from some axe murderer, or a serial nun killer."

"Serial nun killer?" Sandy said with a grin. "Somebody's been watching too much TV."

Virgil laughed. "It sure isn't me. Like I said, I've been busy. But it's a valid question, don't you think? How would you feel about that?"

Sandy considered the question. "I don't think I'd feel differently. Whoever it was helped save my life."

"I'll see what we can do," Virgil said. He gave his wife a kiss, grabbed the report, and said, "Gotta go. Busy day today."

As Virgil walked from the back deck over toward the driveway where his Range Rover was parked he happened to glance down at the pond. His father's cross was covered with butterflies. There were so many the wood of the cross itself wasn't visible. The butterflies were gently flapping their wings and it made the cross look like it had a life of its own, which, Virgil knew, was probably true in one way or another. He was about to turn and climb into the Rover when all at once every single butterfly took flight, and flew straight up and away until they were so high Virgil could no longer see them.

When Virgil looked back down at the cross he

expected to see his father standing there, but Mason was nowhere in sight.

When Virgil walked into the Major Crimes Unit facility, he found all his detectives sitting in the conference room going through the case notes.

"Please tell me one of you guys have figured something out."

"I've figured out I'm not very good with flow charts," Rosencrantz said. "It's like my brain doesn't process information that way." He was standing next to a giant whiteboard staring at pictures of everyone involved with MedCap, Freedom Pharm, and their current case. Hand-drawn colored lines intersected each image connecting different people in multiple ways.

Virgil walked over to the board and said, "Who put this together?"

"All of us," Ortiz said. "We thought the visual might help."

Rosencrantz shook his head and sat down. "Doesn't help me. If anything, it makes the whole thing more confusing."

Virgil clapped his friend on the back. "Don't sweat it, Rosie. Work the info in whatever way is best for you."

Murton walked over next to his brother. "Last night

you said you were going to go home and think. Did you come up with anything?"

"Nope. Too tired. I laid in bed and stared at the ceiling half the night. Felt like I never really slept. Is Becky here yet?"

"Yeah," Murton said. "She's in the computer lab with Nicky and Wu. They think they'll have some solid intel on Lester Poole by this afternoon."

"What about the files from Senator Poole's laptop?"

"There was nothing of note, Jonesy. The military contract files are encrypted, and everything else is generic information. There wasn't anything to indicate the senator knew what his son was up to."

Virgil didn't want to hear that but he also knew there wasn't anything he could do about it. The facts were the facts. He turned and looked at the board, examining the individual pictures and the intersecting lines that ran between each photo. After a few minutes one in particular stood out amongst the rest. He tapped the image with his index finger, then turned back to his detectives. "Why is this guy up here?"

"Because you said you wanted every scrap of information," Ross said. "Right down to the very last detail, if I'm not mistaken."

"You're not," Virgil said. "That's some great work. I wouldn't have thought to put him up there."

"We almost didn't," Mayo said. "But J. Allen Turkis

was the attorney for both Harlan Shaw and Rick Said, and since Getz—who got us to Reed—works for the Said Corporation, we thought Turkis should go on the board as well."

Virgil stepped back, took out his phone, snapped a picture of the board, and began to walk out of the room.

Murton looked at Virgil and said, "Hey, Jones-man, where are you going?"

"Up to my office. I've got to think about something."

"That's what you said you were going to do last night."

"I know. But now my thinking has changed."

VIRGIL WENT OVER THE SCENARIO IN HIS HEAD FOR AN hour. He didn't know if it worked or not. In the end, he knew there was only one way to find out. He picked up the phone, dialed, and when it was answered, he said, "Hey, Mac. Jonesy here."

"I'm aware," Mac said. "I have caller ID. Most people do these days. How's Sandy?"

"She's doing better, thank you. Listen, I'm calling for a couple of reasons. One is to tell you how sorry I am about Senator Poole and his son. We almost had him... Lester, but we were about two minutes too late."

"I heard," Mac said. "And don't beat yourself up,

Jonesy. It sounds to me like you did everything you could."

While Mac's comment had been meant to comfort, it had the opposite effect on Virgil. "You heard about their deaths, or you heard we were about two minutes late?"

"Ah, there's the detective I know and love. And yes, as it happens, I spoke with Sandy this morning."

"Mind if I ask why?"

"She wanted to know if I had a connection with anyone at UNOS."

"What'd you tell her?"

"The truth…which is that I don't."

"Okay," Virgil said.

"You said there were a couple of things?"

"Yes. The other is this: I discovered, some time ago, and almost by chance, that J. Allen Turkis was both Harlan Shaw's and Rick Said's attorney. Are you using him as well?"

"We are," Mac said. "He's been instrumental in the contract negotiations Senator Poole and I had with the DoD."

"So Turkis was hooked in with Poole?"

"Yes. If you don't mind, why are you asking about Mr. Turkis?"

"Because I need to speak with the man about something, and I'm not sure he'll want to disclose what I need to know."

"Well, I'm not sure what you're after, but I'm guessing you could probably convince the man if you handled it just right."

"What makes you say that?"

"Because he's your attorney too."

Virgil could practically hear Mac smiling on the other end of the phone. "Excuse me?"

Mac let out a little chuckle and said, "I was so impressed with his work, not to mention his past relationship with Said and this company, that we've retained his firm to handle all of our legal affairs. You are a stakeholder in the corporation because of the Shelby County drilling operation, which means he is, in effect, your de facto lawyer as well."

"Thanks, Mac. I gotta run. I need to see if I can meet with Turkis. I'm going to call him right now."

"Don't bother," Mac said.

"Why not?"

"Hold on just a moment, Jonesy."

In the background, Virgil heard Mac say, "I've got Detective Virgil Jones on the line. Wants to know if he can get a quick word with you. Sure, I'll let him know." Then, back to Virgil: "He's sitting in my office right now. He has a very short meeting that starts in a few minutes. If you swing by in about half an hour, he's all yours."

And Virgil thought, *Perfect.*

Virgil walked into the Said corporate headquarters, then had to go through the process of signing in, showing his ID, getting a visitor's badge, and all kinds of nonsense. When he finally arrived at Mac's office, his executive assistant showed him in. Turkis and Mac were waiting.

Virgil shook hands with both men, then said, "Sorry if I'm a little late. You've got quite the security downstairs."

"A necessary evil these days," Mac said. "But you shouldn't have had to go through all that. As I said on the phone you're a stakeholder in the company."

"Then why do I have to wear this stupid visitor's badge?"

"Because you've yet to stop in and pick up your permanent pass. I'll have one ready for you by the time you leave."

"Thanks," Virgil said.

"Why are you looking at me like that?" Mac said.

"Because I need to ask you something, and I know you're not going to like it."

"You're going to ask me to step out, aren't you? It must run in the family."

"The truth is, I don't think you'll want to hear this," Virgil said. "It's for your own protection."

Mac let out a sigh, then stood and headed for the door.

"I think I'll go have an early lunch with Nichole. Turk, take care of Jonesy here, will you? He's one of the good ones."

"I'll do what I can," Turkis said. He was looking at Virgil when he spoke, his face as blank as slate.

CHAPTER THIRTY-ONE

ONCE THEY WERE ALONE, VIRGIL SAID, "IT'S GOOD TO see you again, Mr. Turkis."

"And you, Detective. How may I be of assistance?"

"I need a small piece of information you may or may not have. If you do, I believe it will help me with a very big problem."

Turkis was smart enough not to ask about the problem, but he did have something to say. "I want you to know that when you called Mac earlier, I was in the room the entire time. I didn't hear your end of the conversation, but I did hear Mac's. What I'm driving at, Detective, is this: What Mac said about me being your de facto attorney is exactly correct…with one minor caveat."

"Which is?" Virgil said.

"De facto is defined as practices that exist in reality,

whether or not they are officially recognized by laws or other formal norms."

"I'm aware of the word's meaning, sir."

Turkis smiled. "Of that, I have no doubt. But the key to the statement I just made are the words, *whether or not*. Those three words leave plenty of room for interpretation. The very nature of law itself, I suppose. In any event, if you have questions as they relate to your relationship with this company that are inclusive of your part within it, then I can and will help you. If your questions are outside of that realm, I'll only answer if I can."

"Fair enough," Virgil said. "I need to sort of walk myself through it as well, so here goes: You were Rick Said's attorney."

"You know I was."

"And Harlan Shaw's."

"That's right."

"Were you Senator Poole's attorney?"

"Only in the sense that I helped him and this company negotiate the contracts with the Department of Defense. I'm afraid I can't speak further about those contracts or the DoD itself."

"That's fine," Virgil said. "I'm not interested in any of that. The truth is, sir, the Major Crimes Unit is investigating the death of Senator Poole's son, Lester. There are certain aspects of the case I can't disclose, but our problem is a lack of information. That's where I'm hoping you can help us."

"What sort of information are you looking for?"

"Probably the most basic," Virgil said. "That's my way of saying I don't think I'll know until I hear it. What can you tell me about Senator Poole? And before you answer, let me say this: I'm not looking for anything that would violate attorney client confidentiality. I want to know about the man. Your general impressions of him, if nothing else."

Turkis steepled his fingers the way lawyers do and took his time as he formulated an answer. Finally he looked at Virgil and said, "I believe Senator Poole was someone you don't find much anymore in either the political or business arenas. He was honest, loyal to his constituents, and a tough but fair negotiator who wasn't afraid to thoroughly examine both sides of a debate. He was also a loving father, a grieving widower, and a man, who, for a shorter time than I would have liked, one whom I had the pleasure of calling my friend."

"I would imagine if you considered him a friend, you knew his sons as well."

"Yes, of course."

"And your impressions of them?"

"Detective…"

"I'm simply looking for your opinion. Nothing more.

And your impressions of them will remain between you and me."

"Very well. Cut from a different cloth, those two. One was a leopard who couldn't change his spots, and the other remains a chameleon with the ability to blend in with the background as he sees fit."

"Care to elaborate on that?" Virgil said.

"I'm not sure I should. Do you remember the last conversation we had, Detective?"

"Of course."

"Then you'll remember I mentioned Rick Said told me you were one of the smartest people he ever knew. Rick surrounded himself with very intelligent people, so it was quite a compliment. I'm hoping you'll live up to it now. Ask me the important questions."

"Were you aware Lester had filed to run for governor?"

"I was."

"Would he have won?"

"Wrong question, Detective."

Virgil thought back through every conversation he'd had with both Senator Poole, and his son, James, regarding Lester. He looked at Turkis and said, "Would he have used any means at his disposal to win?"

"I'm certain of it."

"Did he have help?"

"Same answer," Turkis said.

"Was the help coming from his brother, James?"

"I can't speak to that, Detective."

"You seem to have a better read on Agent Poole than I do."

"That's because I worked closely with him in the contract negotiations with the DoD."

"Why would a Treasury agent be involved with military contracts?"

"Answer your own question, Detective."

"They wouldn't, as far as I know," Virgil said.

"Correct. So what does that tell you?"

"You just called Agent Poole a chameleon. Are you saying he's with the Department of Defense?"

"No, and he's not a Treasury agent, either. He's with DIA."

Virgil couldn't believe what he was hearing. "He's with the Defense Intelligence Agency?"

"Yes. And he's involved strictly as a means of oversight."

Virgil was getting frustrated, but let out a little laugh in spite of it all.

"Something humorous on your mind, Detective?"

"Earlier you asked if I remembered our last conversation. What I remember most is my comment about never wanting to sit down with you at a poker table." Virgil took out his phone and brought up the picture he'd taken of their suspect board in the conference room. "What's funny is this: I'm about to go all in and show you my cards, Mr. Turkis." He held his phone out. "Take a look at this picture, please."

Turkis took the phone and used his thumb and forefinger to enlarge and manipulate the photograph. If he was surprised at seeing his own face on the board, he didn't let it show.

Virgil waited until Turkis was finished, then said, "Whoever was helping Lester Poole is on that board. I'm sure of it."

Turkis didn't respond with words, but with action. He zoomed in on one of the pictures until it was large enough to fill the entire screen. After that, he simply handed the phone back to Virgil.

Virgil took the phone, looked at the screen, and shook his head. "That's not possible. This man is dead. I was present when it happened. One of my detectives shot and killed him, and his actions saved my life."

"I have no doubt the man is dead, Detective. But no man ever truly works alone, does he?"

"What are you saying, sir?"

"Detective Wheeler is your brother."

"Yes. He's been a part of my family for decades."

"And of your own children, the eldest is adopted as well."

"That's correct. My son, Jonas…his biological parents were killed, and Sandy and I adopted him."

"I'm aware," Turkis said. "Mac and I have been through the history of your family. He considers you a true friend. Just as you did with Detective Donatti, if I'm not mistaken."

"You are not," Virgil said.

Turkis glanced at his watch. "I'm afraid I have to get back to work, Detective. Earn my keep, and all that. But before I do, look at the picture I just pointed out and ask yourself this question: What is the single most notable thing Detective Wheeler and your son, Jonas Donatti, have in common, other than the fact they were both adopted?"

It took Virgil a minute, but he finally got it. When he smiled, Turkis did as well and said, "You see? Our friend Rick was right about you all along."

On the drive back to the Major Crimes Unit facility, Virgil called Becky and said, "We've caught a break...I think. I need you to do something, and I need it done quick."

"Why am I not surprised?" Becky said. "What is it?"

"I need you to get into Kentucky's adoption records. I don't know if they're sealed or not. I know Indiana records aren't because of everything Sandy and I went through with Jonas, but I'm not sure about Kentucky."

"Hang on," Becky said. "I can tell you in about ten seconds."

Virgil heard her clacking away on her keyboard. When she came back on the line, she said, "Bad news. Kentucky requires a court order with cause to view those records."

"How do you know?"

"I Googled it, sharp stuff."

"We don't have time to get a court order. How long would it take you to get in and have a look?"

"Probably about as long as it would take to get a court order."

"Why?" Virgil said.

"Because you and Murt told me to get out of CAB's system like we'd never been there. If we still were, I could use their system to sneak in and it wouldn't come back on us."

"So it can't be done?"

"No...I didn't say that. It can be done, but it can't be done quickly."

"What if we didn't care if Kentucky knew what we were doing?"

"You're talking about a brute force attack on a government institution, Jonesy. Can *that* be done? The short answer is yes, but we're in enough trouble as it is."

"I wasn't talking about you, Becks. Let me speak with Nicky for a minute."

When Nicky came on the line, Virgil essentially had to repeat the conversation he'd just had with Becky.

Nicky listened to Virgil's request and said, "I'm certain we could do it, and there are a number of precautions we can take to make sure it doesn't come back and bite you…or us, but you still wouldn't want it done from your facility here, or at the bar. It's simply too dangerous."

"But the bottom line is you can do it?" Virgil said.

"Oh, yes. Probably wouldn't take more than an hour or so."

"Do it," Virgil said. "The quicker the better."

When Virgil arrived back at the Major Crimes Unit facility, he was bombarded with questions by his other detectives. He held up his hand, and said, "Everyone give me a few minutes, please, then meet me in the conference room. Murt? You're with me."

Virgil and Murton walked down to the computer lab to speak with Becky. "Nicky and Wu get started?"

"They did," Becky said. "I don't know where they're operating from, and to tell you the truth, I'm not sure I want to know. Said they'd be in touch the moment they have anything. Why do you want to know who Agent Poole's biological father is?"

"Because it could be the key to everything. Let's get to

the conference room, and I'll explain to everybody at once."

Virgil stared at the whiteboard in the conference room while everyone took their seats. He was focused on one picture in particular...the same person Turkis had pointed out to him. He turned and faced everybody and said, "I just came from a very interesting meeting with J. Allen Turkis. Everybody remember who he is?"

Everyone said they did, and Virgil continued with, "I asked him about the Pooles...all three of them. His answers were a little vague, but he did lay out a framework and pointed me at someone we should have been looking at all along."

"Who?" Murton said. "We've looked at everyone on the board."

"But we haven't, Murt. We know who everyone is, and we could see them, but we weren't actually looking." Virgil turned to the board and pulled down one of the pictures. "We never looked at this guy."

Mayo let out a little chuckle. "That's because he's dead. Why would we look at him?"

Virgil set the picture on the table and said, "When I drove up to confront the senator and Agent Poole, what began as a heated discussion turned into one that left me believing both men were being honest with me…and in a way, I suppose they were. They simply left out a key fact." Then Virgil laughed at himself and said, "Actually, even that isn't quite right. They gave me the key, but I never followed up on it. I didn't see the point."

"What was the key?" Mayo asked.

"Agent Poole told me he was adopted."

"So what?" Ross said.

"That's about as much thought as I put into it as well, young man. But Turkis got me pointed in the right direction."

"What are you driving at, boss?" Ortiz said.

"I'll let you guys figure it out. I'm going to ask you the same question Turkis asked me. Everyone in this room knows my parents adopted and raised Murt. You also know Sandy and I adopted Jonas after both his parents were murdered. So, here's the question: What's the one thing Jonas and Murt have in common?"

Becky rolled her eyes and said, "Duh. They were both adopted."

"Beside that."

"They're both male," Ross said.

"True," Virgil said. "But narrow your focus. It's one single thing."

"I've got it," Rosencrantz said. "Jonas and Murt kept their family name. Agent Poole took the senator's last name."

Virgil tipped a finger at him. "Exactly."

Rosencrantz leaned across the table, picked up the picture, and looked at Virgil. "So if we're right, Agent Poole is Brent Williams's brother."

Virgil nodded and said, "Yep."

CHAPTER THIRTY-TWO

BRENT WILLIAMS HAD BEEN A THORN IN THE MCU'S SIDE for quite some time. As a good cop gone bad, he'd systematically deconstructed himself when he wouldn't let his suspicions go regarding certain elements of various cases he'd worked alongside the Major Crimes Unit. When Williams was finally fired from his job, he became Harlan Shaw's head of security, a job that ultimately cost him his own life when he got mixed up with Charlie Reed and tried to kill Virgil. Mayo had shot him to death, and after that everyone thought he'd be nothing more than a footnote in a closed case file.

"So what we need is definitive proof that Williams and Poole were biological brothers," Virgil said. "Once we have that, we'll be closer to getting our hands on the recording."

"How?" Ross said.

"I haven't quite figured that part out yet. But it's a step in the right direction."

Murton took the photo of Williams from Rosencrantz and said, "I'll tell you something, Virgil, I'm sort of hoping you're wrong."

Virgil was surprised by his brother's comments and said so. "Why?"

"Because if you're right, this whole thing goes back much further than MedCap. It goes all the way back to the speedway incident, and everything we've ever done right up until Small got her kidney transplant. Who knows how much intel they've got on us? We've bent our fair share of rules over the years."

"There's no denying that," Virgil said. "But we've always operated from a place of serving the common good…of taking the bad guys off the map. I don't have any trouble sleeping at night."

"I don't think anyone in this room does," Ross said. "I know I don't. The question is, what do we do now?"

"Right now we need to wait and see what Nicky and Wu come up with," Virgil said.

They didn't have to wait long.

Becky's phone dinged at her and she put it on speaker so everyone could hear, and answered by saying, "What'd you get?"

"Exactly what Jonesy thought we would," Nicky said. "Brent Williams and James Poole are biological brothers."

Virgil moved closer to the phone and said, "Good work, guys. Listen I need to ask you something and tell you something."

"What is it?" Nicky said.

"When you and Wu were working in the office over the bar looking for any leaks in our system, you didn't talk about anything did you?"

"Nothing of substance, if you know what I mean."

"Good…and I do," Virgil said. "We've been doing a little extrapolation regarding current and past events and have discovered the threat we're facing right now might not be the only one. My advice? It's time for you guys to grab Nichole and head back to the island until we can figure this out. There's no need to put yourselves at further risk."

"We are already one step ahead of Wu," Wu said. "The jet is ready and Nichole is packing as we speak."

Virgil was glad to hear it. One less thing to worry about. "We really appreciate your help."

"Our pleasure, Jonesy. Call if you need us."

Virgil said he would.

After the call ended, Virgil looked at his squad and said, "We still have two very big problems to address; where those recordings are, and how they were obtained in the first place. I want everyone in this room to sit down and come up with ideas. Nothing is off the table…unless, you know, it's a bad idea."

"Most of my good ideas come from sitting around a bar with a pitcher of beer in front of me," Rosencrantz said.

"Me too," Ross said.

Virgil checked the clock on the wall. "Little early for quitting time."

"We're not quitting," Mayo said. "We're looking for a change of scenery."

"And the beer," Ortiz added.

"Guys…"

Murton looked at his brother and said, "It's not a bad idea, Jones-man. We're all wound so tight it's hard to see straight."

Virgil gave it up. "Okay, I guess you're right. But take your summary reports with you. Hell, Murt and I might join you later."

Murton clapped Virgil on the back and said, "Now you're talking." Then he changed his tone. "But why later?"

"You and I have something to talk about."

They ended up in Virgil's office. "What's going on?" Murton said.

"I wanted to tell you about something I saw earlier today before I came in."

They both sat down, and Murton said, "What was it?"

"Remember everything I told you about the last conversation I had with my dad?"

"Sure."

"When I was leaving, I happened to glance down toward the pond and saw his cross was covered with butterflies. And I'm not talking about a couple dozen. There must have been hundreds of them, Murt. There were so many I couldn't even see the wood of the cross."

Murton didn't respond right away, and when he did, it wasn't exactly what Virgil wanted to hear. "If it was a message, I can't make any sense of it."

"Me either. I keep replaying the conversation in my head and I don't know what butterflies have to do with any of it."

"Hit the highlights again for me," Murton said.

Virgil took out his notepad and looked at what he'd written down regarding the conversation between himself and his father. "He said he was trying to lighten my load, made sure we'd look at MedCap, and that everything is relative, and connected." Virgil tossed the notebook on his desk. "He said I have people in my life that have all but painted the solution to our problem on the ceiling and I should listen to them. That's it."

"Didn't you tell me earlier he mentioned Delroy?" Murton said.

"Yeah, but that's not unusual. He comes up a lot in our conversations."

Murton stood. "C'mon, Virgil. Let's go."

"Where?"

"Where else? To the bar. I think Delroy knows something and he's not even aware of it."

"What does he know?"

"Beats me," Murton said. "But it's a place to start."

VIRGIL AND MURTON WALKED THROUGH THE KITCHEN entrance, said hello to Robert, and started to move toward the bar. They were almost to the swinging doors when Virgil glanced down and saw Robert's baseball bat leaning against the wall. The thought of the bat jogged his memory and he turned back to his chef.

"Ask you something, Robert?"

"Yeah, mon. Ask me anyting you like."

"Remember the day when Brent Williams showed up and tried to arrest you after you found the body out back by the dumpster?"

Robert subconsciously reached up and rubbed his eye. "Yeah, mon. Do I ever. What about it?"

"I know Williams assaulted you, and he tore up the bar. But did he ever go up to the office?"

Robert shook his head. "No, mon, no. He too busy making a mess downstairs, him."

"Okay," Virgil said. "The rest of the guys here?"

"Day in da bar. I'm fixing everyone a late lunch. You two want anyting?"

Murton shook his head. "I'm good, Chef. Maybe later?"

"Same here," Virgil said.

"Yeah, irie. You change your mind, you let me know."

Virgil and Murton said they would, then stepped through the swinging doors and into the bar area. And the second they were inside, Virgil got slapped in the face.

THE SLAP WASN'T LITERAL, BUT TO VIRGIL IT FELT LIKE IT was. He saw his detectives seated in a corner booth, a half pitcher of beer on the table. Everyone was sitting quietly with their summary reports, their heads down, their thoughts trained on the problem at hand. But that wasn't where the slap came from. It came when Delroy stepped out of the walk-in cooler.

Murton looked at his brother and said, "What is it, Jones-man? You look like you're about to stroke out."

Virgil shook his head. "I'm fine, Murt. Let's go talk to Delroy."

"Sure," Murton said. "What's the topic du jour?"

"I think I know what the butterflies are all about. If I'm right, maybe the rest of it too."

Virgil and Murton took a seat at the bar, and Delroy drew them each a Red Stripe from the tap.

"How my main men, mon?"

"We're doing well, Delroy," Virgil said. "Do you have time for a little conversation?"

"Yeah, mon. What you want to talk about?"

"How's the walk-in cooler doing? Giving you any more trouble?" Virgil gently elbowed Murton in the ribs as he asked the question.

Delroy shrugged. "It seem to be holding up for now. I tink the caterpillars will probably last another month or so. Day usually go out like clockwork."

Murton dropped his chin, then slowly turned his head toward his brother. "Caterpillars and butterflies."

Virgil bit into his lower lip and said, "Yep."

Delroy gave his friends an odd look and said, "What all dis about butterflies?"

"Long story," Virgil said. "I'll fill you in as soon as I can. Right now Murt and I need to take a peek inside the walk-in. Might be best if you waited out here."

Delroy didn't know what was going on, so he didn't really care. "No problem, mon. Delroy have plenty to do anyway."

Virgil and Murton walked around to the end of the bar by the stairs. Virgil looked at his brother and said, "No speaking…just in case."

"I'm with you," Murton said. He grabbed the handle, opened the cooler's door and they both walked inside.

THE COOLER HAD MOTION-ACTIVATED LIGHTING AND ONCE they were inside, the lights clicked on. Virgil and Murton headed to the far corner where the cooler's electrical panel was located. They looked at it for a moment, then Virgil leaned close to Murton and whispered, "We're going to need a screwdriver."

Murton nodded and walked out. Two minutes later he was back, and went to work removing the screws that held the panel in place. Once the cover was off, Virgil set it aside and Murton pulled a penlight out of his pocket and clicked it on.

And that's when they saw the transmitter. It was tucked behind the circuit board the capacitors were connected to.

Virgil turned to Murton and mouthed, *What the fuck?* He reached up to grab the device, but Murton stopped him. When Virgil looked at him, Murton shook his head, held up an index finger, then leaned in closer to look at the transmitter.

A thin wire was attached to part of the circuit board and the device itself. Another wire covered with metallic tape ran straight up the wall where it disappeared into the ceiling.

Virgil took out his phone and snapped a picture of the whole setup. Then he walked over, put his back against the far wall, and counted the steps from one side to the other. With that done, he looked at Murton, tipped his head toward the door, and both men walked from the cooler and back into the bar area. Neither of them said a word until they were sitting outside on the employee picnic table.

"How'd you figure it out?" Murton said.

"Robert's baseball bat," Virgil said. "When I saw it sitting there, it reminded me of the time Williams showed up and trashed the bar and punched Robert in the eye."

"How did that get you to the cooler?"

"Because I also remembered Delroy used the bat once."

Murton nodded. "That ICE Agent was going for his gun and Delroy busted his arm."

"Yep. And when I thought ICE, it made me think of the cooler and how Delroy keeps referring to capacitors as caterpillars. Dad said he was trying to lighten my load. That's essentially what capacitors do…they carry a load so the system doesn't fry itself. He also told me the answers were practically written on the ceiling." Virgil brought up the picture he'd taken, then handed the phone to his brother.

Murton studied the photo for a few seconds and said, "It looks like the transmitter is getting its power from the circuit board. See how it's wired right in?"

"I know. And the wire up to the ceiling? That area is right below the office upstairs."

"I'll tell you something, Virgil. It's no wonder Nicky and Wu didn't find a bug. They did their sweep at the exact same time the repair technician was out here swapping the capacitors."

Virgil caught on right away. "Yep. No power to the circuit board means no power to the recording device."

Murton laughed, and Virgil thought it odd. "What's so funny?"

"I was thinking about the time we were chasing down Hunter Moon and his crew. We led them to Becky's parent's house by using that appraiser…Doug Stimpler. Remember him?"

"Yeah. What of it?"

"When he was there, he asked me what I did for a living. I told him pest control." Murton stood and said, "C'mon, let's go find a bug."

CHAPTER THIRTY-THREE

Before they went upstairs, Virgil and Murton walked over to the table to speak with the other men. Ortiz looked up and said, "Care to join us?"

"Can't," Virgil said. "We think we found our leak. Murt and I are going up to the office right now to look. You guys stay put, will you?"

"Why?" Rosencrantz said. "We could help you."

"Because I don't want to make any noise," Virgil said.

"I don't think it matters," Murton said. "As long as we don't talk about anything of substance. I say we all go up and look. Chances are we're going to have to move some furniture and equipment."

"I withdraw my offer of assistance," Rosencrantz said.

"Too late," Virgil said. "Murt's right. Let's go."

All six men climbed the stairs, and once they were in the room, Virgil tried to visualize the cooler below and orient himself based on where the wire led to. It was harder than he thought because the office didn't completely line up with the layout of the cooler.

Everyone got down on their hands and knees and began searching the floor. They looked for ten minutes, covering every inch of the office until finally, Murton, who was looking underneath one of the computer racks, cleared his throat to get everyone's attention. He pointed under the array and moved aside so Virgil and the rest of the men could see the tiny microphone.

Once everyone had a look, they all went back downstairs, and Mayo asked the obvious question. "Now what?"

Virgil looked at his brother and said, "Murt, we need to put the panel back in place, but I want to pull the capacitors before we do. We need to warm it up in there a little."

"What do you want us to do?" Rosencrantz said.

Virgil gave him half a grin. "Rearrange the cooler."

"Great. I work in a bar now."

Virgil clapped him on the back. "Not really."

"Then what would you call it?"

Murton laughed and said, "Pest control."

Downstairs, Virgil pulled Delroy aside as everyone else began to set up the cooler. "We're going to rearrange the walk-in a little. In the meantime, clear all the customers out of here. Give everyone a voucher for free drinks next time."

"Why? What happening?" Delroy said.

"I'll explain in a second, but when we're ready, I'll need you to make a phone call."

"Sure, mon. Who Delroy call?"

"The cooler repair technician. We need him to come out and fix the capacitors again."

"But day working just fine."

"Trust me, Delroy." Then Virgil quickly gave his bar manager the basics of what had been happening without going into too much detail.

When he finished, Delroy looked at Virgil, and said, "Dat rasshole. I never did like him, me."

"How long does he usually take to arrive?"

"It never da same. But last time when you were here he said he could make it faster because of all da trouble."

"Okay, hang on a second." Virgil popped the cooler's door, stuck his head inside and said, "How long?"

"Ten minutes or so," Murton said.

"Good enough," Virgil said. Then to Delroy: "Clear everyone out, then make the call. Try to sound mad."

"Delroy not have to try, mon."

AFTER THE REPAIR TECHNICIAN LISTENED TO DELROY'S rant, he assured him that he'd be there in less than thirty minutes. He ended the call, then dialed a number from memory. When it was answered on the other end, the technician said, "I can't be sure, but we might have a problem."

"What sort of problem?"

"I just got a call from the Jamaican. He says their walk-in cooler is acting up again."

"So what? Go out there and do what you've always done. Swap out the capacitors, and get the power going to the circuit board."

"What good does any of it do if you can't access the computer? Isn't that the only way to get the original recordings?"

"Yeah, and I'm working on it. The computer contains the password for the cloud account. Once I have the computer, I'll have access to everything."

"Okay, whatever. It's your issue, not mine, but I was just out there less than a week ago. The capacitors I've been using should have lasted for another three weeks at least."

"You think it's a trap?"

"I don't know. That's why I said we might have a problem."

"I'll tell you what it probably is. It's a coincidence. Something else has broken down and it has nothing to do with our operation."

"So what should I do?"

The voice on the other end of the phone sighed and said, "What I just told you. Fix the problem...whatever it is, and make sure there's power running to our transmitter while you're there."

"It doesn't feel right."

"I don't care if it feels right or not. You're dealing with a bunch of local yokels. Get to work, and get it done."

THE WALK-IN COOLER WAS SET UP THE WAY VIRGIL wanted it, so he pulled everyone aside and said, "Okay, here's how we're going to do this: Murt and I will be inside the cooler and hiding behind the cases of beer. Mayo and Ortiz, I want you behind the bar covering Delroy. Ross, take the top of the stairs, but stay out of sight until the tech is inside the cooler, then work your way down to the bottom of the steps."

"What about me?" Rosencrantz said.

"Grab an apron and pretend you're working the tables."

"I have to be a waitress now?"

Virgil gave him a grin. "Well, I was thinking waiter, but if you want to slip into something more comfortable, that's your call."

Murton laughed. "Not bad, Jones-man. Maybe my work is starting to pay off."

"How about I act like a sad and lonely customer sitting at the bar while drowning my sorrows?"

"That's fine," Virgil said. "Whatever works."

Delroy hurried in from the kitchen area. "He here. Just pulled up, him."

"Okay, everyone get in place. This is just one guy, so he shouldn't be too much trouble, but be careful."

It didn't escape Virgil that his statement was almost the same thing Murton had said about Charlie Reed.

THE TECH WALKED IN WITH A SHEEPISH LOOK ON HIS FACE. He went right up to Delroy and said, "I can't begin to tell you how sorry I am about this. I know the capacitors we've been using aren't the best, but they should have lasted longer than a few days."

"Uh-huh," Delroy said. "Maybe da problem is in da workmanship."

"Well, I understand your frustration, sir. Let me go take a quick look, and I'll come out and talk with you before I do anything."

"Yeah, mon, you do dat."

The tech looked around and said, "It seems kind of slow in here today."

"Maybe dat because everyone tired of warm beer."

"I better get started then."

"Yeah, mon. Maybe you should."

The technician walked into the cooler and over to the panel. He set his bag on the floor, reached for a screwdriver and began the process of removing the cover. Once he had all the screws out, he set the panel aside, glanced back at the door to make sure no one was watching, then turned to inspect the device's power supply.

That's when Murton stepped from behind one of the stacks, held out the capacitors, and said, "Looking for these?"

The tech looked at him, then slowly reached for his bag.

Virgil stepped out from behind the other stack, his Sig pointed at the tech, and said, "If your hand goes inside that bag, it won't be coming back out. Face down, on the ground. Don't make me say it twice."

The tech knew he was beat. He did as Virgil had ordered, and once they had him handcuffed, Murton looked inside the bag. He found a box of capacitors, along with some miscellaneous tools, but no weapons.

"Here's what's going to happen. You're under arrest. The charges will include everything from trespassing on the low end of the spectrum, to conspiracy to commit murder at the other. You have the right to remain silent, but I suggest you forego that at the moment and start talking. What's your name, and who do you work for?"

The repairman visibly deflated. "My name is Walter Silva. I work for a man who would like to see you removed from the planet."

Murton let out a little chuckle. "That doesn't really narrow the list very much, but based on recent events, I'd say you're speaking of Brent Williams's brother."

"How much cooperation am I going to get from you guys if I tell you what I know? And by the way, I didn't conspire to murder anyone. Hell, I haven't even trespassed, as you say. I've been invited here every single time."

"We know how to play ball," Virgil said. "Give us what we need, and we might be able to work something out. If all you've done is plant bugs, it won't be too bad. I give you my word on that. But lie to me once, and you'll go down for everything and anything I can think of."

Silva bobbed his head, and choked out a sob. "I have a family. My wife is dying a slow and painful death. I've got enough medical bills to keep the hospital afloat for the next decade. If I go to jail, my kids will get put into the system. I can't let that happen. My whole family will be gone."

"Then start talking," Virgil said.

"Any chance we could do it upstairs? It's getting sort of warm in here."

THEY WALKED OUT OF THE COOLER, MURTON MARCHED Silva upstairs to the office, and Virgil told everyone else to leave. But his men weren't quite ready to go.

"What gives, Jonesy?" Rosencrantz said. "Every one of us told you that we're in this together."

"It's okay, Rosie. You don't have to go if you don't want to, but Murt and I have this guy ready to open up. I don't want to spook him by having six cops staring him down. Stay or go, but the interview is off limits."

Rosencrantz didn't like it, but he knew he wouldn't change Virgil's mind, so he simply shrugged and said, "You're buying the beer."

Virgil said, "Deal," and then headed upstairs.

SILVA TOLD THEM HE'D KNOWN BRENT WILLIAMS AND James Poole ever since grade school. "Their old man was a piece of work, let me tell you. He'd beat those boys on a regular basis. It got so bad that CPS came and took them away. Then a few years back I ran into Williams…this was right after he'd been demoted. He told me how you guys were trying to screw him over, and that the things you did cost him his job."

"He screwed himself over," Murton said.

Silva nodded. "I don't doubt you, Detective. I'm simply letting you know what the man told me."

"Go on," Virgil said.

"Anyway, he said he had a job for me, that it paid cash, and I'd be able to keep my family afloat. Felt like I didn't have any choice. I needed that money bad."

"You know Williams is dead, right?" Murton said.

"Yeah, that's how I got hooked up with his brother, James. Brent and James had always been close, so I guess that's how Poole got involved in keeping the bug in place. Said he wanted to get revenge for Brent, and help Lester at the same time."

"That doesn't exactly add up," Virgil said. "Lester is dead as well."

"I know, but James didn't want to let it go. He told me he wanted the whole group…including the former governor. All this should have gone away after Lester got killed, but James wouldn't quit."

"So they were running a double game, each man going after someone for different reasons," Virgil said.

"Sort of," Silva said. "Williams wanted you guys out of the picture, Lester wanted the current governor gone, and James wanted the former governor out of commission."

"Okay, most of that makes sense," Murton said. "But I don't understand why Agent Poole would want trouble for Mac."

"Because James provided oversight on the military contracts, and while Mac's company is about to make billions of dollars in revenue, all Senator Poole could get was a consulting fee. He did all the heavy lifting, and Mac's company is going to get all the money."

"How does the transmitter work?" Virgil said.

"It runs off the cooler's power grid, and is hooked into a local WI-FI source. It sends the recordings straight to the cloud."

"Whose cloud?" Murton said.

"Lester Poole's. James has been trying to get his hands on his brother's computer ever since he died. He wants those recordings."

Murton pointed a finger at Silva and got right in his face. "Do not move. My partner and I need to step out of the room for a moment."

Silva shrunk back. "I won't. I'm cooperating here, remember?"

Murton leaned closer. "Not one single inch."

CHAPTER THIRTY-FOUR

ONCE THEY WERE OUT IN THE HALL, MURTON LOOKED AT his brother, lowered his voice, and said, "I screwed up."

"How?"

"It was during our conversation with Mac. He asked what kind of support we were getting from the county."

"I'm aware," Virgil said.

"Then you'll remember what I told him. I said we looked at the Marion County Sheriff's report, and they did everything right."

"I know, Murt. It was a factual statement."

"Yeah, it was factual. It just wasn't complete because I also told him they didn't find one single thing on paper, or on his computer that provided any actionable intelligence."

Virgil thought for a moment, then said, "Lester Poole's

computer must still be sitting in the evidence lockup at Central Booking."

"Yeah, and I'm betting the reason they never found anything on the computer is because they couldn't get it open. I never bothered to follow up. I simply took it on faith they got it open and and there was nothing to see."

"Then the recording dropped off at Cora's office must have come directly from Lester Poole."

"It sure looks like it," Murton said.

Virgil pointed at the office door. "I hope you're right because if you are, we'll have the master recordings of everything that's ever been discussed in the bar office. I'll be right back. Go sit on Silva. I gotta get our guys moving."

VIRGIL RAN DOWN THE STEPS AND OVER TO THE TABLE where his men were sitting. "Rosie, I'm going to text you a number. It's James Poole's cell phone. I want all of you guys to get back to the shop, get Becky working the number and have her ping it, or whatever the hell she does. I want a location on this guy as soon as possible."

"What do you want us to do when we locate him?" Mayo said.

"Arrest him for murder as an accessory after the fact, conspiracy to commit murder, interfering with an ongoing state investigation, lying to a state police officer, and resisting arrest."

"What if he doesn't resist?" Ortiz said.

"Make him."

"Isn't this guy a fed?" Ross asked.

"I don't care if he's the King of England. He's going in the system."

All four men stood and said they'd take care of it. Ross looked at Virgil and said, "What are you and Murt going to do?"

"We're going down to Central Booking to get our lives back…I hope. After Becky gets a location on Poole, have her come to the bar. Let her know we'll need a computer opened up."

BECKY GOT POOLE'S LOCATION WITHOUT TOO MUCH difficulty, then handed the information over to Rosencrantz. "He's at the funeral home. Probably making arrangements for both his father and brother."

Rosencrantz looked at the screen, got the location, and said, "That's only twenty minutes from here. Jonesy wants you at the bar to open a computer, but it's going to take him some time to get there." He explained about the repair tech and the listening device, then finished with: "So keep an eye on Poole's location until we have him. If he starts moving you're going to have to let us know. After that, get over to the bar."

Becky said she would, then all four men went to grab Poole.

Virgil stuck his head inside the office door, looked at Murton and Silva and said, "Everything okay in here?"

Murton nodded. "We're good, Jonesy."

Virgil looked at Silva and said, "We appreciate your cooperation, Mr. Silva. I hope you've told the entire truth."

"I have," Silva said. "I promise you."

"What's your wife's name, what hospital is she in, and what floor?"

Silva gave Virgil the information, then asked why he wanted it. "Because I try to do the right thing, even though sometimes it isn't."

"I don't understand," Silva said.

"I need a few more minutes. Sit tight." He closed the door, then went back downstairs so Silva couldn't hear his conversations.

He took out his phone and the first call was quick and easy. He dialed the hospital and asked for the nurse's station on the proper floor. When the nurse picked up, Virgil said, "Yes, hello, it's Walter Silva. I'm running behind schedule today, but I'm calling to check on my wife's condition."

"Yes, Mr. Silva. I'm afraid there's been no improvement. She's very close to the end now. I think it's time to consider bringing Hospice care into the equation. I'm so very sorry."

Virgil told the nurse he'd think about it, thanked her, then asked to be transferred to the billing department.

"I could do that, and I will if you like, but I have the ability to pull up pretty much any sort of information you need."

"Oh, well, okay. I wasn't aware of that. I'm trying to figure out how to get you guys some money. Can you tell me what my current balance is?"

"Sure. Take me about thirty seconds."

Virgil waited while the nurse went to work on her keyboard, and when she told Virgil the amount, he nearly dropped his phone. "I didn't realize it was quite so much."

"Believe it or not, that's the discounted rate because of your lack of insurance."

"I believe it," Virgil said. "I guess I'll have to see about getting a second mortgage on the house." The nurse didn't have anything to say about that, other than, "Good luck, Mr. Silva."

Virgil thanked her and ended the call.

Then he dialed a different number and when it was answered, he said, "Hello, Patty. How are you?"

"I'm well. How are you?"

"Busy, and I've only got a second, but I need a favor."

"Anything for you, Jonesy, you know that."

"I'm trying to do a good thing for a not so bad guy who got stuck in a no-win situation. How would Said, Inc. feel about making a charitable contribution?"

"What kind?"

"Taking care of a hospital bill. It'll keep a guy out of jail, and his kids at home. The wife is dying."

"How much are we talking about?"

"Half a mil, give or take."

"Is the guy worth it?"

"Who's to say? But I'm trying to get some good karma back, and I think this is a start. The idea came to me when I remembered how your Uncle Rick took care of the medical bills for the Larson family."

"Consider it done. Text me the details and I'll make sure the check goes out today."

Virgil went back upstairs, took out his keys, and removed Silva's handcuffs. "You're right about the trespassing charge. It wouldn't stick. The conspiracy to commit murder was nothing more than a tactic to frighten you."

"It worked," Silva said.

"As for placing the bug, that is a crime, but it's one I'm willing to overlook given your cooperation here today, not to mention the other difficulties you're facing right now."

"You're saying I'm off the hook?"

"Would you be willing to testify in court regarding the things Agent Poole had you do?"

"Yes. Absolutely."

"Then you're off the hook."

Silva started to cry again, and after he'd gotten himself together he looked at Virgil, and said, "Why? I always thought cops were, well, you know…"

"Assholes?"

Silva waved his hands in front of himself. "No, no, not at all. I just thought they never cut anyone a break."

"Everyone deserves a break once in a while, Mr. Silva. Go be with your family."

Silva shook hands with both Murton and Virgil, then left the bar. After he was gone, Murton looked at his brother and said, "Working on your karma?"

Virgil nodded. "Yup. Gotta start somewhere. Let's get over to the Marion County evidence locker and grab that computer."

Mayo, Ortiz, Ross, and Rosencrantz found Poole at the funeral home where Becky told them he'd be, and he went without a fight. The problem was, he wouldn't shut the hell up, tossing all sorts of threats at the four men, including federal prison time if they didn't let him go immediately. By the time they got him outside and over to their squad cars, Rosencrantz was done. He turned to Mayo and said, "Slap me as hard as you can in the face."

Mayo gave him an odd look, then Rosencrantz repeated himself. "Do it, or I'll do it to you."

Mayo visibly swallowed, then said, "Okay, it's your face." He wound up and smacked his friend with an open palm, leaving a nasty red mark across the side of Rosencrantz's cheek.

Rosencrantz shook the sting away, clapped Mayo on the back and said, "Thanks." Then he walked over to Poole, who was still spouting off about being a federal agent, and how much trouble everyone was going to be in. Rosencrantz spun him around, punched him in the face and said, "Stop resisting."

After that, Poole didn't say a word, and they drove him down to Central Booking to be processed.

They arrived with Agent Poole, just as Virgil and Murton were leaving with Lester Poole's laptop.

Virgil looked at Rosencrantz's face and said, "What happened to you?"

"Poole wasn't resisting. We had to help him along."

Virgil bobbed his head in a silent laugh. "Whatever works. Becky headed to the bar?"

"Yep." Rosencrantz checked his watch and said, "She'll probably be there waiting when you get back." He tipped his head at the computer. "You think everything is on there?"

"I sure as hell hope so."

IT TOOK BECKY THE REST OF THE DAY TO GET THE computer opened up, but once she had it, they knew they were out of the woods. She logged on to Poole's cloud account, deleted everything, changed the username and password, then uploaded a bit of encrypted code which would prevent anyone from ever trying to recover any data. It might have been a bit of overkill, but they all knew it was better to be safe than sorry.

Next, the laptop's hard drive was erased, reformatted, locked down with another encryption program, then placed in the bar's microwave until it started to pop and sizzle. Once it cooled, Becky took the computer apart, pulled the hard drive, then looked at her husband, her head tipped to the side, her eyes blinking rapidly.

Murton smiled and said, "Does Mommy need another hammer?"

"Nope. Mommy needs a power drill."

And then they all thought it was all over.

Except it wasn't.

EPILOGUE

When Virgil arrived home, he discovered that the house was empty except for Sandy. He found her in the kitchen making a large salad with all sorts of sticks and twigs, nuts, berries, vinegar and oil, along with a few other things he didn't even recognize.

It was pretty much everything Virgil didn't like on his salad.

Virgil liked very little lettuce, lots of cheese, meat, and at least a half bottle of ranch dressing to wash it all down. He gave his wife a hug and a kiss, then looked at the bowl. "No man-salad tonight, huh?"

Sandy gave him a warm smile and said, "Not tonight. This is better and healthier."

"Well, it might be healthier, but better is sort of subjective, don't you think?"

"I suppose that might be true," Sandy said. "Except

I've invited Murton and Becky over for dinner tonight, and when I asked Becky what they wanted, she reminded me of how much she enjoys my salads."

Virgil didn't really mind, but he felt compelled to offer his opinion on how the boys would feel about dinner. He looked in the bowl again and said, "I don't think Jonas and Wyatt will want to eat the creekside special."

Sandy pinched him in the tit.

"Hey, that hurts," Virgil said.

"That's why you should behave yourself." Then she gave Virgil another kiss and went back to work. "Delroy and Huma, along with Sarah and Ross, are taking all the kids out to dinner—including Ellie Rae. It'll be just the four of us for a couple of hours. Nice, huh?"

"You bet," Virgil said. "What time are Murt and Becky coming over?"

"Any minute now. Set the table for me?"

"Sure. Say…is everything okay?"

"Of course. Why wouldn't it be?" Then before Virgil could answer, Sandy asked another question. "How was your day today?"

"It was fine. We got a bad guy locked up, and my guess is he'll be going away for a very long time."

Sandy glanced out the kitchen window and saw Murton and Becky holding hands as they walked across the backyard. "That's great, sweetheart. Here come

Murton and Becky. I'm going to go freshen up just a bit. Get some drinks going?"

"Happy to," Virgil said. "But listen, I want you to know since we just finished everything up with this case, I still haven't had a chance to speak with Becky about the UNOS search. I'd rather handle it later, if you don't mind. I've had enough work-related talk for the day."

"That's fine," Sandy said. "In fact, I've decided I never should have asked to begin with. The last thing in the world I'd ever want is for something to happen to Becky because of me. I'll be back down in ten minutes or so."

Virgil opened a bottle of wine for Becky and Sandy, then took out a couple of rocks glasses and poured himself and Murton three fingers of whiskey.

"Where's Small?" Murton said.

"Freshening up. She should be down any minute. I hope you're not very hungry."

"Why?"

"Because Sandy's making one of her special salads. It looks like she went out to the woods and scraped the forest floor with the bowl."

"I like Small's salads," Murton said.

"Me, too," Becky added. "In fact, it was my idea."

Virgil gave her the brow. "How can you tell me you love me and suggest rabbit food for dinner?"

Becky laughed and said, "I could ask you the same thing every time you try to grill chicken."

"Yeah, yeah. Let's go sit outside, huh?"

When Sandy walked out onto the back deck, Virgil looked at her and almost dropped his drink. She had on a dress he'd only ever seen once before in his life. It was the same dress she'd worn the night they'd all convinced Virgil to give up the pills…so long ago now. It was a full-length white gown that flowed around her body with the slightest of movements. Her long blond hair was braided loosely in the back, her feet were bare, and in that one perfect moment, Virgil couldn't ever remember seeing a more beautiful sight.

He stood, walked up to his wife, and said, "You look amazing."

That got Virgil a warm smile. "Thank you. Is that wine for me?"

"It is," Virgil said.

"Would you mind if I had something a little stronger?"

"What did you have in mind?"

"How about some of that whiskey you guys are drinking?"

"Sure," Virgil said. "Sit down and I'll get you a glass."

Less than a minute later Virgil was back with his wife's drink, and everyone sat and talked about nothing of substance for a while. When there was a natural break in the conversation, Sandy looked at Becky and said, "I'd like to ask you to forget about the UNOS request I made earlier. I shouldn't have put you in that position, and I'm sorry. I'd like to drop the whole thing."

Sandy's statement caught Becky off guard, but she handled it like a pro…or so she thought. "That's fine. It's probably for the best."

"I agree," Sandy said, her voice taking on a hollow tone.

Becky held Sandy's gaze and said, "What changed your mind?"

Sandy reached into a small side pocket of her dress and pulled out the digital recorder Virgil had placed in the gun safe. She set it on the table, hit the Play button, and said, "This." Then she stood, took her glass of whiskey, and walked down toward the pond as the audio began to play.

…BECAUSE MY BROTHER'S WIFE IS GOING TO DIE IF THE woman who shot her doesn't. She's brain-dead as it is. All we'll be doing is helping the process along…

Virgil had heard enough. He reached over, turned the recording device off, then stood to go speak with his wife.

But no matter the intimate relationships that exist between husbands and wives, or the unspoken rules of marital engagements, Murton had plans of his own. He grabbed Virgil's arm to stop him. "Jonesy…"

Virgil tried to pull his arm free, but Murton held fast. Then he slowly stood and said, "Virgil, do you trust me?"

"Of course I do."

"Then let me."

"It's not your place, Murt."

"Yes, it is, Virgil. Don't you see? I started it. That means I intend to finish it." He pointed toward the pond without taking his eyes from his brother. "That woman down there…the one we all cherish? She and I have a particular bond, one which goes right to the heart of the matter when it comes to life and death, and I know you know what I'm talking about. She's your wife, and I mean you no disrespect, but I'm asking, as your brother and your friend…let me. I think maybe I need it as much as she does."

"Let go of my arm, Murt."

Murton let go, and to his credit, Virgil stayed on the deck because he knew his brother was right.

MURTON TOOK HIS GLASS OF WHISKEY WITH HIM, PULLED a chair over by the cross, and sat down next to Sandy. He didn't speak because it wasn't his conversation to start.

"That day," Sandy said. "That terrible, awful day. I sometimes wonder how I manage. It lives in my dreams and follows me like a shadow on the sidewalk during my waking hours. I don't really dwell on it, but it's always there. I don't know how to put it behind me."

Murton didn't have to ask which day Sandy was referring to because he already knew. It was the day Sandy had killed Murton's biological father, Ralph Wheeler, to save her own son. "It's not the kind of thing you put behind you, Small. It's the kind of thing you put away."

"He was your father, Murt."

"Mason Jones was my father. Ralph Wheeler was a drunk, a coward, and a murderer. If you hadn't shot him, Virgil would have. If Virgil didn't, I'd have found a way. I have a lot of people in my life who I love, but only two who I consider saviors. The man whose spirit lives in the cross behind me is one. You're the other. Mason saved me from Ralph when I was a boy, and you saved me from him when I was an adult. You're my hero, Small. You always will be. It's why we did what we had to do in order to save your life."

"And you would have spent the rest of *your life* in prison, Murt. Maybe worse."

"And I'd have woken up with a smile on my face

every single day until they strapped me down and stuck a needle in my arm."

"Did Virgil know?"

"Only after the fact. He didn't know, know, but he knew. He was also smart enough not to ask me about it."

"Becky?"

Murton nodded. "With me the entire time. She sort of muscled her way in."

Sandy put her elbow on her thighs and her face in her hands. "You and your wife risked your lives to save me. You could have lost Ellie Rae."

"Losing our daughter to you and Virgil wouldn't have been a loss if it saved your life."

Sandy looked up at her brother-in-law, tears streaming down her face. "She was really gone? Lisa Young?"

Murton nodded. "There was no question. She was completely brain-dead. You were dying and she was being kept alive by machines. What purpose would it have served to lose you both?"

"And no one else matched?"

"No one. We were out of options. It was either sit there and watch you die, or do something about it. I chose the latter, and I'll tell you something else: I'd do it again tomorrow."

"How can I ever thank you, Murton?"

"Don't you get it, Sandy? You thanked me in advance. You thanked me when you got Virgil off those pills. You thanked me by saving your son instead of Ralph Wheeler. You thanked me by being with Virgil, which brought Becky, Ellie Rae, and for a short time, my grandmother into my life. All I did was try to balance the books."

"I think we can call it even now."

"That might be a debate for another time. Or maybe not. Who knows what the future holds? I do know this, though: Virgil is worried sick that the stress of you finding out what happened will cause you to lose your kidneys. Don't let that be the case, and take it easy on my brother, will you? He wasn't trying to deceive you. He was trying to save you in the only way he knew how."

Sandy wiped the tears from her face and finally smiled. "I don't get to give him any grief?"

"I wouldn't," Murton said. "Not after everything I've seen him do time and again to save us all."

Then Sandy's smile turned to a laugh and she said, "Well, earlier I did get to pinch him on the tit."

Murton laughed right along with her. "So how about we leave it at that?"

"I love you, Murton Wheeler."

"I love you too, Small."

Sandy stood, then held out a hand for Murton to join her. Murton took her hand and gave it a kiss, but stayed in his seat. "I think I'm going to sit for a few more minutes. Finish my drink and gather my thoughts. I'll be right up."

"Don't be long."

"I won't." Then Murton watched Sandy walk all the way up to the deck, where she wrapped her husband and Becky with a long, warm embrace.

He was still watching when Mason said, "Well done, Son. Well done indeed."

When Murton heard the voice, he turned so quickly he almost fell out of his chair. Mason wasn't there, but a single butterfly sat atop the cross, its wings flapping gently in the fading remains of the day.

Thank you for reading State of Remains. If you're enjoying the series, then there's good news: Virgil and the gang will be back soon in **State of Suspense.**

- You felt the Anger.
- You experienced the Betrayal.
- You took Control.
- You faced the Deception.
- You accepted the Exile.
- You fought for Freedom.
- You understood the Genesis.
- You held on to Humanity.
- You braced for Impact.
- You defined Justice.
- You captured the Killers.
- You lived the Life.
- You mastered the Mind.
- You fed the Need.
- You found the One
- You made your Play.
- You examined your Qualms.
- You discovered what Remains…
- Now, it's time to withstand the Suspense!

Visit ThomasScottBooks.com for further information regarding the Virgil Jones Mystery Thriller Series, release dates, and more.

Scan me with your Smart phone!

— Also by Thomas Scott —

VIRGIL JONES SERIES IN ORDER:

State of Anger - Book 1
State of Betrayal - Book 2
State of Control - Book 3
State of Deception - Book 4
State of Exile - Book 5
State of Freedom - Book 6
State of Genesis - Book 7
State of Humanity - Book 8
State of Impact - Book 9
State of Justice - Book 10
State of Killers - Book 11
State of Life - Book 12
State of Mind - Book 13
State of Need - Book 14
State of One - Book 15
State of Play - Book 16
State of Qualms - Book 17
State of Remains - Book 18

JACK BELLOWS SERIES IN ORDER:

Wayward Strangers

Updates on future novels available at:
ThomasScottBooks.com

ABOUT THE AUTHOR

Thomas Scott is the author of the **Virgil Jones** Mystery Thriller series, and the **Jack Bellows** series of novels. He lives in northern Indiana with his lovely wife, Debra, and his trusty sidekicks and writing buddies, Lucy, the cat, and Buster, the dog.

You may contact Thomas anytime via his website ThomasScottBooks.com where he personally answers every single email he receives. Be sure to sign up to be notified of the latest release information.

Also, if you enjoy the Virgil Jones series of books, leaving an honest review on Amazon.com helps others decide if a book is right for them. Just a sentence or two makes all the difference in the world. Plus, rumor has it that it's good for the soul.

For information on future books in the Virgil Jones series, or to connect with the author, please visit:
ThomasScottBooks.com

And remember:
Virgil and the gang will return soon in State of Suspense!